PAINT

the first Stock Car Racing Mystery

"The planning, sleuthing, humor and the wide array of characters give this first in the series an extra special start. The thrill of the race and the excitement are contagious. Even if you don't know a lot about NASCAR, this installment will bring you full circle. There is good information at the end of the story for all enthusiasts."

—*Mystery Morgue*

"Glad and Ruby are a modern-day Nick and Nora. Set in the South, readers are treated to a taste of Southern hospitality in Ruby's family. Racing fans are sure to appreciate all of the references to the sport. There are colorful characters in *Swapping Paint*, as I imagine there are in the racing world. This series promises to be a winner!"

—*Fresh Fiction*

"*Swapping Paint*, told in the third person from the perspective of Glad, is a madcap comedic whodunit that engages the audience due to the antics of the lead duo as he gladly prefers to watch the goings-on while she takes the wheel at speeds that NASCAR drivers envy. . . . Fans of racing and mysteries will enjoy this speedy turn around the track as Joyce and Jim Lavene provide a superb racing thriller."

—*Midwest Book Review*

"One doesn't have to be a NASCAR enthusiast to be swept up in Joyce and Jim Lavene's *Swapping Paint*. But die-hard fans will certainly revel in all the inside references and banter that gives this book so much of its bounce and brightness. Half the fun of this story is watching Ruby, a voluptuous Southern belle, have her way with Glad, who's seventeen years her senior and thoroughly smitten with his down-home darling."

—*ForeWord*

HOOKED
UP

ALSO BY JOYCE & JIM LAVENE

Swapping Paint: A Stock Car Racing Mystery

FORTHCOMING BY JOYCE & JIM LAVENE

The Telltale Turtle: A Pet Psychic Mystery

OTHER SERIES BY JOYCE & JIM LAVENE

Sharyn Howard Mysteries
Peggy Lee Garden Mysteries

A STOCK CAR RACING MYSTERY

HOOKED UP

JOYCE & JIM LAVENE

MIDNIGHT INK
WOODBURY, MINNESOTA

FIRST EDITION
First Printing, 2008

Book design by Donna Burch
Cover design by Kevin R. Brown
Cover driver image © Ian Spanier / The Image Bank / Getty Images

Midnight Ink, an imprint of Llewellyn Publications

Library of Congress Cataloging-in-Publication Data
Lavene, Joyce.
  Hooked up: a stock car racing mystery / Joyce and Jim Lavene.—1st ed.
     p.   cm.
  ISBN 978-0-7387-1110-2
  1. Stock car racing—Fiction. I. Lavene, James. II. Title.
PS3562.A8479H66 2008
813'.54--dc22

                                                                    2007032453

Midnight Ink
Llewellyn Publications
2143 Wooddale Drive, Dept. 978-0-7387-1110-2
Woodbury, MN 55125-2989, U.S.A.
www.midnightinkbooks.com

Printed in the United States of America

ONE

"Who's that sleeping in my bed?"

"Shh! You'll wake him." Ruby drags me away from the bedroom door, *my* bedroom door, where some strange man is sleeping in our bed. I have just enough time to see that he's also wearing *my* pajamas.

"Wake him? I should get my gun out and shoot him! How did he get in there? And what's that big black thing on the bed?"

Ruby keeps walking down the hall toward the kitchen of our 2000 Holiday Rambler Navigator. I follow her statuesque form, admiring the sway of her hips even as I work myself into a fine temper, as my Polish grandma used to call it. I mean, a man should have some inalienable rights. One of those should be *not* sharing his pajamas and his bed.

"He's a cat, Glad. His name is Malibu. Bill, his owner, was stranded out on the road. Mama and I picked them up. Bill was exhausted." Ruby pours a cup of coffee. "He needed a place to get himself

1

together. He said he hadn't had a good night's sleep in days. What else could I do?"

Those big blue eyes turn on me, so wide and innocent. But I'm not backing down. There are some things that should be private. "When did you pick him up? Your dad and I were right behind you the whole time. I didn't see anyone hitchhiking."

"He was at the last rest stop. You were too busy flirting with that woman in the '57 Chevy. Remember?" She smiles sweetly.

I vaguely remember the woman. The car was fantastic. It had everything. If I had time for something that sweet, it would be the car, not the woman. "I wasn't flirting with anyone. I can't even look at a car without you thinking I'm looking at another woman?" I put my arms around her waist and pull her close. "I don't need another woman, sweetie. You're all I want and all I can handle."

She pouts and I kiss her sexy lower lip. Then I shake my head. "But you aren't getting out of this that easy. You can't pick up some bum from a rest stop and put him in our bed. And you gave him *my* pajamas. Don't you think that was taking kindness to an extreme?"

"Well, he couldn't wear *my* pajamas! If you could've seen him, you'd know why I did it."

"If I'd seen him, I might have given him a few bucks, but not the key to my RV."

"Glad, the good book says to give no matter what the person seems to be like. Remember the parable about the lepers?"

"Not right now. But I don't think it says anything about putting a stranger in your bed after you give him your husband's pajamas."

"Let me call Mama." Ruby edges away from me. "She'll back my story. She thought it was the right thing to do."

"While we're at it, let's call Oprah and see what she thinks." I can't believe she doesn't see any harm in what she's done. "This is our bed and my pajamas. I don't care if the queen of England thinks it was the right thing to do."

"Fine." The word barely slips out of her pretty lips. "If that's the way you feel about it, I hope you're never alone, hurt, and exhausted and have no one to turn to."

"I hope not too. But I'm not real worried about that right now. I'm going to get that guy out of my bed. Maybe you could find some disinfectant and someplace we can burn my pajamas."

"Oh, you're so dramatic! Everything will be fine after we wash the pajamas. You'll see."

"And while we're at Wal-Mart getting new pajamas, we can pick up a mattress cover to put on the bed." I start back toward the bedroom.

She stops me. "I'll go. I created the problem, and I'll take care of it. I don't want Bill to be upset when I tell him my big oaf of a husband has no Christian charity."

"Tell him whatever you want to. Just get him out of here." She's not going to make me feel guilty about this. No telling who this guy is or where he's been. I have to sleep in that bed tonight, if we eventually make it through this line of RVs waiting to get into Dover International Speedway.

It's the Thursday morning before race weekend at the Monster Mile. Dover, the next race after Lowe's, isn't a bad drive from Charlotte, North Carolina normally. Ruby and I make this circuit every year. I might have skipped the race this year, since my driver, Joe Nemechek, isn't driving. I'm only a spectator, not a fan, when

3

Front Row Joe isn't driving. When he's at a race, I'm out there with him. He may not win all the time, but he's one hell of a driver.

Now, Joe is a different story. I'd give *him* my pajamas, no problem.

Jimmie Johnson will be here, of course. He's good on this track, and he knows it. Ruby pulls for Jimmie, so she's happy anyway. I don't want to know how she would feel about sharing her bed and pajamas with him. Some things are better if you don't talk about them.

Ruby's parents decided to join us on this trip. Her father, Zeke, hasn't been to a race since he was confined to a wheelchair a couple of years ago, but he decided he wanted to see his son race at Dover. He can't drive his RV anymore, and Ruby's mom has never driven it. That's how we decided to split up. If I'd known Ruby was going to take on passengers, I would've driven our RV and let her drive her parents' 1987 Coachman Shasta 280.

I don't have anything against Ruby's parents. They have their quirks, but I suppose they're like any other in-laws. Louise, Ruby's mom, has for some reason never called me by my name. She just calls me "Ruby's husband." Ruby's father once chased me out of his yard with a shotgun. Seems he didn't care for the idea of his daughter marrying a Yankee.

Until I met the Furr family, I didn't realize people were still fighting the Civil War. Or, as they call it, the War of Northern Aggression. In Chicago, where I grew up, we were too busy fighting each other to remember anything that far back.

I pour myself a cup of coffee while I wait for Ruby to get the stranger out of our bedroom. I didn't think it would take this long. I think I could've had him out in about five seconds. But I was a cop for more years than I like to think about, and I might not be as dainty and delicate as Ruby.

There's a knock on the door, and Louise steps inside. "There you are. I brought these by for Bill. Where's Ruby?"

"Asking Bill to leave." I reach for the plate of brownies in her hand. "I'll take those. Thanks."

She holds them back and glares at me. "I *said* they were for Bill. What do you mean, Ruby's asking him to leave? Where will he go?"

"I don't care." I really can't believe Ruby and Louise are so touched by this man. What did he do that was so appealing? And thinking about the two women finding him so attractive makes me wonder what's going on back there in the bedroom with him and Ruby.

"All you people are the same." Louise says "you people," but she means Yankees. "This poor man needs our help. The good book says we have to give."

"Hold that thought." She's still got the brownies in her hand. They smell really good. Once we take care of Bill, maybe I can sweet-talk a few from her.

I'm normally not worried about Ruby being with another man. She's loyal down to her Royal Carnation Pink toenails. It's the men I worry about. My Ruby is a very desirable woman.

In this case, though, I'm starting to worry that Bill might've hypnotized Louise and Ruby when he met them at the rest area. Nothing else makes sense. Okay, I don't believe it was *really* hypnosis, but I do know there are drugs that can cause this kind of behavior.

Louise is glaring hard at my back as I walk to the bedroom, but I figure I can take her staring. It's when she follows me that I start getting nervous.

The bedroom door is closed. My heart starts beating fast. I trust Ruby. She's the best thing that's ever happened to me. I know she wouldn't do anything to hurt me—at least not on purpose.

But my last marriage ended when I found my first wife in our bed with her aerobics instructor, which pretty much signaled that our relationship was over. Standing here, wondering what I might find going on in my bed this time, is chipping a few years off what life I have left to live. I don't know if I can take finding Ruby in bed with Bill.

Fortunately, my pistol is still in the glove compartment of our Ford Ranger, which is still attached to the back of the RV. I wouldn't trust myself to have it in my hands at this moment. All the training in the world can't prepare you for something like this.

"Well? Why are you still standing there?" Louise demands from behind me. "Open the door."

She's right. I know she's right. But I can't bring myself to open the door. Every man has his limitations. This is mine.

I step to one side. "You open it."

Louise rolls her eyes and briskly steps forward. "You are one weird boy. What's wrong with you anyway?"

I don't answer. I *can't* answer. I can still see my ex-wife the day I came home early from work. It's not a thing a man forgets. Trust me. And her aerobics instructor wasn't even wearing my pajamas. He wasn't wearing *any* pajamas.

I take a deep breath, and Louise opens the bedroom door. She peers inside and catches her breath. I'm too far on the right to see whatever she sees in the room. Short of pushing her out of the way, I'm stuck with her interpretation. "*What?* What's going on?"

"Oh, Ruby!" Louise shakes her head. "What are you doing?"

That's it. I slam the door open all the way with my forearm and step into the room. There are no lights on, and the blinds are drawn on the door and window. The shadows merge on the bed, becoming Ruby's form and the large black cat I saw before.

"Isn't he adorable?" Ruby asks her mother. "He's so friendly too. Aren't you just so friendly?" She talks gibberish to the cat. "And you're so soft and fluffy."

I glance around the room, my old cop senses taking control of my brain. I don't see Bill anywhere. I check the bathroom, but he's not there. I check the closet, but he's not there either. This is a nice RV, but you can only hide in so many places. "Where's Bill?"

"He was gone when I got back here," Ruby explains. "He probably heard you talking about him and left."

"I hope you're satisfied," Louise says. She shakes her head and reaches down to pet the cat. "He's a beautiful animal. Didn't Bill leave a note or something about coming back for him?"

"I didn't see anything. All I could find were his ragged old clothes and Glad's pajamas that I gave him."

"Then what's he wearing?" I notice the bottom drawer of my dresser is open.

"Oh, he took those old jeans you should've given to Goodwill last year and that old Talladega T-shirt. And those nasty moccasins you've been wearing since before I met you."

"In other words, your helpless stray stole my clothes. Did you check to see if he took anything else?" I take out my cell phone. "I'm calling the police."

"You put that thing away, Ruby's husband," Louise chimes in. "I'm sure you have plenty you can share with that poor man. You didn't see him. Someone had beaten him. He was lucky to escape with his life."

Ruby stares at me too, and I put the cell phone away. "I think both of you have lost your minds." I say this in the *kindest* way I can. "Let's at least put the cat outside."

Both women yell "No!" at the same time. Louise drops the brownies on the bed as she rushes to her daughter's side to protect the cat. Ruby clutches the animal to her ample bosom—a place usually reserved for me.

"Come on," I say. "You can't be serious. What are we gonna do with a cat?"

Louise and Ruby glare at me while the big black monster creeps away from Ruby and starts licking the brownies. So much for me eating them.

"I'm sure Bill will be back for him," Ruby assures me as she and Louise laugh at the animal's mischief. The cooing and baby talk that follows (directed at the cat) is almost enough to put me off of ever eating again.

"I'm sure Bill has already forgotten his furry friend." I reach for the cat.

The animal looks up at me and hisses. Large white fangs protrude from his pink mouth as half-inch-long claws show in the front paw he uses to scratch my hand.

"No wonder he left it here." I pull my mutilated hand back and look at the damage. "That cat better have a rabies shot. Good thing I had that tetanus booster last year."

"Calm down, Glad." Ruby gets off the bed and hands me a tissue. "He's wearing a collar with his name and his shot record on it."

"I hope it has an address on it too, because it can't live here."

Before I can acknowledge that my ultimatum will be largely ignored, RV horns start blowing. It means traffic is finally moving. I have to get back up to the Furrs' RV. For good measure, I add, "I'd like that thing to be gone when I get back."

Ruby and Louise glare at me, and the cat snarls. Not a great beginning for race weekend.

I slam the door on my way out and stalk up to Ruby's parents' RV. Zeke is waiting for me at the door. "Where the hell have you been, Glad? I thought I was going to have to get out and push this thing. What's going on that couldn't wait?"

I don't know where to start, but it all tumbles out as I pull the RV forward. Soon I'm actually close enough to see our parking spaces, and I pull the Coachman into one of them. It will be another hour before it's all set up, but that's another story.

Zeke agrees with me. "A man shouldn't have to share his bed with a stranger," he says. "Unless she's a pretty little honey."

I appreciate Zeke's support. At least someone besides me isn't crazy. But I don't want to think about Zeke being in bed with Louise, much less a pretty little honey. "Thanks. Louise and Ruby are nuts about this guy. I don't know what happened. But I'm sure not keeping that cat."

"Damn straight! A man has to be king in his castle."

It's kind of scary to be on Zeke's side. If it wasn't for the scratches on my hand, I'd seriously rethink my position. "I'm gonna start setting up. You want me to take you outside?"

"I can get outside by myself, thank you," Zeke says, turning on me faster than a pit crew can change a tire. "You get things set up. I'll take care of myself."

At least Zeke and I agree on some things sometimes. I'm never sure what Louise is thinking.

By this time, Ruby has pulled our RV into the space beside us. I decide to work at getting back on her good side before I set up anything. Ruby is one of those people with a long memory. I could find myself sleeping in one of the Furrs' captain's chairs tonight if I'm not careful.

Outside is chaos. Everyone is moving at the same time. Late-arriving drivers are getting their cars in place for practice runs, and fans are getting RVs set up while they yell at friends across the parking lot. A hundred different vendors are setting up their striped tents.

Dover is a tighter track than Lowe's, with more restrictions. No tents or open fires for campers. I guess they're more worried about the fun getting out of control. And it's true that a hundred thousand or so people *can* get out of hand. I respect that, but at the same time I miss the freedom and the tent campers. They can be a rowdy, fun group.

Ruby steps out of the Navigator with Louise right behind her. Louise gives me an evil look and then goes inside her RV.

I ignore her and go over to Ruby. "Let's not stay angry over this." I come up from behind and put my arms around her. "I love you. I know you did what you thought was right."

"Even if it wasn't?"

At last she's beginning to see the light. I guess the evil spell, or drugs—whatever it was that Bill and his cat did to her—is over. "That's right. We all do wrong things for good reasons. I don't hold it against you, sweetie."

"Thank you, honey. You're such a wonderful husband. So kind and forgiving." She smiles at me, and I fall for it.

"That's okay. As long as we're on the right track."

"We're on the right track." She moves away from me with a snap. "Unfortunately, we're at different tracks. *Your* track is sleeping in the truck tonight while Malibu and I share our filthy, disgusting bed that probably saved a man's life."

"Ruby…"

"Excuse me." She brushes by me. "I'm going to level the RV."

"Fine. I'll unhitch the truck and get your parents' RV set up."

She's mad, and there's nothing I can do about it right now. I'm not sleeping in the truck, but it won't be a good night anyway.

"Hey! My two biggest fans!" Ruby's brother, Bobby, speeds up in his hooked-up 1966 Mustang with his friend, another rookie driver, John Paxton. "You made it. Where's Mama and Daddy? I hope you had a good trip."

"Hi, Glad! Hi, Ruby!" John shakes my hand as Ruby squeals and runs over to hug him. She adopted him after meeting him at Lowe's. He's another one of her sob stories. Something about dead parents and barely being able to keep his race car going. He doesn't have a big team like Roush sponsoring him, and that can be a problem.

I admire Bobby's ride for a minute (who wouldn't?), and then I retreat to unhitch the truck. Let Ruby explain what happened. I've got my money on Bobby backing me and Zeke. He wouldn't want Bill in his pajamas either.

At that moment, we hear the first scream. Information runs like dust off a track through the spectator crowd. There is no grapevine here. It's more like instant messaging.

"Someone's dead on the track!" a man in a golf cart yells as he drives by.

"Someone fell off the DuPont bridge," a woman shouts from the cab of a Chevy Silverado.

I look back at Ruby, and she's already in the car with Bobby and John. I run and jump in the back seat next to her. The tires squeal as Bobby pulls in front of oncoming traffic to head up to the track.

The multistory grandstands loom over the campground, with the Dover Hotel and Casino rising to the left of it. Traffic is still fierce, drivers clogging the main road into the track. Bobby takes a look at the scene and shakes his head. "We'll never get in this way, even with my pass."

"Let's park here and go through the side gate." Ruby points toward the open gate.

People are rushing toward the grandstands. Already, security is beefing up its presence, trying to keep everyone out. We have only a few seconds to get in before they have it locked down.

Bobby pulls the Mustang right up to the gate, and we jump out. I realize this is all impulse and slow my gait. *What the hell are you doing?* I've seen enough bodies to last me a lifetime. I don't need to see another one.

"Come on, Glad," Ruby urges, already at the gate. "We'll miss it."

"It's a dead body, sweetie. I'll sit this one out. You can tell me about it later."

"Never mind him, Ruby." Bobby holds the gate open. "Let's get down there."

I realize when I see their two blond heads disappear around the corner, with John right beside them, why I was going. *Remember what happened in Charlotte?* my stupid voice of guilt and anxiety asks. *Remember the mess Bobby and Ruby were both in that time? That's why you need to go.* "Hold up!" I yell. "Wait for me!"

They don't wait, of course. But years of chasing suspects through the back alleys of Chicago don't fail me, and I catch up with the three of them. There's some wheezing and heart pounding going on that wasn't there when I was twenty-five, but for a forty-two-year-old ex-cop, I'm not in bad shape.

People are filling the grandstands, rushing up to the fence that borders the track. The DuPont Monster Bridge, which crosses one side of the track, is empty, waiting for the movers and shakers with invitations who will sit behind its glass walls during the race.

Underneath it is a body. From the angle of the legs and arms, I can tell he's in bad shape. His face is turned upward, his open eyes staring at the blue sky beyond the bridge. I estimate the fall at about thirty feet. The chances are the crowd is right and the man is dead.

Ruby and Bobby stare at the scene until Ruby gets a strange look on her face. She steps away from her brother and puts her hand on mine. "Glad, do you recognize that shirt?"

TWO

I'D KNOW THAT SHIRT anywhere. I got it from 'Dega about ten years ago. For a while, it was my lucky shirt. Every time I wore it, Joe won a race. It lost its charm when Joe lost at the Brickhouse 500. Too bad. It was good while it lasted. I probably haven't worn it in a year or so, but it doesn't deserve to go out this way.

"I suppose those are my jeans and moccasins too?" I speak to Ruby, but I'm looking at the dead man on the track.

She's looking at him too. "I'm sorry, Glad. I didn't know this would happen."

"It's okay." I put my arm around her. "It's not like I ever planned to wear them again."

People around us are taking pictures of the scene. I see security begin to move into place, ushering rubberneckers out of the grandstands. It won't be long until they reach us. The sound of sirens has gotten louder, meaning the real pros are here to take over.

I'd rather not be here when they get here. I hope there's nothing in the pockets of those jeans that ties us to Bill. It's not that I don't want to help, but I don't want to get involved. We went through this at Lowe's. We must be under some kind of weird curse this year. It's our silly season, I guess.

"Let's get out of here, baby," I urge Ruby. Bobby is taking pictures with a camera the size of a box of matches.

I tap John on the shoulder. His face is as white and stricken as that of any rookie cop seeing a dead guy for the first time. "John? You okay, buddy? Let's get out of here. I think we've all seen enough."

"Bill," he mutters. His eyes don't move from the grisly scene below us. "Oh my God! It's Bill."

I'm wondering if everyone knew this guy. Did he ask Bobby and John for a ride as they went by?

Bobby looks up. "Your brother?"

John makes a strangled sound in the back of his throat and heads down to the track.

"That guy is John's brother?" I watch the young rookie stumble over the grandstand seats.

Ruby makes an excited dolphin noise that can sometimes only be perceived by dogs. I happen to be tuned to her frequency. The noise usually means she forgot something and has to go back for it. I'm hoping it doesn't mean that in this case.

"Glad! I just noticed something important!"

So much for hope. "Ruby, we have to get out of here. They might ask us questions if we don't. You don't want Bobby to get in trouble, right?"

Too late. She pushes past me and stands at the fence again. "We have to help John. And look at his face. Something's wrong."

Bobby and I both look at John's face—as much as we can see of it anyway. I can tell Bobby doesn't know what he's supposed to be looking for either.

"That's his brother," Bobby says. "Of course he's upset."

"I'm not talking about *John's* face," Ruby answers. "Look at the dead man's face."

I look at the dead guy on the track. He was lucky he fell face-up. I've seen jumpers fall face-down. Not a pretty picture. Bill could still have an open coffin if his family wants it that way.

Bobby shrugs. "What about it? He looks dead to me. And kinda busted up."

I agree with him. "At least he looks like he's at peace."

Ruby frowns at both of us and taps her foot impatiently. "You don't get it. His face should be a mess. I told you he had cuts and bruises all over his face when I saw him before. He's wearing your clothes, Glad, and he looks like Bill, but he can't be Bill."

Bobby glances up at the security guards coming our way. "Could we talk about this outside the track? If Mr. Hamilton hears about this, I might not be able to qualify."

"All right," Ruby agrees. "You have pictures anyway. That's all the proof we need."

"Proof?" I venture. "Proof of what?"

"That something isn't right. That can't be Bill, even though it looks like him."

"*And* he's wearing my clothes?"

She plucks the camera out of her brother's hand and flounces off in front of us, heading for the exit. Bobby smiles at me and shakes his head. I can only hope this isn't the beginning of something I'd

16

rather not experience. Ruby has a way of getting things in her head that it would take a pry bar to get out.

"We have to talk to the police," she announces when we get outside the grandstands. "Poor John. What a homecoming."

"You knew he was from Dover?" I didn't know he was from Dover, but I guess John and I haven't talked as much. Once Ruby discovers someone, she knows everything about them.

Bobby jumps in his Mustang and revs the engine. "What did you say, sis? I can't hear you. Sorry, I have to go."

I watch as his car burns rubber leaving, and I wish I was still in the back seat. I hope I misunderstood Ruby's last words. But what are my chances?

"We have to go to the police," she repeats. "We can't pretend we didn't notice and that something strange isn't going on. John deserves to know the truth."

"Sweetie." I slide my arm around her waist and nuzzle her flower-scented hair. She changes shampoos every week, and most of the time I don't know what I'm smelling. But this week she's wearing jasmine, my favorite. I try to impress her with my knowledge and subtly throw her off the track she's racing down at two hundred miles per hour. "I love when you use that jasmine stuff in your hair. It really smells great. Let's go back to the RV and lie down for a while before we get started setting up."

She stares at me like I've lost my mind. "Glad, we have to do this. The police have to know. You wouldn't have liked it if someone was withholding information when you were a detective. Maybe someone killed Bill. We don't know. But he and John deserve our honesty."

And our bed and pajamas. "Ruby, the police don't want to know that Bill's face should be messed up. They aren't going to care.

17

Unless they find something suspicious, this will be a simple suicide. The guy was in bad shape. You said so yourself. He probably jumped off the bridge. It's a trick of the light that you can't see the scratches and bruises on his face that you saw up close."

She holds up Bobby's camera and wiggles it in front of my face. "We'll see. I'll download these pictures to the laptop and take a closer look. If his face is clear, like I think it will be, *then* will you go with me to talk to the police?"

What can I say? It's a logical argument. Ruby and Louise may have been the last people to see Bill alive. If they say his face was messed up and the pictures don't corroborate their statements, something *is* wrong. I can't imagine what it could be, since she identified Bill and he's wearing my T-shirt. I really don't want to think about what it could be.

"Okay. *If* you and your mom both look at the pictures, agree that it's the same guy and that his face isn't bruised the way you saw it an hour ago, we'll talk to the police. But the two of you have to agree."

I don't know what the chances are they won't agree. Ruby and Louise agree on almost everything, except marrying me.

Ruby stalks back to the RV while I follow behind, trapped in her tailwind. She whips out the laptop at the same time as she calls her mother. It amazes me that she's so geared toward technology. If I can hold a cell phone and walk at the same time, I'm doing good. I hated computers when I was on the job. I sure don't want to use one now.

Louise doesn't bother knocking. She runs past me after coming up the stairs and grabs Ruby's hand excitedly. "I heard about the man who fell off the bridge. Are you sure it was Bill?"

Ruby smiles at me in a superior way. Louise looks back and frowns. I amble to the refrigerator for a beer. I need something to take the edge off.

Louise can hardly contain herself when Ruby tells her what she suspects and that Bill is John's brother. Talk about tainting a witness. Now Louise is going to agree whether she thinks it's true or not, just to spite me.

The two women hover over the laptop as Ruby downloads the pictures. I collapse in my chair with my Bud, but a screeching howl and two sets of sharp claws greet me. I stand up quickly, and the cat hisses at me but doesn't get out of the chair.

"You little—"

"You hurt Malibu, Glad." Ruby comes to *his* rescue.

"I've got inch-long claw marks in my butt and you're worried about *me* hurting *him*?"

"Look at the size difference." She compares me to the cat. "You sat on him. He was only defending himself."

"Poor little baby," Louise says, taking the cat from Ruby. "You'll be safe here. I won't let that big brute hurt you."

With the cat between them, both women groan as they look at the pictures Bobby took before he got to the track. Lots of women in tight jeans and bikinis. That's Bobby for you.

"There he is." Louise points to the screen. "Of course that's Bill. How awful. Poor John. That boy has been through so much."

Ruby pulls it up closer so Bill's face is filling the screen. "Now, Mama, did you notice any bruising on Bill's face when we picked him up?"

"Of course I did! That man was a mess. No way is that the same man. He looks like the same person, but he couldn't have healed that fast."

Ruby looks back at me. "I told you. I don't know how or why, but that's not Bill."

"What about my clothes and shoes? How do you explain him wearing those if it isn't Bill?"

Louise shrugs and Ruby shakes her head. "I can't," she says. "But I know what I know." Louise nods.

That makes sense to me. "All right. Let's go talk to the police."

Ruby glances at the mirror hanging over the sofa. "Let me brush my hair and put on some lipstick. I don't want anyone to see me looking like this."

Louise and I stare at each other wordlessly, with the cat purring in her arms. His green eyes shift to me, and I know what he's thinking. I've got news for him. I don't care if Bill is dead. We're not keeping that damn cat. Maybe John would like to have him to remember his brother.

I finish my beer, crush the can, and put it in the recycle bin. Ruby comes out of the bedroom about twenty minutes later with lipstick, brushed hair, new clothes, and new shoes.

"Mama, will you sit with Malibu? After all he's been through, I hate for him to be alone." Ruby strokes the thick black fur and coos at the animal.

"Of course I will. I'll have to take him back to the Coachman. Your daddy was getting a little snackish when I left. By now, he'll want a full meal."

"That's fine. Thank you. Maybe Malibu will eat something too. That should make him feel better."

Once Ruby has everything set up with her mother, she joins me outside. I can't help but admire her long, tanned legs in her jean shorts. Ruby is a gorgeous woman any man would be proud to have at his side. I suppose I feel particularly lucky because I'm so much older than her. She'll be twenty-six on her next birthday.

The last two years with her, since we were married on the track at Sonoma, have been like heaven. It may not seem like it at this moment, but mostly we see eye to eye. We both love NASCAR, beer, RVs, and having a good time. We both love the life we lead following the drivers' circuit from Florida to Pocono.

I hope I can reason with her about the cat. Living in an RV would be difficult with an animal. At least that's my approach. I hope she doesn't think about all those people we know who travel the circuit with pets.

"How will we find the person in charge?" Ruby asks as we approach the Earnhardt Grandstand.

Dover police are everywhere. I see a few Delaware State Police officers too. Security guards are blocking the entrances to the grandstands while police appear to be questioning people.

"We'll tell an officer we have information," I say. I wonder if she's losing her nerve. "We don't have to do this, you know. We could go back and finish setting up and let the police figure this out."

She stares at me. "Glad, sometimes I don't believe you ever were a police detective. Either that or they do things much differently in Chicago than they do in Midland. Where I come from, people help the police. We don't hold back information."

I don't correct her, but people withhold information everywhere. "That's fine. I thought you might be having second thoughts. That's all."

To demonstrate how wrong I am, Ruby walks up to an officer, taps him on the shoulder, and tells him she has information pertinent to the case. The officer looks her up and down (a little too closely for me) and then pulls out a notebook. "Give me your name and where I can reach you. If the captain needs something, she'll call you."

"I have really important information," she insists. "I think the man on the track may have been murdered."

If she expected the officer to do more than blink, she's disappointed. "I'll be glad to take your name and cell phone number if you have one. The captain is busy right now. But I promise she'll call you."

Ruby looks at me. "You were right."

I shrug. "I had this job for a long time. You get all kinds of weirdoes around a crime scene. Leave your name and number. If the captain has any questions about what happened, she'll call."

The officer nods in acceptance of this wisdom. He keeps his pen poised above his notebook, but Ruby turns on her heel and leaves without giving him the information.

I follow her after a quick I-don't-understand-either look at the officer. He shrugs and puts his pen away. Ruby doesn't realize she did him a favor. If no one gives you any information, you don't have to do any paperwork.

But she's definitely unhappy. "I know something is wrong, Glad. But they could think they have this whole thing wrapped up before they call me. I have to do something else."

It would be too good to be true that they would have the whole thing wrapped up that fast. I can't look at her face, all pouty and upset, without wanting to make it better. Besides, I tell myself to salvage my pride as I scan the grandstand openings for lax security, there's the matter of the cat. The best way to get rid of it without Ruby feeling guilty is to find one of Bill's relatives in case John doesn't want it.

"I think I can get us in." I grab her hand and give it a squeeze. "See that gate? There's no one stationed there. I think we can sneak in and go have a talk with the captain."

She smiles and hugs me. "Great idea! I knew I could count on you."

"Always." I kiss her, and then we walk casually toward the grandstands. With everything going on—drivers coming and going, cars being delivered, snack vendors, and curious fans—the police can't see everything.

We make it inside the gate and turn our attentions to the empty grandstands and then to the track, where a group of people, including John, are standing around looking at Bill. One officer is up on the bridge looking down as they measure from the top of the bridge to the track. I don't see official crime scene officers as of yet, but they can't be far away.

Two men in suits are pacing around the scene. I make them as Dover Speedway officials. They probably want this over today. Tomorrow is practice. If Bill's death is ruled a suicide, they might get their wish. I can't imagine they'll want to hear what Ruby has to say. No matter what, it will complicate an already bad situation.

We're lucky. No one notices our approach until we're on the track. We see a woman with dark hair cut short, about 125 pounds, an ex-smoker (my guess—she keeps rummaging through her pockets). She finally locates a stick of gum and crams it in her mouth. She's wearing plain black slacks and a black shirt. No high heels either. Good, sturdy walking shoes. She's gotta be the captain. She's the only woman down here besides Ruby.

I realize I know her. Or at least I *knew* her, a long time ago. We took some training at Quantico about twenty years ago. It was a very pleasant two weeks.

Ruby tightens her grip on my hand as the officer on the bridge calls everyone's attention to us. "Here we go," she says. "I hope I look okay."

"Beautiful as always." I smile and kiss her hand.

"Excuse me, sir, ma'am." An officer from the group around Bill hurries to meet us before we can reach the crime scene. "This area is off limits. I'm with the Dover Police Department. This is a crime scene. I'll have to ask you to go back the way you came."

"I realize that, Officer—" I read his nametag, "—O'Neal. I'm Detective Glad Wycznewski, Chicago PD. This woman has some information you're going to want to hear."

I'm not sure who looks at me with more surprise, Ruby or Officer O'Neal. Ruby knows I don't like to broadcast my former employment. And the one thing O'Neal wasn't expecting was a homicide detective. Sort of fun all the way around. Not that I wouldn't change it for being back in our RV right now.

"Of course, Detective." O'Neal shakes my hand. "Are you here for the race?"

"Yeah. I heard about your problem. It sounds like you'll need all the help you can get."

O'Neal smiles. "I think this is just a suicide, Detective. Not that we don't value your input. That's my captain over there." He points to the dark-haired woman, who's looking his way with an impatient frown. "Captain Barker."

24

Ruby has been remarkably quiet. She lets go of my hand as we approach the group on the track. She holds her blond head high and strides forward like a Viking goddess going to war in her cut-off jeans and red tank top. Just looking at her makes me wish we were alone somewhere.

"Why are you escorting these people here when I asked you to keep them away?" Captain Barker asks in an irritated voice.

O'Neal rushes forward to placate her. "This is Detective Wycznewski, ma'am. He's from Chicago. He says he has information."

The captain only looks a little less put out. Nothing worse than a visiting detective who throws himself in the middle of your case. She looks again, and her eyes open wider. "Glad? Is that you? It's been a long time. You look good. How have you been?"

Ann Barker holds my hand a little longer than is comfortable for a friendly handshake. Then she covers it with her other hand. "You're a long way from home."

Ruby glances suspiciously between me and her. I know I'll have to deal with this later. "I'm fine. You're looking good yourself. You made captain, huh?"

"Yep. I was the last one standing. What brings you to Dover? Do you know this man?"

"In a manner of speaking."

"*I* knew him." Ruby nudges me out of the way and holds out her manicured hand. "I'm Ruby. Ruby *Wycznewski*. I met this man a few hours ago. His name is Bill. I gave him a ride in my RV. At least I gave someone who *looked* like him a ride in my RV."

Ann glances up at me. "Let me guess. Your wife? She's psychic, right?"

"My grandma was a little psychic," Ruby confesses, digging us in deeper. "But this doesn't have anything to do with being psychic." She tells Ann her story quickly and concisely.

Ann ignores her and turns to me. "So they're still letting you carry a badge?"

"Not anymore. I'm retired. But that doesn't lessen what my wife has to say."

"Of course not. She knew this man, gave him *your* clothes, and now she can identify him, but it's not really him. Is that about it?"

"That's right," Ruby agrees quickly. "I know it doesn't make much sense, but it's true."

Ann smiles in the lopsided, cute way I remember. No sparks there, but a nice memory. She gets that too-patient attitude officers get when they want to get rid of a civilian. "And we appreciate you coming forward. Officer O'Neal will escort you off the track. Please find the exit and stay out until they announce the area has been cleared."

Ruby's head shoots up, her gaze catching mine. "Do something, Glad."

"I think I've done all I can do, sweetie. Let's let the captain find her own answers."

"Thank you." Ann's brown eyes ask the question before her words do. "When did you leave Chicago PD?"

"A few years ago."

"You were there a long time. You should've come here with me. I wouldn't have kicked you out."

"I left. Personal issues."

She takes my hand again. "I hope we can find some time to exchange war stories before you leave."

"I'd like that. But you have an investigation on your hands. I know what that's like."

"Not really much of one," she admits. "Besides your wife's statement, I think it's open and shut. Bill Paxton committed suicide."

"You know who he is?" Ruby demands. "Why didn't you say so?"

One of the men in suits turns to face us. He's standing close to John. "We're trying to keep things quiet."

Ruby's mouth drops open. I'm a little surprised myself. The man facing us looks exactly like the man on the ground, except he has scratches and bruises on his face.

He holds out his hand to Ruby. "I want to thank you for the kindness you've shown my brother John. He's told me so much about you."

John sniffs and wipes his face with his hand. "Bill always had problems. I can't believe it's come to this."

"Who are you?" Ruby's pretty blue eyes narrow as she focuses on the older man.

"Forgive me. I'm Bill's twin brother, Phil Paxton. I own the casino and hotel next door."

THREE

"WHAT WAS *THAT* ABOUT? Who is she, Glad?"

I knew it wouldn't take long. As we're escorted from the grandstands, Ruby stops thinking about the dead guy and starts wondering about Ann. It's inevitable. "She's someone I knew a long time ago. I wasn't even married the *first* time yet when I knew Ann."

"Is that 'knew' in the biblical sense?" Her eyes are bright with more questions than I can answer. "Did you sleep with her?"

"I don't think that's relevant right now."

"You're jealous when I talk to Junior. Don't give me relevancy. Just answer the question. Did you sleep with her?"

What does a man say in a case like this? If I answer yes, she's going to want to know all the details, including the big question: *How do I measure up to Ann in bed?* If I answer no, she probably won't believe me and she'll keep trying to worm it out of me. Either way doesn't sound like much fun to me.

I choose the honest path. "Yes. But it was a long time ago. I hardly remember it, barely recognized her. We were only together a couple of weeks. It wasn't a love affair. Just someone to hang out with during some training sessions."

"You might feel that way, but she obviously still has some feelings for you."

"Look, sweetie, I think she was surprised to see me. I'm sure she's married and has kids by now. Maybe even grandchildren." I hold my breath, hoping she's going to buy it.

"You're probably right." She takes my arm and snuggles close to me as we walk toward the RV. "*I* wouldn't forget you, darlin'. She probably wishes she would've snapped you up when she had the chance."

You know how you see a cartoon guy saying, "Whew!" while he wipes his forehead and a ton of sweat flies off? That's me right now. Not that I have anything to hide. I never thought to mention Ann when I talked to Ruby about my past. Really, I'm amazed she remembered me. And flattered.

"No way that wasn't Bill," Ruby says, changing the subject. "I'm not stupid. He can call himself Phil if he wants to, but the bruises and scratches were in the same place. That's Bill."

Kasey Kahne is signing autographs in the parking lot beside his number 9 Dodge Charger. Hundreds of fans are pushing to get close to him. They've already forgotten the dead man on the track. I wish it was going to be as simple for me.

"I understand what you're saying," I say, trying to calm Ruby down. "But the police aren't seeing what you're saying. You've got this big shot telling them his brother is dead on the track. Unless there's some hard evidence, they're going to take his word for it."

"There has to be some way to prove he's Bill." She shakes her head, her big, blond curls bouncing. "I can't believe it. He seemed like such a nice man. He was so down and out. He acted like he hadn't eaten in days. I'm not usually so gullible."

I hate to contradict her. But when it comes to hard-luck cases, she's about as gullible as they come. Like with John. She talked to him for a few minutes and the next thing I knew, he was coming over to her parents' house for dinner after the race in Charlotte. She set things up with him and Bobby so he could race in Dover. She's a very giving kind of person.

I admit to being surprised she'd let Bill sleep in our bed and wear my clothes, but picking him up in the first place sounds like her to me.

We reach our RV through a growing sea of NASCAR fans. There are signs everywhere, from "Junior is #1" to "We Love Kurt!" People are still pouring through the gates. RVs are on all sides of us now, and the police cars aren't visible anymore from where we stand. A man's death is easily swept aside by the excitement of the race.

I'm getting dark here. Sometimes it's easy to get caught up in the emotions of my old life, which took such a disastrous turn. I try to stay focused on all the good now, particularly Ruby. That was one of the reasons I left the job in Chicago. I didn't want to deal with it anymore.

"There has to be some way." She paces back and forth in front of the RV while I unhitch the truck. "What do you think he did, Glad? Killed his brother and took his place? We have to talk to John. There must be some way to tell them apart besides the bruises."

"It seems odd to me that one brother owns a multimillion-dollar casino complex while his twin is hitchhiking on the road and his younger brother doesn't have enough spare change for a cup of coffee." I give the hitch one last tug and the truck bounces down on its wheels. "Usually the apples don't fall that far from the tree."

"What are you two doing out here?" Zeke comes around the corner in his wheelchair and glares at us. "I've needed to use the commode for the last half hour. It's not connected. I can't get into a Porta-Potty. What the hell am I supposed to do?"

"I'll take care of it." Even though a part of me wants to tell him to buzz off because Ruby and I are still talking, I know the reason he agreed to come to Dover is that he knew he could depend on us for help.

"I'll get it, Glad," Ruby volunteers. "You take care of ours and I'll see to Mama and Daddy's."

That works for me. It gives her something else to think about besides the dead man, whoever he is, and Ann. Not that I think she should forget about the dead man. At this stage, I agree with her. Something *is* wrong. But I don't know what more she can do about it. Without some kind of physical proof, there isn't a case against Phil. Or Bill.

I mull it over while I connect the water and sewer to the RV. The connection seems fine, but the only way to test it is to flush the toilet. Thinking about Bill and Phil, I forget about the damn cat in the bedroom. But he doesn't forget about me.

I'm fine until I flush the toilet and then start to walk out of the bathroom. There's a step down from the bathroom to the bedroom. Without looking down, I start to walk out. The black menace formerly known as Malibu is stretched across the doorway. I manage to step over him, but that isn't good enough. The cat screeches and digs his claws into my leg. In turn, I trip and fall, managing to be sprawled on the blue carpet when Ruby finds me.

"All done." She stares down at me. "What are you doing down there?"

"I tripped over the cat. Why is it here, anyway? I thought it was too traumatized to stay by itself and left with your mother."

"Mama forgot that Daddy is allergic to cats. She took him home, but she had to bring him back. I was coming to check on him." She scans the room and sees Malibu limping toward her. "Oh Glad, he's hurt! You must've stepped on him. I hope you didn't break his paw."

"I didn't step on him. I stepped *over* him, and he clawed me. Ruby, that cat is going to have to go. The RV isn't big enough for both of us." I wish I'd thought to tell her I'm allergic to cats. Zeke is smarter than me sometimes—especially when it comes to knowing what the women in his family are going to do.

Ruby picks up Malibu and cradles him in her arms, petting him and fussing over him. I'm still on the floor, without so much as an offer of a hand to help me up.

I might as well get over it. She takes the cat in the other room and I get up on my own, sorely tempted to limp a little. I'm sure I must deserve some sympathy by now, but I know she won't fall for it. She probably won't even notice.

"I've got it!" she says before I can sit down. "We can take Malibu to 'Phil' and see how he reacts."

"The cat or the man?"

"The cat. Cats have a special way of recognizing the people in their lives. If Malibu acts like he knows him, it could be a way of getting to him."

"The cat or the man?"

32

"The man. 'Phil' might even be pining for Malibu, since he's really Bill. They had a good relationship. I can't believe he doesn't miss him, even if he is a killer."

"Or Malibu was the one who clawed up his face in the first place and Bill was searching for some good-looking, soft-hearted blond to leave him with." I smile at her from where I'm sitting, making sure I check the chair for furry pests before I sit down.

"You didn't see them together. They were inseparable. You could tell they were soul mates." She sighs and pets the cat while he's standing on the counter eating tuna.

"Okay, let's try it."

"You mean it?"

"Sure. This whole thing is pretty screwy anyway. What have we got to lose?"

She runs over and hugs me. I tug her down into my lap and kiss her, forgetting for a moment about the cat, the dead guy, and even the race. She has that effect on me. When she's around, it's like we're the only two people in the world.

The cat doesn't see it that way. Don't ask me how he manages to do it, but somehow he jumps from the counter to my shoulders, where he digs as many claws as he has through my shirt and into my skin.

I shoot up from the chair, yelling, and Ruby tumbles to the floor. The cat screeches and runs under the sofa.

"Oh, we scared him!" She crawls to the edge of the sofa and tries to entice the little monster out from under there.

"*We* scared *him*?" I don't think I even want to know what convoluted thought process brought her to that understanding of the situation. But it occurs to me that confronting "Phil" might be the best way to get rid of the beast, short of putting him in a Porta-Potty for some unsuspecting visitor to find. John lives on the road like we do and probably wouldn't be able to handle the cat either—not that I'd wish it on him.

"There you go." She helps the cat out from under the sofa. "It's okay. Glad didn't mean to scare you. Tell him you're sorry."

I look up at her. Is she talking to *me*?

"Glad, if you don't tell Malibu you're sorry, he'll never learn to trust you. I had a pet chicken once. He had the same problem. He was always underfoot. Eventually, he grew to trust us and he knew we wouldn't hurt him. After that, he quit pecking people's hands and getting caught in Betsy's hair."

"That's really touching, sweetie. But if you think I'm giving that little monster a chance to scratch me again, you're crazy. What happened to the chicken?"

"Daddy killed it and we ate it."

I wait for the punch line. There isn't one. "I'm sorry."

"It's okay. That's what happens to chickens."

Some demon imp takes hold of me. I'm almost laughing, but I manage to keep a straight face. "I bet it was a lot easier for Zeke to get him out to the chopping block."

Ruby looks up at me and clutches Malibu tightly to her. "Don't even think about it! A chicken is different. Let's take Malibu to the casino and see how he reacts to 'Phil.'"

I don't argue with that. Either way, I come home with one less cat. Even if "Phil" denies he's Bill, I can still give him the cat. I'm sure he'll want his brother's beloved pet.

After Ruby tidies up and puts on more lipstick, we head out for the casino. The beast and I stared at each other in the living room the whole time she was getting ready. He knows I want to get rid of him. I know he wants to scratch out my eyes. At least we have an understanding.

We turn on the air conditioning before we leave. It's going to be a scorcher. No sign of clouds in the bright blue sky. A PA system is announcing all the events coming up for the race. There's truck practice and qualifying for the Busch series this afternoon, as well as a spotter meeting. That's something I've always wanted to do. Standing up at the top of the grandstand, watching the race and calling it as I see it. Sounds like fun to me.

Large trucks airbrushed with drivers' names, numbers, and cars are lined up to get inside and hit the garage. It will take as much time as the mechanics have right up to the race to set up and fine-tune the cars. Drivers will walk around and talk to the fans, have lunch with sponsors, and have thousands of photos taken. But the real work isn't seen by the fans. The drivers are pretty faces, but the cars are the real show.

"Look! There's Bobby's car!" Ruby points to the three Hamilton Team trucks in line. The painting of Bobby's face on the side of the truck is larger than my whole body. He's staring out at the hot-dog-eating crowd.

"Hey, Ruby!" Junior hails her after leaving a crowd of fans who are still watching him and waving. "I thought I'd see you here. Zeke and Louise with you?"

"Yeah, we finally convinced Daddy to get out of the house. He couldn't stand to miss Bobby driving in the 400."

"I'm glad to hear it." He looks at me, nods, and puts out his hand. "Glad, good to see you again."

"Earnhardt." I perform the same ritual. "Good to see you too."

Like Ruby said, Junior isn't the only driver she grew up with. He's just the only one I have a problem with. Not that he's ever acted like he was interested in her. They're always like brother and sister. I don't know what it is. Maybe it has something to do with a rumor I heard about them having dated.

"Is that your cat?" He puts his hand on the beast.

"His name is Malibu." She holds the cat up a little so Junior can see him. "Isn't he gorgeous?"

I realize this might be another way to get rid of the animal. When Junior tries to pet him, as his hand is lowering to do at this moment, the beast is going to scratch him. That might be enough to make Ruby give him up. I don't matter as much. I'm only her husband, not her high school sweetheart who happens to be a famous driver. I wait for it almost breathlessly.

But it doesn't happen.

Malibu looks up, yawns, and meows a little as Junior pets him. He even rolls over to let him pet his stomach. What's up with that?

Junior and Ruby exclaim over how beautiful the cat's green eyes are and how soft his black fur is. It makes the many scratches and bites I have on my body burn and itch. When I can't take it any-more, I clear my throat really loud, and they all (including the cat) look up at me.

"That's right," Ruby says. "We're on our way to the casino to try to prove Bill murdered his brother Phil."

"Isn't that Paxton's family?" Junior asks, still petting the cat. "That wouldn't surprise me. There has been bad blood in that family for as long as I've known them."

"Really?" Ruby pushes him for answers. "Is that why John was stuck in Charlotte with no way to get here?"

"I didn't hear anything about that. But I've heard some talk around the track." He shrugs. "I guess he must be your new cause, right? Always the same Ruby. Take care now. I'll see you later."

Ruby (and the cat) hug him, and we walk away. Now I know the cat only hates *me*. All the more reason to get rid of him—I'm the one who has to live in the RV with him.

The casino parking lot is full of buses from senior-citizen homes. I suppose this would be a big draw for an outing. In comparison with racing, I probably wouldn't even look over this way from the track. But to each his own. I know plenty of race fans who run over here after the events at the track are over for the day.

Inside, everything is plush carpet and glittering lights. There are slot machines everywhere. I'm not much of a gambler myself, but there seem to be plenty of people who are. A man in a red jacket approaches us as soon as we walk in and politely tells us we can't bring the cat into the casino.

"This isn't really my cat," Ruby explains, flashing the big smile that always goes a long way in getting her what she wants. "We need to speak with Phil Paxton. This is his brother's cat."

"I'll check that out, ma'am." He nods. "Wait here."

"Do you think he'll let us in?" Ruby strokes the cat.

"I don't know. If you're right and this is really Bill pretending to be Phil, I think he would. On the other hand, if this is Phil and there's nothing strange going on, I don't think he will."

"Don't look now," she whispers. "I must be right."

"Mr. and Mrs. Wycznewski! I'm so glad to see you." Phil (or Bill) welcomes us with open arms. The man is unremarkable. Medium height. Medium build. Thinning brown hair and brown eyes.

I also don't see anything of John in the twins' faces. The younger man is one of the hot-shot, glamorous rookie drivers that Zeke and many of the old-timers love to hate. They say they are too pretty and too willing to get their pictures taken. It's not about the racing for them, according to Ruby's father.

He shakes my hand and turns to Ruby. "What a beautiful cat! We don't normally allow animals, except seeing-eye dogs, into the casino. We spent a lot of money upgrading this place recently. New carpets and slots. You understand."

"We're not actually here to gamble," I tell him.

"We're here about the cat," Ruby finishes. "This is your brother's cat. Here." She pushes Malibu at him and then stands back, waiting for some monumental event that will prove once and for all this man is Bill.

Malibu is startled and scratches Phil, gives a loud howl, and then jumps down to the floor and runs into the casino.

Ruby is completely confused. "I don't understand. Why would Malibu do that? It doesn't make any sense. The two of you had such a good bond. I thought he'd know you."

Phil takes out a handkerchief and holds it to the scratch on his face while he puts his wounded hand to his mouth. "Bill and Malibu had a wonderful relationship. The cat has always hated me."

By this time, the cat is running wild across the top of the slots, jumping from one person to another and knocking one old man with a walker to the floor. Phil signals for his security people to come in and help catch the animal.

I'm happy Malibu hates Phil as much as he hates me, even though it lessens the chances he's going to take the cat off my hands. At least Malibu didn't cozy up to him like he did to Junior and Ruby. Now I know it's not just me.

The security guards are like the Three Stooges. They're knocking over more than the cat is, smashing drinks on the floor and making old women scream as they dive under machines to try to catch him.

Ruby snaps out of her daze and runs to help. Malibu sees her and makes a flying leap from a low-hanging light fixture right into her arms. Probably doesn't put a scratch on her either.

The casino is in chaos, with people trying to get out the front door and security guards nursing scratches and bites. To make matters worse, Ann and her officers come through the door, looking for Phil.

"What's going on in here?" she asks as several old people limp past her.

"It's nothing." Phil is gracious, especially considering the situation. "Mrs. Wycznewski brought my brother's cat in to show me he was all right. We had a little accident after that."

Malibu hisses at Phil and Ruby moves a little farther away. "I thought Malibu might want to be here with Bill—I mean, Phil. I guess I was wrong. I'm sorry."

I watch her hurry out the door with the cat. "She was trying to prove her point," I say to Ann on the side.

"Which was ... ?" Ann asks.

"That Phil is really Bill." I shrug, not apologizing for Ruby. She had her shot.

"Of course he's not," Ann replies. "We've known Bill was a troubled man for some time. Phil did what he could for him. I'm afraid this is a terrible end to a tragic life."

Phil steps in and offers me his hand, the one that isn't scratched. "I'm sorry the two of you got involved in this. Let me give you a few free games. Maybe that will make your wife feel better about all this."

I shake hands with him and can't help wondering what the game really is. I know something is up, even if Ann is too blinded by Phil's position in the community to ask a lot of questions. My gut tells me Ruby is right. The cat may not have recognized him, but that doesn't mean everything is as it should be. "Thanks. Would you like to have the cat to remember your brother?"

He folds the bloody handkerchief and puts it in his pocket. "Not on your life."

FOUR

ANN STOPS US AS we walk through the shiny glass door that leads to the front parking lot. Two men are scrubbing the fountain as a limousine dodges another group of senior citizens. "Glad? What's going on? You're a better cop than this."

"Ruby saw one of these twin brothers before the man on the track died. She gave him a ride in our RV. He looked like he'd been beaten and his clothes were ragged. He left this cat with her. That's what's going on."

Ann glances at Ruby and then pulls me to the side. "This is a high-dollar part of Dover. The Paxtons are *very* influential."

"Does that make them above the law?" I ask, quietly but fiercely.

"Damn it, you know it doesn't. But if Phil says that's his brother over there on the track, it's probably his brother. What possible reason could he have to lie?"

Ruby is about ten feet away, tapping her sandaled foot on the concrete. It won't be more than a minute before she joins us and probably lets the cat jump on me for good measure. "Because Bill has taken Phil's place as head of this fancy casino?"

Ann shakes her head. "You don't have any proof of that."

"I have Ruby. It's only been five years since I was a detective. In my day, witnesses meant something."

"I'm not saying she's lying," she hedges. "I'm saying she's probably mistaken."

A little put out and obviously out of my mind, I stalk back to Ruby, grab the cat from her, and take him to Ann. I don't know if he's too surprised to react or if he's afraid I'm going to kill him, but whatever the reason, he lies still in my arms for once. "Look at the tag, Ann. She's not mistaken about the owner. I still have Bill's clothes in my RV. Maybe you'd like to check them out."

She purses her lips. "I don't think so. We're ruling Bill Paxton's death a suicide. If you want to stay here for the whole race, I think you should keep your mouth shut. Don't confront Phil Paxton again."

"Yes, ma'am. We won't get near him again."

"I'm sorry, Glad. I wish … there's nothing more I can do."

I turn away without saying anything, then give the cat back to Ruby. She keeps up with my long, angry strides. "What was that all about?" she growls. "Another minute of whispering like that and Malibu and I would've *both* been on your back."

"Ann wants to make sure we aren't going to accuse Phil of murdering Bill again. The police are calling it a suicide. Case closed."

"What? How can they do that? Did I not clearly tell them about Bill? Don't they understand what happened?"

"I think they do." I watch a nice blue 1965 Plymouth Barracuda go by. That was my favorite car when I was a kid. I was never lucky enough to have one, but I drooled over many of them in parking lots. "They don't want to act on it."

"That's crazy. Why won't they investigate?"

"Take a look at the casino. It's a multimillion-dollar attraction. You wouldn't want to investigate it on the word of a nobody from another state either. If you're wrong or she can't prove you're right, it could cost her her job."

"But we *can* prove it!"

"How? I thought that was what we tried to do. The cat acted like he didn't know him. Do we have any other evidence?"

She thinks for a minute. "We have Bill's clothes. Maybe they have DNA on them or something. He was bleeding. Maybe there's some blood on his clothes. Wouldn't that work?"

"If we could give the police reasonable suspicion, it might get them a warrant to check Phil's DNA and blood type. But if he's guilty, he could make it harder and fight them."

"But my word doesn't count as reasonable suspicion?" She strokes the cat's fur and he meows as we cross the street.

I put my arm around her shoulders. "Sorry, honey. I'm afraid it doesn't."

"Then what can we do?"

"Enjoy the race?"

She grimaces. "How can I, when this is so wrong?"

"Perhaps I could be of assistance." A tall, gaunt man with an English accent and a black bowler approaches us. He looks like Alan Napier, the man who played Alfred in the old *Batman* TV series. He hands us each a business card. "Forsythe Whitaker, at your service."

I look at his card and back at his face. "Were you listening to our conversation?"

"I'm afraid so. Sometimes a private detective must do what he can to solve his case."

"I'm Ruby Wycznewski." My wife shakes his hand. "Are you from this area?"

"Not originally, Mrs. Wycznewski. But I have lived here long enough to know the lay of the land, so to speak. About thirty years, actually."

"Please, call me Ruby. Are you *really* a private detective?"

"Yes, ma'am. I have been licensed in Delaware for several years. Took it up as something to do upon retirement."

"That's wonderful."

I tug Ruby away from him. "Thanks for your time. I don't think we'll need your services."

"Glad!"

"I believe we can both be of service to one another," Forsythe assures me before I can get away. "You want to rid yourself of that cat. I want to solve the mystery of where ten million dollars disappeared. This may be one and the same."

"Ten million?" Ruby's blue eyes get bigger. "How does that fit in with one of the Paxton brothers being dead?"

"It's a very long story. Perhaps we could find a shady spot and have a bit of lemonade."

"I think we should do that," Ruby says. "Our RV is right over there. I have lemonade in the fridge." She takes his arm and leads him toward our home before I can stop her. It would be a good time for the cat to rise up, screech, and bite him. Of course, the beast lies there and doesn't open his eyes.

"Can I come too?"

They both turn back and look at me. Ruby shakes her head. "Quit being so distrustful and get up here. Forsythe, this is my husband, Glad. He'd like your help too, but he used to be a police detective, so he can't act like he wants it."

"Pleased to meet you, sir." Whitaker tips his hat in my general direction.

This doesn't change my mind about him. Private eyes, even well-mannered English private eyes, are nothing but a pain in the ass. They're always getting in the way, always thinking they know something the police don't. If I had a dollar for every PI who told me he knew the answer to a homicide, I'd be sipping my beer on the Du-Pont bridge during the race.

But it's too late for that. Not only does Ruby take him into the RV, she asks her mother, father, and brother to join us as well. At this point, I'd almost rather spend time with the crazy cat. Once all of the Furrs get going on this, it will be a free-for-all.

I let them sit around the kitchen table and drink lemonade as Ruby explains everything she knows about what happened to Bill (or Phil). Zeke and Louise are horrified by the situation. Bobby takes it in stride. I salute them with my Bud bottle as Whitaker starts his story.

"Five years ago," he says, "there was a bank shipment to the casino in the amount of ten million dollars. The money never made it. Phil and Bill Paxton had recently purchased the casino at that time. The FBI, State Police, and every governmental agency you can imagine investigated. The truck carrying the money was found. But the money has been missing all these years."

Whitaker pauses. I can tell he's told this story many times. He sips his lemonade as his breathless audience waits for him to finish.

Good showmanship, but nothing I can see as related to our problem with the cat—I mean, the dead man.

"As you can imagine, the company that insured the money was extremely put out. They hired many private detectives—some from this area, some not. I was one of those detectives. I followed the case right to the penthouse the brothers shared. Mark my words, they found a way to steal that money."

Malibu is sitting on the cabinet, licking his fur. If he could laugh, I know he'd be joining me. "But you couldn't prove it, right?" I say.

Whitaker looks at me as though I'm an evil schoolboy. "I could not prove my case at that time. But with this new occurrence, I believe there may be light at the end of the tunnel."

"What do you mean, Mr. Whitaker?" Louise asks with bated breath.

"I believe, dear woman, the money has finally got the best of the brothers. I believe Phil murdered Bill for his share."

I slap the arm of the chair where I'm sitting and missing all of the start-up activities associated with the Dover race. "Then that's where you and Ruby part company. Because she believes Bill murdered Phil. She didn't know about the money, but I suppose that would be the missing motive."

Bobby salutes me with his own bottle of beer. "All right! You go, Glad! Where does John come in for his share? Because I'm telling you, that boy needs more than one pair of jeans."

"The younger Paxton doesn't seem to be involved. He was still in school when this happened." Forsythe takes another sip of lemonade. "I would think he would be quite disturbed if he believed his brothers had this hoard of money they refused to share."

"I'd be ticked even if there *wasn't* ten million," Bobby comments. "John told me his brother who owns the casino and hotel does okay for himself. But he doesn't want to share it."

"I think Bill must have killed Phil because he got tired of waiting for his share of the money," Ruby conjectures.

Louise narrows her eyes, looking surprisingly like her daughter. "Exactly! That's why Bill was in such a hurry to get here!"

Ruby jumps up from her seat and hugs her mother. "How terrible is that? And we brought him here. He probably couldn't take the stress anymore, bless his heart. Phil should've shared."

I've heard a load or two of crap in my time. This one is either the best or the worst of the lot. "None of you have any proof. Just because the cat doesn't like the brother that's still alive doesn't prove anything. He doesn't like me either. Whitaker, you can't even make the brothers for the robbery. There's no way any of this leads to a murder conviction."

Louise frowns at me. "Ruby, your husband is so negative. I wouldn't want him to be around if I was sick. He'd probably put me right in the ground."

Bobby laughs and stands to go. "Glad, why don't you come with me before you kill my mama. I'm gonna go watch them work on my car. Are you in?"

I finish my beer and nod. "Yeah, I think so. Let's go, kid. I want to see what's happening on the track."

I give Ruby plenty of time to stop me. She sits at the table with her fellow conspirators, her pert little nose in the air, ignoring me. That's fine. Eventually, she'll see I'm right. If Whitaker had anything, the feds would have checked it out already.

Everyone at the table is silent until Bobby and I step out the door. Immediately, I hear them start talking all at once. Bobby slaps me on the shoulder before he jumps in through the window of his Mustang. "Don't let it get to you. They aren't ignoring you because you don't know what you're talking about. They're ignoring you because you aren't saying what they want to hear."

I must be drunk, because that kind of makes sense to me and it came out of Bobby's mouth. Maybe driving fast is good for him. Maybe there's some Zen thing about it.

I eye the passenger-side window of the Mustang as Bobby guns the engine. No way I'm going to squeeze through that opening. Maybe a hundred years ago, when I was Bobby's age. Time and gravity have a way of putting a man in his place.

I open the door and climb inside. Before I can shut the door, Bobby peels out, leaving the smell of burning rubber behind us. A crowd laughs and applauds as the Mustang races toward the infield gate.

"Watch this." Bobby holds up his pass as he keeps his foot on the gas, passing the security guard with reckless abandon.

This might seem like a bad trait in some ways, but being reckless, driving to the edge, is what racing is all about. Because he's not afraid to push it, Bobby has a good shot at being the next face promoting Pepsi and a hundred other products.

We follow the road to the infield garage area. It's not as big as at Lowe's or Talladega, but Dover has its own charm. There's no camping on the infield, which suits me fine. It will be another eight years or so before I win the draw and a chance to hang around at Lowe's with the drivers and campers in their million-dollar RVs.

After what happened last time I won the pot, I'm not in any hurry to win again.

I look at the track, following the Monster Mile around and under the distinctive DuPont bridge. I've been here out of season for the horse racing they hold here. They build a natural dirt bridge to bring the horses across the track. It's something to see.

Dover is a high-banked concrete track, the only one in the circuit. The surface is grooved and tough on the drivers. They either love it or hate it. Usually it has something to do with whether or not their car can win here.

The track is good for racing, but it's easy for a driver to get caught up in someone else's wreck. I've seen good cars go down this way. It's not a good track for loose handling. The car and the driver have to be tight. Too tight, though, and it doesn't work. It has to be just right.

"Whatcha lookin' at?" Bobby asks. "The real thing is right here. Let me introduce you to our lead mechanic, Floyd Frazier. Floyd, this is my sister's husband, Glad."

Floyd slips a greasy hand my way. "What kinda name is Glad?"

"Polish." I take a rag from Bobby to clean my hand. "What are you running?"

Floyd runs through the specs. "This here is a Dodge Charger, 358-cubic-inch engine with 800 horses that will flat out haul ass. We run an 830-cfm Holley four-barrel carburetor and put Bobby behind the wheel because he knows how to put his foot down and leave it there."

There's a lot of good-natured laughing and talking between Bobby, Floyd, and the other mechanics.

"Sounds good." I can hardly hear myself talk with the engine roaring, but I'm not kidding: it sounds great.

"Glad, this is my crew chief, Lance Maxfield." Bobby grabs another Team Hamilton member sporting a blue jumpsuit with Bobby's biggest sponsor, Cheerwine, emblazoned on it.

"Good to meet you." Maxfield shoves his big hand my way. "We're expecting great things from Bobby this season."

"He's got big shoes to fill," I say. Everyone knows Bobby is Zeke's son. Zeke Furr is a legend in the industry. He never raced much professionally, but he's helped the sport and the drivers a lot.

Maxfield laughs. He's a big, burly man whose hearty slap catches Bobby unaware and almost sends him flying. "Yeah. Bobby can fill them if anybody can. I gotta go. No roughhousing," he warns his driver.

Bobby salutes him. "You got it. I'm as tame as a kitten."

The garage area is starting to come alive as the car haulers make their way to the infield and the pit crews start setting up. The excitement is building as we all wait for the first rounds of practice tomorrow.

Bobby is helping Floyd with the engine. I can see Mark Martin by the number 6 car, off to our right. He looks like a man with car problems. On the other side, I see Ruby's favorite, Jimmie Johnson, and the number 48 car. He's the favorite to win this weekend. He swept here last season, and most people see him doing it again.

Every driver has his favorite track, usually the one he wins on the most. I wouldn't say Dover is Jimmie's favorite track, but he seems to like it pretty well. Of course, Joe isn't here to challenge him, but I'm going to try to enjoy myself anyway. I like David Stremme. He's a young rookie, but I like his style. I might pull for him this race.

No way can I cross over to the dark side and help Ruby cheer for Jimmie.

As I'm checking out the cars around me, trying to decide which crew chief looks satisfied with his car and which doesn't, I notice Phil (or Bill) standing out on the track under the bridge. He's almost exactly where his brother was lying before the boys from the morgue came for him.

He looks up at the bridge on turn three. The bridge doesn't cross over to the infield. It's more like a skybox suite that gets a great view of the race. Phil stares at the bridge for a while, then starts looking down at the track. I figure maybe he's trying to understand what happened to his brother.

Then he gets down on all fours and rubs his hands against the concrete. Clearly, he's looking for something. Did his brother (I give up trying to figure out which one is which) lose something that was recognizable to him? Sometimes that kind of blunt-force trauma can knock rings off fingers and make gold crowns pop off teeth. Anything is possible.

If the crime scene team did its job, there's nothing left for him to find. That's what it looks like. He stands up finally, visually doing another sweep of the concrete he's already searched. I can tell from his face that whatever he's looking for isn't there. There's as much frustration and anger on his features as on the faces of some of the crew chiefs whose cars aren't running right.

He looks up at the bridge again and then makes for the skybox. Obviously, whatever he's looking for could be at wherever the other brother fell from. The skybox is enclosed in glass. No glass on the concrete. It's an easy assumption that the dead brother fell from the top of the bridge. I wonder if the living twin realizes it.

He goes carefully up the stairs to the bridge, looking around himself as though he suspects someone could be watching him. He opens the door with a key he takes from his suit pocket.

I can't see what he's doing in the skybox. The glare from the setting sun is reflected back at me. But in a few minutes, he comes back out, closes the door, and locks it. He looks up at the top of the bridge. He's figured out that the dead guy had to have taken a header from up there. He's a genius.

Will he climb up to search for whatever's missing? There's a tiny ladder leading up to the top, probably for cleaning. He starts up, then changes his mind. This is obviously a job for a lesser being. Or it's something that needs to be done when there are fewer people around.

I'm not sure which, but I have that same feeling in my gut: something is wrong. Maybe the old English PI doesn't know his head from an exhaust pipe, but something is definitely up here.

Not that I didn't believe Ruby, but believing and proving are two different things. I'm wondering if whatever the living twin is looking for would prove what happened to his brother. Whatever is up on the top of the skybox could be the key to the murder, and maybe even the ten-million-dollar robbery.

Another car with problems starts up and dies out. The mechanics around me wince and armchair-diagnose the problem. John gets out of the car and opens the hood. Bobby is busy with Floyd, so I stroll over there to offer my condolences on his brother and the car.

"Thanks." John leans over the engine. "I never thought anything like this would happen to Bill. Phil's another story. I always expected the police to find *him* dead in some alley."

Is that a hint of anger in his voice? "I take it you don't get along with Phil?" I ask.

"You could say that." He looks up at me. "Pass me that ratchet, huh?"

"Sure." I hand him the tool. "He seems a little hard to get to know."

"Say it like it is, Glad. He's a sneaky bastard. I'd be afraid he'd steal the fillings out of my teeth if he got a chance. It was different when he and Bill ran the hotel and casino together. Bill was the kind of guy people did things for just because they liked him."

I can testify to that. He sure had Ruby and Louise eating out of his hand in a short time.

"It all changed after that Brink's business."

"I'm not up with the local gossip. What Brink's business?" I hand John an orange rag.

"They say Bill and Phil hijacked a Brink's truck and got away with millions." He shakes his head. "I don't believe it. If they did, I never saw a penny of it. But that might be because Bill had a breakdown around that time. Maybe he couldn't handle the guilt. I don't know. He dropped out. Moved out in the country somewhere, no phone or much contact with Phil or me."

"But you think Bill knew about the money?"

"Maybe. If there *was* any money. Personally, I think it's all talk. Bill couldn't take working with Phil anymore. He called it quits. A legend was born."

I look at his red Ford Taurus. It's not in the greatest shape. Everyone knows he has financial problems. I suppose he'd rather think his favorite brother would've shared if there were really millions to share. "Think you'll have her ready to race tomorrow?"

53

"You know me." He grins beneath the oily smudges. "I'll get her ready. We'll race and see what happens."

"I'll be looking for you."

"I know you will. You and Ruby have been great to me. Hey!" he says, checking out the car again. "Want to take a drive around the track?"

FIVE

"WHAT DO YOU MEAN, Phil was looking for something?" Ruby demands when I get back from my four laps around the track in John's car.

What hair I have is standing straight up on my head, and there may be bugs on my teeth. What a ride! It never fails to excite me. We only did about 130 miles per hour around the track. I could've gone for 160 and not complained. I won't ever be a NASCAR driver, but I sure as hell feel like one after taking that ride.

I've driven a race car before, since almost every track has a driving experience set up. At Dover, it's the Skip Barber Dodge SRT Thrill Ride. It's the ultimate experience for a fan. You get the real feel of what it's like to be your favorite driver.

I'm afraid my suspicions about Phil looking for something on the track and in the skybox took a back seat to my opportunity to try out the track. Ruby is looking at me like I forgot her birthday. Zeke and Louise are gone. Whitaker too. No sign of the black beast either. I know he must be here someplace.

"Sorry, sweetie, I forgot," I tell Ruby. "He was there looking for something. He started to climb up to the roof of the bridge, but something changed his mind."

"We may still have time." She races toward the bedroom and comes out with a pair of sneakers. "Whatever is up there may be the answer to this whole thing. We have to get up there before him."

Guilt makes me agree. She's probably right anyway. I was hot on Phil's trail until John asked me if I wanted a ride. "That's what I thought too. He probably didn't want people to see him up on top of the bridge. There might be too many questions. But he'll probably only wait until dark."

"Which is coming up quick." She stuffs her feet in the sneakers and ties the laces. "Why are you agreeing with me? I thought you didn't think anything was up with this?"

"I didn't say that. I said the police would ignore us, which they did. I said there was no proof of foul play, which there isn't. Just because something *seems* wrong doesn't make it so."

"But maybe we can attack it from another direction," Ruby says. "We have a motive for Bill to kill Phil. Maybe we can prove it happened."

Which is convoluted thinking, but I'm feeling pretty low right now after forgetting everything for the thrill of the ride. So I agree. "Maybe whatever is up there on the bridge has something to do with Whitaker's theory about the money."

"Exactly." She looks up and smiles at me. It's like a big spear of sunlight stabbing me in the heart. "Ready to go?"

"I'm with you, baby." I pull on my Nemechek ball cap and pick up a flashlight, and the two of us head out the door.

It's not that late yet. Of course, it never is. There's a blaze of lights on the casino next door. People are drifting back and forth between the campground and the slots. A band is playing at the hospitality tent, and a long line of fans are still waiting at the souvenir trailer. No one will be asleep before midnight. Most of the nighttime activities will go on until dawn.

There are lights on the outside of the grandstands, but everyone is too busy partying in the campground to notice when we sneak through the gate again. There are lights on the infield as well, where the teams are still working on their cars for practice tomorrow. But again, they're too preoccupied to see us.

The bridge is hidden in shadows. Chances are I can get up there without anyone paying any attention. We hurry to the stairs going up to the seating area. The tiny ladder Paxton shied away from looks even smaller in the twilight.

"Do you think it's safe?" Ruby stares up there.

"I guess so. Someone probably has to go up there all the time and pressure-wash it or something. I'll go."

"How will you know what you're looking for?" She steps away from the ladder.

I can't help but notice she isn't arguing with me for the chance to go on the roof of the bridge. "I'll pick up anything that looks like it doesn't belong up there."

"Be careful." She hugs me and kisses me like this may be my last moment on earth.

"Easy, honey. I don't plan to check out yet. There are too many payments left on the RV."

"You mean we don't have life insurance to pay for that?" she hisses as I walk by her. "I don't have your resources, you know. I'd have to go back to work at a salon."

"Ruby, this isn't the time to worry about it."

"When would be a good time? If a big wind comes up and blows you off the bridge, it will be too late. You'll be down there on the concrete like Phil."

I start up the ladder past the stairs. "You're not making this any easier. A little encouragement would go a long way."

"Just be careful," she whispers. "We can talk about your life insurance when you get down. Don't you dare fall."

The steel ladder is slippery with dew. I find some footholds on the bridge, but it's hard to use the flashlight. I don't want Ruby up here, so I put the flashlight between my teeth and shine it on top of the bridge as best I can.

"Hurry, Glad. I think I hear security guards coming this way."

I can't answer, but I make a grunting noise I hope will be enough to keep her on the ground. I look off the side of the bridge. The concrete track looks like it's a long way down in the dim light.

It hasn't been that long since Phil (or Bill) was lying down there, staring up at the sky. The speedway was lucky the fall was written up as a suicide. A murder victim on the track would have shut down the race.

Or maybe it wasn't luck. Ann couldn't have made it any clearer to me that she's in the owner's pocket. I don't think there was a serious attempt to investigate the incident. How long was the crime scene team here? Usually, a preliminary takes hours.

I'm thinking all of this to distract myself from looking down and realizing what a fool I am to be up here in the first place. I don't see anything on top of the bridge. Maybe Paxton already came up here.

To make matters worse, the Dover curse starts working a little early. A light rain starts falling. Nothing heavy, kind of like the mist tents they use to help people cool off, but it's enough to make precarious footing worse. My tennis shoes weren't meant for holding on to wet metal.

"Glad, are you still up there?"

I'm really happy I can't answer her with the flashlight in my mouth. Where else would I be? Surely not at home watching TV and drinking a beer. Why would I do that when I can do this?

I'm about to pack it in and edge back to the ladder and down when something catches the light. It's small, and at first I'm not sure if it's part of the bridge. I can barely reach it and still hold on to the side. I stretch as far as I can and put my fingers on it. It's cold, metallic. I close my hand around it and drop the flashlight. The long beam falls silently until the flashlight hits the concrete. Then it crashes loudly and the light goes dim.

Lucky for us, someone starts revving an engine and the sound of the crashing flashlight is lost in the din. I hold whatever I found and suddenly can't move.

"Glad, get down here before you kill yourself instead of killing that poor flashlight. I don't care if Bill or Phil was murdered if it means losing you. Please come down, honey."

I know I can't stay up here, splayed on top of the Monster Bridge for everyone to find tomorrow morning. I can't call for help and I don't want Ruby to save me. I have to push myself back off of the bridge. It's not that far. I can do it.

Slowly (it feels like inches at a time), I slide back across the wet metal, not attempting to stand. The rain starts coming down full force, and I'm soaked in a few seconds. All I need is some lightning and I'll be like a big, Polish lightning rod.

And don't you know, that's what happens. The rain is pelting down. The wind picks up and starts pushing at the bridge. I can hear the pit crews making fast time to get into the garages. Lightning flashes in the dark sky around me, and thunder shakes the bridge.

I'm close to the ladder now. I can feel it with my one foot dangling off the edge of the metal. I can also feel Ruby's hand (I hope it's Ruby's hand) guiding my foot to the first rung. I push one more time and both feet are on the ladder. Right now, I don't care who else is up here. I'm going down.

It's Ruby, of course. Before I can get all the way off the bridge, she's hugging me and kissing me. "I thought you were a goner for sure. Don't ever do something stupid like this again."

Because I don't mind the hugging and kissing, though I wish she'd wait until we were both on the ground, I don't remind her this was *her* idea. I know I told her about the situation, but the only reason I'm up here is because I knew she'd go if I didn't. "Don't worry, baby, we're too hooked up for that kind of thing to kill me."

We both climb down the stairs, and the feeling of solid ground makes me giddy. Ruby is pressed against me like a wet towel. I can live with that. She can't get too close.

"Did you find anything?" she asks after she realizes we're safe.

"I did." I hold out whatever it is so one of the track lights shines on it. "I think it might be a key."

"Hold it right there!" The sound of footsteps running up the grandstand is followed by flashlight beams and several security guards. "What were you doing out there?"

"We got lost." Ruby pushes herself in front of me like a mother tiger protecting her cub. In the light of the flashlights, I can see what the other men see through her wet T-shirt. They're smiling. I'm not.

I strip off my T-shirt and wrap it around her, then put my arms around that. "Is there some law that says fans can't be in the grandstands at night?" Lightning flashes behind me, and thunder rumbles. "During a thunderstorm?"

"It's against the rules," one faceless man explains. "You can be thrown off of speedway property for this."

"You'd do that to newlyweds who only wanted to celebrate their first time together on the track?" Ruby's voice is beguiling and seductive. I'm happy I can't see her face. This is embarrassing enough as it is. She shouldn't have to lie for us.

One of the men answers a call on a radio. I can't see him with the flashlight beams shining in my face. Everyone stands still while the rain beats against us. The man with the radio nods and answers, "Yes, sir."

I don't need him to tell me, but he's going to anyway. "You're coming with us. This looks bad, so you better just keep your mouths shut."

"You got some cement overshoes?" I wise off. "Maybe you could throw us in the fountain."

I know this probably undid all of Ruby's guile, but I don't care. I'm tired, hungry, wet, and getting angry. Bring it on.

"Come with us," the lead security man says. "Mr. Paxton will deal with you."

Ruby and I walk between the group of seven or eight men. By this time, we're completely soaked. It's not Daytona, so it's chilly being out here.

I know we were someplace we weren't supposed to be, but I'll be damned if I'm going to act like a whipped puppy about it. They can let us go or call the police as far as I'm concerned. I'm not going through theatrics for a misdemeanor trespassing charge.

The shiny piece of metal I got from the roof of the bridge is burning a hole in my pocket. I'm pretty sure it's a key. No way of knowing what it's for. Maybe there really is ten million in a safe-deposit box or something. In that case, these security bozos were probably about to look for it themselves.

Not surprisingly, they escort us into the hotel and up an elevator to the top floor. A luxurious penthouse suite with way too many mirrors and gold cupids for my taste opens up before us.

Ruby leans close. "What a place."

I hope she means that in a bad way. I couldn't live in a place like this. Next thing you know I'd be wearing old brocade smoking jackets and slippers all the time. The idea of it makes me shudder.

Paxton is waiting for us in the heart of the suite, a huge room with white and gold furniture and cabinets full of old dishes. He's not wearing a smoking jacket, but I can tell he recently took one off. "I'm so sorry about this mix-up. You're both soaked. You must be freezing." He looks at the lead security guy. "Show our guests to a room where they can dry off."

The security guy nods and grunts. I'm sure he'd rather kick my face in. But he takes us to another room, almost as big as the one we leave, and shuts the door with him and the goon squad on the other side.

Ruby doesn't waste any time. She rushes to the big windows that overlook the casino and racetrack. "If we can get one of these open, we can make a rope out of the sheets and climb down to the street."

I have to laugh at the idea. "What do you think they're going to do, sweetie? Shoot us and dump us in the river?"

She shivers and takes off my wet shirt. "We're talking ten million dollars here, Glad. Anything is possible."

I'm afraid looking at her in her wet T-shirt and shorts is making me think of other things besides ten million dollars or the key in my pocket. I don't suppose they'd give us a few minutes of privacy. No doubt Paxton wants to know if we found anything on the bridge. Too bad. Just the sight of my sexy wife is enough to get me revved up.

"Ruby." I slide my arms around her and kiss the side of her neck. "We might be able to fool around for a few minutes before they get back."

She looks at me like I've lost my mind. "Glad, get real. We're about to be killed. I don't mind the idea of dying while we're making love, but I'm opposed to other people watching and then shooting us. We've got to get out of here."

Her response isn't as enthusiastic as I'd like. But I'm not jumping out a window with a sheet tied around my waist. "Okay. That's fine. I really don't think you have anything to worry about." I look around the room. It's obviously a guest room. No personal mementos or anything marking it as belonging to any one person. There are two long, heavy, white terry bathrobes on the bed. They look like they've been laid out for visitors.

"I know you aren't thinking about putting one of those on, are you?" She follows my line of sight.

"At least they're dry." I pick one up and hand it to her. "If I were you, I'd put one on too. I know you don't want to go out there and talk to Phil or Bill looking like *that*."

She gives a little shriek and runs into the bathroom. I've finally managed to distract her from jumping out the window. "Why didn't you tell me? I look like a raccoon, and my hair is ruined."

"I was thinking more about your shirt, sweetie."

"Why? You can't see anything more than you can during a wet T-shirt contest," she argues from the bathroom over the sound of a hair dryer. I don't know how she managed to locate the appliance so quickly.

"Whatever." I sit down on the bed after putting on the heavy robe. "These are nice, huh? I bet they're expensive." The robes have the hotel insignia on the pockets, like the suit coats the goon squad is wearing.

"They want to buy us, Glad," she yells back. "I'm not for sale. Especially for the price of one of these robes."

She comes out of the bathroom with a clean face and a new hairdo. Ruby is fussy about her hair and makeup. I guess it comes from being a stylist.

"You look great, honey."

"Thanks." She sits down beside me on the bed. "So what did you find?"

"This." I pull the key out of my pocket and show it to her. It's too big to be a safe-deposit-box key. "It looks like a locker key."

Ruby picks it up and looks at it. "How are we going to know if this is what he was looking for?"

"I don't know. Unless we show it to him, I don't know how we'll find out."

"Well, that's not going to happen." The key disappears into the neckline of the white robe.

I move one side of her robe and smile. "I hope you have something on under there, or the key is going to slide down to the floor."

She smiles back. "Don't worry about it. I know how to keep it where I want it."

I move the side of the robe a little more. "Come on, baby. Show me where you put it."

"No. Go away. We're about to die and all you can think about is looking at my breasts." She slaps playfully at my hand.

"I can't think of anything else I'd rather see before I die." I pursue my objective as Ruby giggles and tries to fend me off.

But the door opens after a discreet knock, and the head security goon tells us Phil is waiting with drinks by the fireplace. I'd like to tell him what he can do with his drinks and his cabinets of old dishes, but I suppose the only way we're going to get out of here is to confront him.

"Later." Ruby giggles again and kisses me.

"You bet." I follow behind her as we walk out of the room. The only thing better than the view in front of Ruby is the view behind her.

"I see you dried off and found some robes." Paxton is standing next to the white and gold fireplace with a brandy snifter in one hand. He is indeed wearing a red velvet smoking jacket now.

It's all I can do not to laugh. I guess a guy like me, who lives in an RV and hoards old T-shirts, probably seems like a backwoodsman to him. "This is all real nice, Phil. But what do you want?"

"Please have a drink," he answers. "I have brandy or whatever you'd like to have."

"I'd like a cup of coffee," Ruby says. "Plenty of sugar and milk if you have it."

I glance at her, wondering why she's sitting down and drinking coffee with this man, who she thinks is a killer. She was just about to jump out of a window to get away from him. She looks back at me and mouths something (I don't get it), then shrugs. I have no idea what she's trying to get across.

"Glad?" Paxton says. "Would you like some brandy?"

"No, thanks. I'll take coffee too. Black, no sugar."

A slightly built young man in a plain black suit rushes to get our coffee from a silver urn on a table near the wall. We all sit down together like old friends. I wish I had a beer.

"So you two were out on the track." Paxton comes right to the point. "No one is supposed to be out there without special clearance."

"Which I assume your security men had?" I don't plan to play around with this either. "Strange they were out there, since they aren't speedway security. I thought we'd be coming to see Denis McGlynn, the track security chief."

"I suppose normally Denis's manager would handle this problem," Paxton admits. "But I have a special reason for bringing you here."

"What's that?" Ruby tastes her coffee and shudders. Probably not enough sugar for her. My wife has a sweet tooth.

"I'm looking for something my brother may have dropped before he died. It's something important to me. A family heirloom, so to speak."

He waits for us to confess we found something. He can wait a while longer.

"An heirloom?" I ask. "Did your brother die with it?"

"I'm not sure. I think it may have been on him."

"Wouldn't it have been better to send people out to look for it during the day instead of at night?"

"Practice is tomorrow, and the fans will be all over the area." He waves his hand dismissively. "I thought it might be lost if I waited."

"What makes you think we have it?"

"Because one of my men saw you up on the bridge. I realize you probably didn't know my brother may have dropped the heirloom before he died. I want you to understand how important it is for me to find it. I'll pay handsomely for it."

Ruby shoots to her feet. "Heirloom? Let's call it what it is. Your key to the stolen ten million dollars."

SIX

SILENCE FOLLOWS RUBY'S OUTBURST. Even the fake fire in the fireplace is quiet. The young man in the black suit is gone, but I don't think we're alone with Paxton. Somewhere in the shadows there are bound to be a few of the guys who brought us here.

I hope this isn't about to get ugly. I wish Ruby had stuck to the plan, or at least what *seemed* to be the plan. She sat down, had coffee. I thought we were going to BS our way through this. Now I don't know what happens next.

I'm not fool enough to think I can fight off all these security guys. I hope that's not going to be a requirement to get both of us out of here.

Paxton laughs. Kind of one of those surprised, nervous laughs. "Don't tell me you believe that urban myth about the missing millions. People have been looking for that money for years. Why would it suddenly appear now? And what would my brother's death have to do with it?"

Ruby starts pacing. Not a good sign. It means she's thinking. "Maybe you've kept it hidden all these years. Maybe Phil stole it from you."

"I *am* Phil. How could I steal it from myself?"

"I know you're Bill," she responds. "Even though the cat didn't like you."

"So that's what this is all about." He sounds relieved. "You want me to take my brother's cat. That's fine. Bring him up here and I'll find a home for him."

"It's not only about the cat," Ruby says, even as I get ready to go get the cat and bring him up here. "I think it's something more. I think you murdered your brother."

"That's ridiculous. Why would I kill Bill?"

"You didn't. You killed Phil."

Phil (or Bill), totally missing the logic behind Ruby's allegations, looks to me for help. "What is she talking about? I don't understand what's going on."

I shrug, not planning on helping him. "My wife thinks something is wrong. She hasn't quite figured out what it is yet, but she will."

I can tell he's angry. His stance changes, and his hands tighten into fists. I'm on guard as he turns away to face the fake fire. "I think you'd better go."

I get to my feet. "That works for me. I'll bring the cat up to you."

"Fine."

I grab Ruby's arm before he changes his mind and say, "Thanks for listening. Sorry about your brother."

"We can't leave," Ruby argues as we head for the door. "We have to get to the bottom of this."

"I don't think accusing him of killing his brother is going to make him confess." I have one hand on the doorknob.

"One more thing," Paxton calls out. "If you found something up there on the bridge, I expect it to be returned with the cat. I hope that's clear."

"Crystal." I nudge Ruby through the open doorway.

"We can't give him anything," she says. "He's a killer. He'll probably kill the cat."

"We're not giving him anything. We'll work it out." I slam the door closed behind us and hurry her through the hall. "Let's just get the hell out of here, huh? We can worry about the details later."

In the elevator, knowing there are cameras everywhere, I shake my head when she starts to speak. "This isn't the place, sweetie. We'll talk when we get home."

The hotel lobby is quiet, but the two front desk clerks watch us leave (probably wondering why we're wearing these robes). I don't look around or give Ruby a chance to look around. I push us both through the lobby and out into the night.

The rain has stopped, and there are plenty of people out looking for a party. Music is still coming from somewhere, even though the band in the hospitality tent is gone. I've heard that speedway management plans to make some changes so there's more to do, more fan-friendly. I think it's a good idea.

"Ruby! Glad!" Our friends June and Andy Anderson turn around and greet us after knocking on our front door. "We were wondering where you'd gone off to. They're having a barbecue a few doors down. It's free. Wanna come?"

"Hey, Andy," Ruby says as she hugs June. "Not tonight. Thanks anyway."

"What's wrong, honey?" June asks. "I love those robes. How did you get them?"

"It's a long story." I sure don't want to explain it right now. "But Ruby's right. We've had a rough night. We'll see you tomorrow."

"Practice!" Andy reminds me. "I see Bobby's here. Wish him luck for us."

For once, I'm happy to see my old friends wander back toward their RV. I hope we can sneak inside before anyone else sees us.

But Forsythe Whitaker catches us as we reach the door. "I looked for you everywhere. I saw the security guards take you in. Is everything all right?"

I really don't like this man. I wish he'd leave us alone. I know Ruby would say my feelings are left over from the job, but I don't think that's it. It's something personal about him that I don't trust.

"It was terrible," Ruby starts to explain.

"And we'll fill you in tomorrow." I open the RV door and propel both of us inside, closing the door in Whitaker's face.

"That wasn't nice. He's just trying to help," Ruby tells me. "Oh, Glad!"

I turn around to find our home has been vandalized. Cabinets and drawers have been emptied, cushions and pillows strewn everywhere. In the bedroom, our clothes have all been thrown around. It's like the aftermath of a hurricane.

Ruby shakes her head as she walks through the rooms. "They even killed my air fern. The only plant I didn't kill. I can't believe it."

On a hunch, I ask her, "Where did you put Bill's clothes?"

"In the bathtub. Why?"

I check out the bathroom, and the bathtub is empty. I slap the side of the door as I realize we should have bagged them and put them somewhere safe. Someone else thought of the idea that who-ever Ruby picked up left DNA evidence behind.

"Where's Malibu?" Ruby starts through the RV, calling the cat.

I know we aren't lucky enough to have had the beast stolen as well. Sure enough, he emerges from the closet, meowing and call-ing back to Ruby.

"Oh, poor baby." She picks him up and cuddles him close. She looks at me, and her blue eyes get big. "Glad, we better check on Mama and Daddy. Someone might have gone after them because they were with us."

"I'll do it," I volunteer. "Don't touch anything. I'm calling the police."

I check on Ruby's parents next door. They're fine—too busy watching an old spaghetti Western with Clint Eastwood to be aware of anything else. I tell them about someone breaking into our RV, and Zeke whips out the pistol he keeps in his wheelchair. "Let's go find 'em, boy. This is America. We don't put up with no trash vio-lating our property."

It's not the response I'm looking for, though I should've ex-pected it. "It's okay, Zeke. I called the police. Thanks anyway."

He nods. "That's fine. But if you need an extra hand, just let me know."

By the time I go back to my RV, Ruby is entertaining Dover's finest with coffee and cookies. The two young officers are looking at Ruby more than the report they're filling out.

"Good evening, officers." I slide into the kitchen, and they hast-ily start working again.

"Where were you when this occurred, Mrs. Wycznewski?" the one with the pen asks her.

"She was with me," I answer for her. "Where we were has very little bearing on what happened here. Maybe you should bring in a crime scene team to look the place over."

His smile fades. "Is there anything missing? I see you still have your microwave, DVD player, TV, and police scanner. Seems like someone would have taken those things, don't you think?"

"Are you saying you think we messed the place up for the fun of it?" I'm growling now. I've had about enough for one night.

"Oh, for goodness' sake!" Ruby quiets the discussion. "We were at the hotel for a while. When we came back, the place looked like this."

There's a knock on the door. I don't know who it is, but they might as well join the party, I think as I go to answer it. Ann is on the other side. She's still dressed like she was this afternoon, so I know she hasn't been home yet. Even a suicide verdict is a difficult proposition.

She nods to the officers, who stand up when they see her. "You two can go. I'll take care of this."

The officers make a quick retreat, one of them stashing an extra chocolate-chip cookie in his pocket before he leaves. Ruby offers Ann a cup of coffee, and we sit down at the breakfast bar.

"I didn't expect a homicide detective to be slumming on a breaking-and-entering call." I sip my coffee and take a chocolate-chip cookie.

Ann sighs. "What's going on, Glad? I got a call from Phil Paxton a few minutes ago. He says you took something from him. Is that true?"

Ruby slams the coffeepot down. I wince as I imagine shards of glass spraying around the kitchen. Miraculously, the pot stays together.

"Let me handle this," I tell her. Ruby gives me her Southern Death Ray look, which can kill at less than thirty paces. She stalks out of the kitchen and slams the bedroom door, probably consoling herself with the evil cat. I'll be lucky if I don't sleep in the truck tonight.

I explain the whole thing to Ann again, this time including watching Paxton on the track, being marched up to his hotel suite, and coming back to find our RV trashed and Bill's clothes gone.

I leave out the information about the key we found. I know that's rotten. How would I feel if I were investigating a crime and someone left something that important out? And maybe if she *were* investigating, I'd tell her about it. Lord knows *I* don't want to solve whatever is going on between these brothers.

She looks at me blankly, then sips her coffee. "None of that makes any sense."

"Come on, Ann! Where are those twenty years of instincts? Something is wrong here. I know you have to feel it."

"You know, you never called me. You said you would when we left Quantico. Did you forget about me and marry this pretty baby instead?"

I'm still in outrage mode, and I'm having trouble shifting gears. I've been patronized, pushed around, and violated tonight, and she wants to talk about a two-week relationship we had twenty years ago? I'm afraid I can't make that turn as fast as she can.

"Never mind." She shakes her head. "Don't answer that."

Now I'm *really* confused. I don't know if I should talk about what happened between us or if I should go on about this Phil/Bill thing.

Ann saves me. "Phil Paxton is Phil Paxton, not his brother. He's a big chief around here, Glad. He gives to every charity in the state and bought bulletproof vests for every officer in Dover. Everyone knows him. Everyone likes him. No one is going to buy him hurting his brother or being part of any cover-up." She glances around the RV. "They sure won't believe he broke into your home."

I'm really happy I didn't tell her about the key. "What about the missing clothes? Someone broke in here and, as your competent officer pointed out, didn't steal anything of value. But Bill's clothes are gone."

"I don't know what else to say." She gets up from her stool at the bar. "Stay away from Paxton. If you have something of his, I'll take it with me right now."

She holds her hand out, palm up. I'm thinking, *Not on my grandmother's Rambler.* If I give her the key, it will disappear like Bill's clothes. "I don't have anything of his. I tried to tell him that at the hotel. Whatever he was looking for out there must be gone."

"It better be. Don't make me have a detective come out and talk to you, Glad. This time has been a professional courtesy. Next time someone will be here in an official capacity." She backtracks again and leans forward for a quick kiss.

It's just a peck on the lips, but I'm hoping Ruby isn't peeking around the bedroom door. "You're making a mistake, Ann. You know I wouldn't go through all this if there wasn't something to it."

"Goodbye, Glad. I don't want to see you again." She smiles slyly. "Unless you decide to take on someone more like you."

75

I don't have an answer for that. I rush to look at my mouth in the chrome on the microwave the instant she steps out the door. I'm not sure if she was wearing lipstick. I don't want Ruby to find out for me.

There's nothing on my mouth except cookie crumbs. I only have a second to find that out before Ruby comes back out of the bedroom. "All right! I'm not going to be sent to my room like a little girl! If you two can be in here talking, or whatever you're doing, so can I!"

"She's gone." I walk toward Ruby and try to put my arm around her. "Let me explain."

"Like that's going to happen." She turns her back on me and starts straightening the living room.

"Honey, I haven't seen this woman for twenty years. She said herself I never called her."

"So you were talking about old times?" She fluffs up a pillow with unnecessary violence and throws it across the room.

"No." I'm not sure how to answer this. "Yes. Well, *she* was, anyway. It was a long time ago. I got married a short time later. I forgot about her. It was nothing serious."

"But *she* remembers. Just like a man. Totally forget the person you bonded with for two weeks. Put it out of your mind and go on with your life."

She doesn't make it sound like a good thing. I was thinking it was good I forgot Ann, at least in Ruby's book. "I thought she did the same thing. I didn't realize she took it that seriously."

She looks up, blond curls flying. Her wonderful, generous, forgiving blue eyes scan my face, staying briefly on my lips. For one terrible moment, I'm afraid I missed some lipstick Ann left behind. I don't want to try to talk my way out of *that*, but my mind starts coming up with a thousand excuses for what happened. None of them are true. Who'd believe the truth?

She finally gives in. "Let's forget about it." I take the first deep breath since she came out of the bedroom. "What did she say about Bill and Phil? Did you tell her about the key?"

I'm really confused by now. I hope my answer is what it's supposed to be. "No. I didn't tell her about the key."

With a whoop of surprise and happiness, she rushes into the kitchen and jumps on me, wrapping her legs around my waist. "Baby, you are the best!"

With her mouth and other parts of her impressive anatomy pressed against mine, I'm inclined to agree with her. At least I'm not confused anymore. This is where I belong.

Too bad the moment is over so quickly. Ruby stares at me and says, "We have to figure out what that key is for."

I start walking toward the bedroom with her still snuggled up against me. "Not tonight, sweetie. I think we have to throw everything on the floor and go to bed."

She kisses the side of my neck and whispers, "Okay. Let's do that first."

Friday morning, NASCAR Nextel Cup Series practice day, dawns bright and clear. I step out in my khaki shorts, put up the awning on the RV, and take out the grill. By the time I have Ruby's wind chimes hung and the chairs and table in place, the grill is ready to go.

I feel pretty good about things, especially last night. Not the part with Phil and Bill, the part with me and Ruby. Despite the cat scratches on my ass, things went really well, at least after I closed the black beast in the closet. I'm ready to face a new day with a large slab of my famous grilled bacon and a few dozen of Ruby's flapjacks.

Some friends of ours who we see at several races across the country stop by to sit and chat. Bart Macklin is from Salt Lake City, and Don Jenkins is from Aurora, Illinois. They each have their favorite drivers and their cars inscribed on their coffee mugs.

Bart pulls for Kurt Busch, and Don pulls for Jeff Gordon. Don's whole RV is a shrine to Gordon, including a piece of Gordon's number 24 car from a race where it wrecked. I couldn't believe it when Don was lucky enough to sneak down and get it from the track that day. No telling what it would be worth on eBay. I was excited for him, even though Gordon doesn't mean anything to me. The man was hot at one time, but he's obviously running scared now. A driver has to be on the edge to be successful. He has to like to go fast and not be afraid. The older the driver gets, the more races he wins and the less likely he is to take chances. It's the way it goes.

Ruby joins us with a pot of coffee and a mound of flapjacks. Zeke and Louise holler for us (as they call it), then come over for breakfast.

This is the way life is meant to be. Sitting around a table with your friends and family in the sunshine, the smell of high-test gasoline sprinkled on the breeze. I could sit here forever if Joe would drive by at about 180 miles per hour. Wow, what a thought!

"The grandstands are open," Don says around a mouthful of bacon. "I thought we'd head over that way. The Busch Series practice starts at nine."

"Cup Series at ten," Bart adds.

"Sounds good to me." I smile at Ruby, and she frowns back at me.

"Remember the other thing we have to do, honey?"

I really don't. What other thing? I'm not going to admit to this forgetfulness, though. I don't want Ruby to think this is some kind of senior moment. "Oh yeah. Maybe that won't take so long. We could meet Don and Bart over there."

She smiles. It's the right answer. "That could work. We'll see."

Don and Bart each have another cup of coffee and then leave, Zeke and Louise with them. Ruby and I clean up (most of it is paper and goes in the trash) while I try to remember what we're supposed to do this morning.

"I've got the key." She pats the pocket of her jean shorts. "The sooner we find out what it goes to, the better. Your little girlfriend will be surprised when we blow this case wide open."

Right. *That's* what we're supposed to do. Go see a locksmith who can tell us what this key opens instead of watching practice with our friends. No wonder I blanked it out. I vaguely remember agreeing to it early this morning, before we went to sleep.

After everything is secure and locked up (I don't want to clean up a mess like that again), we get in the truck and head toward the mall in Dover. Ruby has already looked up a locksmith on the Internet. Lucky for us we have a computer. Otherwise we might have had to stay at the track and watch practice.

Dover isn't a very big place. I can't say I know it very well. Except for a few bars and a nightclub or two, I haven't wandered around very much. I'm not really looking for a lot of outside amusement when I come to a race. I come to watch the cars go around the track and to hang out with my friends. We go out some, but there's enough to do at the speedway for me. Don and Bart like to play the slots a little.

Obviously, I'm the only one who feels that way. There's a line of trucks and cars waiting to get out on U.S. Highway 13. Buses are coming in and veering off toward the casino. No wonder they have a traffic cop directing the intersection. That was probably my least favorite job as a rookie. Standing in the middle of the street in the rain and the snow, angry drivers swearing at me and honking their horns. Thank God I'm out of that now.

I'm thinking about what Ruby said about life insurance. She'll get some of the pension I draw from my fifteen years, but that won't be enough to live on. The RV will be paid for if I die, and the investments my uncle manages for me will pass on to her. Do I need life insurance too?

I sneak a look at her pretty face. She's a lot younger than me. The chances are good I'll kick before she does. Especially if I keep climbing up on slippery wet bridges in the middle of the night. And that's if I don't get shot or run over by a monster truck while investigating someone's unfortunate death. Ruby seems drawn to them, and I'm bound to be there with her.

I put those thoughts aside as we pull into the mall parking lot. I glance at my watch. How long could this take? A good locksmith should know exactly where this key goes.

As I open the truck door, I notice a red Buick pulling in about three spaces down. I saw that car pull out after us back at the track. I mess around, adjusting the rearview mirror, keeping the car in the corner of my eye. There are two men in the front seat. Neither one of them make a move to get out of the car.

"What are you doing, Glad?" Ruby comes around to see what's keeping me.

"Don't look now, but somebody is following us."

SEVEN

"Where?" She cranes her neck in the most obvious way possible to see the men in the Buick. "What do they look like? Did they follow us from the speedway?"

"I think so." I take her arm and we walk quickly to the entrance of the mall. By now, if they don't know we're on to them, they must be morons. I'm assuming Phil sent them to follow us in case we tried to find out about the key. "We're going to have to lose them if we want to find out anything."

"Why?" She stares behind us. "Let's confront them. That way they'll know we're on to them."

"That's not the way this works." I walk quickly behind a Dumpster and take her with me. "We wait until they walk by, then we get back in the truck and look for another locksmith."

"That's ridiculous! That could take all day!"

I glance around the corner of the Dumpster. The two men are standing outside their car now, one talking on a cell phone. Probably telling Phil what's going on. It's obvious to me that he's worried we'll find out what this key opens. How far he's willing to go to keep that from happening is anyone's guess.

"I say, are we looking for something out here? Is there a problem?"

Whitaker is standing behind us looking out at the parking lot. He keeps turning up like the proverbial bad penny.

"Someone followed us here," Ruby tells him, even though I wish she wouldn't. I know she trusts him—probably that damn British accent. What is it with women and that accent?

"Really? Do you know who they are?"

"No. Maybe *you* do." I face him, prepared to interrogate.

"What do you mean?"

Ruby turns on me. "Yeah, Glad. What do you mean?"

"I mean, why is he here? He just *happened* to be at the mall the same time as us? That's wearing a little thin."

"I was, in fact, shopping inside." Whitaker holds up his bag. "I needed new socks and ended up buying new shoes as well."

"That's me!" Ruby laughs. "I go in for one thing and come out with another. The only problem is, when you live in an RV, you have to throw something out before you bring in something new."

"Excuse me." I stare in what I hope is a significant way at her. Sometimes it's like we're telepathic. This isn't one of those times. "If we're finished talking about shopping, maybe your friend can explain how he knew we were here."

"That is fairly easy." He grins. "I saw the two of you walk 'round the Dumpster as I was coming out the door. I waited, and when I didn't see you come back, I thought I should offer my services in case you were in trouble."

"See?" Ruby admonishes me. "There's nothing suspicious about that."

I glance around the corner of the Dumpster. The two men and the car are gone. "Okay. This is too much for me. I'm going to watch practice."

"What about what we're doing?" Ruby's glance darts to Whitaker and back to me. "What about the *thing*?"

"The thing?" I laugh. "Oh, the *thing*. I don't know. I don't think we should do what we were going to do right now. I think we should go back to the speedway and think about it some more. Preferably while we watch the cars go around the track."

Whitaker sniffs. "If you need some privacy, I can walk to the other side of the Dumpster."

"That would be fine." I fold my arms across my chest. I read somewhere the gesture means I'm in control. I don't feel like it, but maybe Whitaker read that article too and will get that meaning from it.

He raises his chin and sniffs again. "Very well. Do call me if you need me."

When he's gone, Ruby shouts, "How can you think he has anything to do with the key?"

"He admitted he's looking for the money. I think he'd be interested in the key. I think he might have sent those guys to follow us. When they spotted us, they called him and he conveniently came out of the mall. He didn't need them anymore, so they left."

"That's ridiculous! Why would he tell us about the missing money at all if he was worried about us finding it? Wouldn't he have kept it a secret?"

"I don't know. All I know is I'm missing practice and we can't take this key into the locksmith today. We have to find another way of doing it. Whether it's Whitaker or Phil, or even Bill, someone would know we have the key, and it wouldn't take much to get it back from us."

She looks tough and puts her hands on her hips. "It's in my bra. Just let someone try to stick their hand in there. They'll come up short a few fingers."

I love her naiveté. I could show her how easy that would be, but I don't want to go there. Let her have an illusion of safety from the world she understands. I know if there's really that much money at stake, whoever is trying to get it won't stop because the key is in her bra.

I put my arm around her and kiss her. "Let's go back and re-hash this. For right now, we're stalled."

"Okay. And I won't say anything else to dear Forsythe. I think you're wrong about him, but better safe than miserable, as Granny always says."

I've met Granny. She lives on a few hundred acres up in the mountains of North Carolina, where she scared off the rattlesnakes by looking at them. She's close to a hundred years old and she still plows her fields with an old mule. She can say whatever she likes.

"Sounds good." I kiss Ruby's head right where one blond curl always hangs at her temple. "Don't worry, sweetie. We'll find out what's going on."

"I'm not worried. We make a great team. Nothing can hide from us."

So we hop back in the Ranger and drive through an hour of traffic to get back to the speedway again. People are really coming in now. Not everyone likes to get to the event early. I like to get the best parking space I can. I feel bad for all those RVs still coming in. They'll be parking in the back lots, where they'll have to wait for a shuttle or walk a mile to get to the race.

The Busch Series practice is over, but that means the serious part is ready. I can't wait to see how the cars stack up. I can be objective at this race, since Joe isn't here. I can look at Gordon's Chevy and see how it compares to Johnson's Chevy. I can look at Mark Martin's driving next to Kurt Busch's and see how they both measure up. Everything is in place for qualifying tomorrow. The cars probably won't get any better, although they may get worse.

"I'll get the beer and the cooler." I turn off the engine after we park by the RV. With any luck, Bart and Don saved us some seats. Otherwise we'll be up in the nosebleed section.

"Great!" Ruby darts from the truck. "Let me get rid of my pocketbook and get some sunblock."

We both have our agendas. I can take care of mine, which will be hers in a short while when she gets thirsty. This is what it's all about. I'm ready for it.

Thankfully, no one has broken into the RV again. They must think we have the key with us. That would be a logical assumption. I race for the cooler under the cabinet, then turn back to pop open the fridge. Greeting me there are two green eyes narrowed above a snarling mouth with sharp teeth.

The cat is standing on top of the fridge, kind of draped down enough so I can't open the door without moving him. I'd like to move him into the street, but Ruby wouldn't be happy with that. So I try talking to the beast. "There's a good boy. Get down before Glad has to show you his mean, ugly side that he's put on hold since you scratched him in bed. Come on, you mangy little monster. Get off the fridge."

He snarls and hisses at me, one extended paw raking the air where my face was a few seconds ago. He's pretty clear about not moving. I'd call for Ruby, but I don't want to let her know I can't deal with this. It's just a dumb cat, for God's sake. I've handled drunks, burglars, murderers, and dope addicts. I'm not going to let this big furry thing beat me.

I pick up a Popsicle stick from the counter and throw it across the room. "Go get it, boy. Go on. Fetch the stick."

The cat swats at me again.

I pick up an old tennis ball that's always floating around. I throw it across the room. "There you go. Chase that."

The cat hisses and snarls at me.

"Glad, have you seen my hat?" Ruby calls from the bedroom.

"In the top of the closet," I respond. "I was trying to keep it from getting flattened."

"Thanks."

I can only think of one other thing that might draw the cat off of the fridge. I open a fresh can of tuna and set it out on the counter. Before I can turn around and offer it to Malibu, he jumps off the fridge and onto my back. All four feet have claws that dig through my shirt and into my back. What makes it worse is that he's positioned himself in such a way that I can't reach him to get him off without losing a considerable amount of flesh.

"Oh, that's a good idea." Ruby sails into the kitchen, takes the cat off my back, and puts him on the counter in front of the tuna. "We'll probably need to get him some real cat food soon. He's growing on you, isn't he?"

It's impossible for me to answer that question without going off on how much we don't need a cat, especially an impossible monster like this one. So I smile and hope blood isn't seeping into my 1996 Pocono collector's T-shirt. "Let's go. I hope to see some of practice."

I open the door and stop. There are about fifty people standing outside. A suit is in front, nearest the door. Behind him are several uniformed officers, and behind them are security guards from the speedway and the casino. I think the people behind *them* are looky-loos who want to know what's going on.

"Where's the FBI?" I ask who I assume is the lead detective.

"What's going on out there?" Ruby comes to the door, takes one look at our uninvited guests, and drops her hat as she puts her hands up in the air. "We surrender!"

"Relax, sweetie." I put her hands down. "They don't have their guns out."

"I have a search warrant for Mr. Paxton's property." The suit hands it to me. "You can go ahead and give it to me, or we can rip your place apart."

"You mean like Paxton's men did last night? I told Captain Barker they were looking for something."

The suit steps closer to me. "Mr. Wycznewski, give the man what he wants. I don't want to have to do this. Why are you antagonizing him?"

"I don't know." I shrug. "I get off on giving everyone a hard time, I guess."

"Are you willing to hand over the property?" The suit takes a step back and raises his voice to be sure Paxton can hear him. The officers behind him take a step forward. The security guards, not wanting to be left behind, take a step forward too. If they weren't threatening me, I'd find it hilarious.

"Oh, here!" Ruby takes the key out of her bra and hands it to the suit. "It took us a couple of hours to get this place cleaned up last night. It's not worth doing it again."

He looks at the key and frowns.

"You didn't know what it was?" I smile at his dawning awareness of what property we were holding.

He looks up at me and shakes his head. "Let's get this over with."

Paxton marches forward, the ranks parting for him like Moses with the Red Sea. The detective puts the key in his hand.

"Oh well." Ruby looks at me. "I guess we'll never know what the key is for."

"That's okay." I put my arm around her. "Let's get them off our backs and enjoy the race like we came here to do."

But Paxton points at me unexpectedly. "I don't know what you're trying to pull, Wycznewski, but this is *not* what I was looking for. I want the key you found on top of the bridge yesterday." He turns to the detective. "You have a search warrant, Lieutenant. I expect you to use it. If you can't find my property, arrest them."

"Mr. Paxton, I can search their RV. But I can't arrest anyone for finding something, especially when you won't tell me what that something is."

"It's not necessary for you to know everything, Lieutenant. Just do your job."

"I could do my job better if you told me what you're looking for."

He stares at him like he's a fly on his windshield. "I'm looking for the key. This isn't it. They know what I want. I'll be in my office."

Neither one of us believes this is happening. There was a key on top of the bridge but it's not the right key? "If this is the wrong key," Ruby asks me, "what kind of key is it?"

"I don't know. I guess we'll have to get out of the way and let them do their job." I kiss the side of her face. "At least we can go to practice."

"Whoa!" The lieutenant stops us from walking away. "You didn't read the warrant. It includes a search of your persons as well. Officer Franks will go with you, Mr. Wycznewski. Officer Reynolds will search your wife."

"Can he do that?" Ruby asks me.

"He can. But he's risking us suing his ass for wrongful persecution. I'm sure the lieutenant is aware of that."

"Hand over the damn key and you can go on your way and I can go home," he promises.

"I gave you the only key we have besides truck keys and RV keys," Ruby argues. "We found that key where Bill was looking for it yesterday. This is some stupid game he's playing."

The lieutenant shrugs. "Have it your way. You first, Mrs. Wycznewski."

Ruby huffs and stomps into the bedroom with Officer Reynolds and slams the door shut.

"This way, sir." Officer Franks points to the living room. "We'll wait in here until Officer Reynolds is finished."

I'll never forget the look on Ruby's face when she and Reynolds finally emerge from the bedroom. The last time I saw her look like that was when Junior bump-drafted Jimmie's car. It's a combination Angry Samurai and Sheena, Queen of the Jungle. It bodes well for no one.

I can't say my own experience with Officer Franks is pleasant, but I take it in stride. At least there's no body-cavity search. It could be much worse.

"He's clean," Franks tells the lieutenant.

"So is she," Reynolds responds.

"I guess we'll search the RV." The lieutenant throws up his arms. "We don't have much choice."

Malibu meows from the top of the fridge. Ruby grabs him and puts him into the big beach bag she always carries. "I hope there's no law against taking my cat with me."

"Not at all." The lieutenant nods at her. "I'm sorry for this. I wish you'd give Mr. Paxton what he wants without the fuss."

"We tried." Her teeth are clenched so tight you can hardly understand what she's saying.

"All right." He looks at his officers. "Let's find the key."

Ruby stalks out of the RV. I expect the cat to jump out of the bag, but he stays hidden in the brightly colored material. "Of all the nerve!" she fumes as we walk toward the grandstands. "That woman enjoyed seeing me naked. I'm sure she goes that way. I feel pretty sure she was coming on to me. How could something like this happen? It's like we don't even live in a free country anymore. People can make you take your clothes off, search your house, steal your food. There's no justice. I can't believe it."

I let her rant. She might as well get it out of her system. I understand the procedure. I've strip-searched, or ordered it to be done, dozens of times. I still feel violated now. But it really breaks my heart when Ruby is finally talked out and she turns to me with tears in her eyes.

"That poor man will never get any justice." She lays her head on my shoulder. "What can we do?"

"I think we've done about all we can, honey." I put my arms around her and hold her close. "I don't know what game Paxton is playing. Maybe he didn't want the police to know that was the key. This whole thing is crazy."

"I know." She lifts her head and kisses my chin. "I'm sorry. You were right. We shouldn't have gotten involved. Let's forget about it."

Up in the stands, Andy sees us coming and waves to us. We sit down beside him and he fills us in on all the problems the drivers have had so far. Jeff Gordon's number 66 Best Buy car ran a couple of laps and then went off the field in a cloud of smoke. Jeremy Mayfield ran too loose and almost hit the wall on the third turn. Johnson's number 48 Lowe's car ran perfect, even though he kept telling his crew chief, Chad Knauss, he was having problems with the steering.

"This should be some interesting qualifying," Andy says with a smile.

"How is Bobby doing?" Ruby asks her parents, who are sitting there too.

"He'd be doing a helluva lot better if it wasn't for those damn stupid engines they're using nowadays," Zeke tells her. "When we used to race, they didn't have all that crap on the car. It's a wonder they work at all."

"He's not going to qualify tomorrow if he doesn't pick up some speed," Louise replies with as much knowledge of the sport as her husband. Together, they've been involved with racing for probably a hundred years.

"Yeah," Bart agrees. "He acts like he's afraid in the turns."

Down on the concrete track, David Stremme has his turn. Every aspect of the race, including what the track is made of, is crucial to the driver. Concrete is different from asphalt. Most of the tracks in the NASCAR circuit are some form of asphalt. Dover is the only concrete track. That's why they call it the Monster Mile. It's a grueling four hundred laps for man and machine.

"That new guy from hereabouts is up next." Bart puts on his glasses and reads the program. "John Paxton. He didn't do too well at Lowe's. Maybe he'll do better here."

Louise looks skeptical. Zeke offers his opinion. "The boy doesn't have a good car. Maybe if that stingy brother of his helped him out, he'd have a chance."

"John is definitely the youngest, best-looking brother," Andy says. "No wonder he started driving."

"He's also the nicest brother," Ruby tells them. "Bill was nice too. Or at least I think he was."

Everyone in the grandstands is waiting for Paxton's car to emerge onto the track. Nothing happens. People start talking about the possibilities of what could be wrong, from engine blowout to bad brakes. Still nothing happens.

The whine of the PA system catches everyone's attention. "The number 11 car, driven by John Paxton, has been disqualified. Car number 102 will be driven by Chad Lee."

The number 102 car spins up on the track and starts running hard for the first turn. Fans are watching the time. It's not as important today as it will be during qualifying tomorrow. But sometimes one of these young guns can come out and take the pole from the more experienced drivers. Now that's exciting.

"Hey!" Bobby joins us to watch his competition. "Did you all hear the news?"

"You mean how you're afraid to go fast around the turns?" Bart laughs and nudges Andy with his elbow.

"Don't pay him no mind," Zeke says to his son. "Just put your foot down when you're out there, boy. You're never gonna win like you've been driving."

Bobby frowns. "I'm not afraid to go fast around the turns. I had some trouble with the car. And I was talking about John disappearing."

The conversation gets louder as we all start shouting so we can hear over the roar of the number 102 car. To add to the problem, Malibu decides at that moment to escape from Ruby's beach bag. He jumps down across the seats, heading for the track.

EIGHT

RUBY AND I FOLLOW the cat as best we can. Not being a four-legged feline, we can't jump from seat to seat, across people's heads, and up their backs. But we can follow the trail of cursing and shouting that shows where Malibu has been.

Despite the fact that I'd like to get rid of the little beast, my heart stops as he reaches the bottom of the grandstand and heads toward the track. A human can't reach the track from here. There's a high fence preventing parts of cars from flying up and hitting fans. But a cat might be different. He could probably scale the fence in less time than it takes for a pit stop and be on the track with Chad Lee as he's going 130 miles per hour.

Ruby stops beside me and clutches my arm. "Glad!"

"I know." We start down the rest of the grandstand. Malibu looks like he's confused, frightened by the roar of the engine. Ruby starts calling him, but he probably can't hear her.

The cat veers back toward the grandstand. I reach the bottom as he darts through a hole underneath the seats and runs toward the back side. I step down into Dover's famous mud that surrounds the grandstands area after a rain and miss grabbing the cat by half a second.

Swearing, I run to the exit area with Ruby following me. Going outside the track will be no safer for the animal. The cars and trucks going by might be moving slower, but they can still squish a cat.

He's black, so he hides pretty well in the shadows. I call him as I come around the Allison Grandstand, but I don't see him.

"I'll come around from the Petty Grandstand," I tell Ruby. "You flush him out this way."

Breathless, she agrees, calling "Kitty, kitty" as she runs. I move into the shadows of the Petty Grandstand and come back to the right. I even call "Kitty, kitty" like Ruby, except I can't reach those upper decibels.

Surprisingly, I find the little monster a few minutes later. He's curled up in a tight ball, meowing like he's calling someone. I know he's going to rake my hand with his little claws, but I can't wait for Ruby and take a chance on him bolting again. I reach down and pick him up carefully, and he doesn't hiss at me. Even more amazing, he doesn't scratch me. He curls up against me and starts purring.

I pet his head and try to sound reassuring as I promise tuna and playtime if he'll stay put. Then I notice something on the ground behind where he was cowering.

"You found him!" Ruby reaches for the cat and baby-talks as she takes him from me. "Did he hurt you? I'm sure he didn't mean to."

Another surprise: she's talking to me. "No. He seemed happy to see me."

"You see?" She kisses the top of Malibu's head. "He likes you."

"Yeah. We'll see." I lean down and pick up the driver's helmet I find on the ground. It's got a number 11 and sponsors' logos plastered on it. "Look at this. It's John's helmet."

"What do you think it's doing under there?" Ruby nuzzles the cat as she looks at the helmet. "Is that blood on the side?"

"I really don't want to know. It's bad enough when *you* find things that don't make sense. Now we have a cat that wants to investigate."

Ruby kisses him. "He's my kitty Watson."

"What does that make me?" I ask as I reach for my cell phone.

"I think that makes you Inspector Lestrade."

"Nice."

The police don't have far to come. After all, they're probably still ransacking our RV. I recognize the two officers who meet us under the grandstand. I wonder if they're as tired of seeing us as I am of seeing them.

I tell them everything that happened and show them where I found the cat and the helmet. We're all standing around in the mud while practice runs scream by on the track.

"You say this driver, John Paxton, is missing?" one officer (thankfully not Officer Franks) asks me. "How do you know he's missing?"

"We heard it in the grandstands." I know I wouldn't be convinced by that evidence, but it seems to be true. "He's Phil Paxton's brother. It looks like he could be hurt."

"I think that might be blood on the helmet," Ruby points out.

"You two stay put," he tells us. "I'll have to call this in."

"Yeah. I know."

All right. I admit it. My curiosity is piqued. First one brother dies under suspicious circumstances, and then another disappears. In the middle of this, the third brother is desperate to find a key that would seem to be part of a ten-million-dollar fraud scheme. I think the game is definitely afoot.

The officer finishes his phone call, takes our names and numbers (like he doesn't already know who we are), and tells us we can go. By this time, it's afternoon and hotter than inside Joe's car running full blast. Thousands of fans are milling around, and the beer truck is giving away glasses of Bud Light. I think it's time to pause and reflect.

Ruby and I walk back toward the RV, where the search is finishing up. The lieutenant is gone, but Officer Reynolds is talking with Officer Franks outside. They see us coming and break off their conversation.

"Find anything?" I ask.

"Nope. We searched pretty good too." Franks puts his hand on my shoulder and leans in. "Look, Wycznewski, we don't want to bug you and your wife. You don't want us crawling around in your stuff. Why don't we call a truce and you give Mr. Paxton what he wants."

Before I can answer, Ruby lets loose. "I gave him what we had. If you don't believe me, ask Paxton why we bothered to take the key to a locksmith this morning. We thought we had what he was looking for. Probably the key to wherever that ten million dollars is being stored. If that wasn't it, my husband risked his life up on top of the Monster Bridge for nothing. We can't give you something we don't have."

Breasts heaving in her pink tank top, I think she's pretty convincing, but I add, "Maybe you should find out if the key we gave Paxton is the real thing. Maybe he's throwing you off by accusing us of not giving the right key back to him."

Franks shakes his head. "Why would he do that?"

"Because ten million dollars buys a lot of stuff," Ruby tells him sagely.

I can't tell if he's really convinced or just tired and ready to go home. He seems to take it in, then nods his head and says goodbye.

"That was pretty good," I tell Ruby as we brace ourselves for destruction and open the RV door.

"Thanks. This whole thing stinks."

"Yeah." We both kind of pretend like our home isn't wrecked. It is, of course. The police did as good a job as whoever searched it to begin with. Wordlessly, we start cleaning up. Ruby puts Malibu on the counter with what's left of the tuna.

"Something is up with these three brothers." She puts away pots and pans, bowls and plates. "But we may be wrong about Paxton the casino owner being the bad guy."

"How's that?" I put chairs back in place and stuff papers and maps back in the glove box.

"If this ten million dollars isn't an urban myth, suppose someone else wants a part of it."

"Or all of it." I move into the living area to clean up.

"And that someone kills whichever brother died on the track. He demands the money from the casino Paxton, and when he doesn't get it, he kidnaps John, who is a dupe in all this." Ruby finishes her theory with a flourish as she puts the last of the frozen food back in the freezer.

"Impressive. I like Forsythe Whitaker for the bad guy."

"No way. He's a nice man."

"Just because he has that accent doesn't make him nice."

"It's not just that," she argues. "It's intuition."

"Well, who do you like if not Whitaker?"

"I don't know yet. But I think we should take a ride out to the rest area where I picked up Paxton number one and see what we can find out. Maybe someone else saw him out there."

"We have three hours before final practice or any other events. Let's eat lunch on the way."

Ruby looks around the RV. "What about the mess?"

"Don't worry. It will still be here when we get back. Unless Malibu decides to clean it up."

The cat hears his name and meows loudly. He jumps from the counter straight at me. I wince but I catch him. He doesn't scratch me. I pet his little ears and he purrs. "Maybe you're right. Maybe he likes me now."

"Of course he does. He knows who his mommy and daddy are now."

I put the cat back on the counter. "That's about all I can handle. We seem to be stuck with the cat, but I won't be his daddy."

Ruby takes my arm as we leave the RV. "Why not? He can be like our baby. A little furry baby who eats tuna."

"And has claws. Like Rosemary's Baby."

She punches me in the arm playfully. "He's not evil. He's a small animal that's easily frightened. He only lashes out when he's scared."

"Was he scared last night when we were making love?"

Ruby rolls her eyes and grins. "With all the noise you were making, he probably thought you were trying to kill me. He was being protective." She looks at my ass. "How *is* your backside today?"

"Pretty good." I smile and squeeze her hand. "Want to cop a feel in the truck?"

"Maybe. We'll see."

———

We eat lunch at Atwood's and head back the way we came on Highway 300. Ruby picked Paxton up at the last rest area before we got to Dover. At least the race traffic is gone now, but it's still a long way back.

The rest area is a clean, modern facility. One woman with reddish blond hair and bad eyebrows is working behind the welcome desk. I remember her from when we stopped here. I'm afraid she looks a little like she has a caterpillar stuck to her forehead, between her eyes.

"Hello. Can I help you find something?"

Ruby leans against the desk and smiles as she looks at the woman's nametag, which reads, *Miss Margaret Finch*. "Hi, Margaret. I was wondering if you noticed a homeless man up here early yesterday morning. He was medium height, ragged clothes, looked like he was in a fight."

The woman looks at Ruby like she's asking her to swallow a bug. "There are homeless people up here from time to time, but they *never* come in the building. I never leave my post while the rest area is open. So it's doubtful that our paths would have crossed."

She's lying. I can see it in her eyes. Will Ruby pick up on it?

Ruby sighs and hangs her head a little. "I stopped here and that man stole my diamond bracelet. I was hoping not to have to go any further than this. I guess I'll have to talk to the state board of tourism. I hope that doesn't reflect on you."

Margaret flutters her eyelashes and runs her hand through her hair. "I'm sorry I can't help you. I hate you lost your bracelet. Maybe you should contact your insurance company. Maybe they could reimburse you and you could buy a new bracelet."

"I wish I could do that," Ruby sighs. "But it wasn't insured. I got it from my mama on the way here. It belonged to my grandmother, who recently passed away. We didn't have time to insure it."

"That's too bad."

"Yes, it is. But you see why my only chance is to find that man. If you haven't seen him up here before and have no idea where he came from, I'm going to have to call in whoever I need to so I can get my grandma's bracelet back."

Now Margaret is affronted. "I assure you, I wouldn't know who he is. Even if I'd noticed him, which I didn't, I wouldn't speak to him."

Ruby smiles in a way that reminds me of Malibu. Maybe that's why they get along so well. "He mentioned you."

"What? Why would he do that? What did he say?"

"He said he knew you. He said you'd helped him before."

By now, Margaret is extremely upset. She starts to cry. "I couldn't help it. I felt so sorry for him. He's been up here before. He lives near here. I can't believe he'd steal from you. He seems like such a gentleman. I love his cat. Now I'm sorry I gave him something to eat."

"That's okay." Ruby hands her a tissue. "I just need to know where to find him."

Margaret blows her nose and points out the door. "He lives in an old place about half a mile from here. It's practically falling down. I've taken him home before, after he used the phone. I'm sure there must be some explanation. Bill certainly isn't a thief."

"I hope you're right. What happened to him? He looked like someone beat him up."

"I'm not sure. I've never seen him like that. I asked him what happened before he made his phone call. He wouldn't tell me."

"Did he ever say who he was calling?"

"He mentioned having a brother. I knew they couldn't be close or he wouldn't let Bill live that way."

"Thanks, Margaret. That's a really pretty name. I have a cousin named Margaret who was runner-up for the Miss North Carolina crown a few years back."

"Really?" Margaret laughs a little nervously. "My uncle lives in Forest City. Is that far from you?"

Now it's become a gabfest. Margaret wants to know how Ruby does her hair, and Ruby is giving Margaret tips on makeup. I tap Ruby on the shoulder and remind her of our deadline. "We better go look for the bracelet, sweetie."

"You're right, honey." She smiles back at me, then at Margaret. "Don't worry. The tourism board won't hear any of this from me."

"Thank you, Ruby. I know this seems like kind of a dead-end job, but I meet a lot of interesting people."

"And potential husbands," Ruby quips.

"That too." Margaret blushes and looks away.

Ruby and I walk out together. I take out the truck keys and congratulate her. "I have to hand it to you. How did you know?"

"Her nameplate on the desk." She saunters to her side of the cab. "Any woman her age who still has the 'Miss' in front of her name is looking at any man who comes within two miles of her. She probably thought Bill might measure up one day."

"I don't believe it." I laugh as I start the engine. "Beauty-parlor tactics. Why didn't I ever think of that?"

"Maybe because you never worked at a beauty parlor," she drawls. "Don't mistake beauty and good grooming for stupidity, darlin'."

"I never do."

We leave the rest-area parking lot and head in the general direction of Margaret's pointing finger. There's a dirt road going off into the woods that surround the facility. Margaret is standing outside the building, nodding and pointing.

The road is more like a path for an all-terrain vehicle. Even then it's so grown up with weeds it doesn't look like anything has come down here in quite a while. I take it nice and slow. The Ranger wasn't built for off-road. I have good tires, which helps a lot, but I'd be better off with a dirt bike.

"What would Bill be doing back here?" Ruby asks. "I know you didn't talk to him, but he was well spoken, intelligent. I can't imagine him living out here."

"They said he had problems." I negotiate a pothole the size of the truck. "Maybe he couldn't handle living the life he left."

"Then why is Phil the one with the scratches and bruises? Unless it was always Phil, and Bill was the one running the hotel and casino."

"I don't know, honey. The whole thing makes my head hurt. I wish we weren't involved." I look at her pouty smile and add, "But we are. We'll have to figure it out. Then it will probably make sense."

"Thanks." She smiles at me, then yells, "Watch out for that turn!"

I swing wide when I see the sharp turn that's more like an angle in the road. A few more feet and we'd have been in the trees. My truck definitely wouldn't like that.

"Look!" Ruby points. "There's an old house, just like Margaret said."

I shake my head. "She's pretty good to get that Subaru back here."

"You know, women *can* drive."

Wanting to avoid the discussion about why there aren't women drivers in NASCAR, I agree. "You're an excellent driver."

"Damn straight!"

"You would've made a helluva race-car driver."

"Yes, I would."

"Looks like we're here." I turn off the truck and open the door. "Shall we check it out?"

"You played me back there, didn't you?" Blue eyes glare up at me from her pretty face.

"No, ma'am. I would never disrespect you that way."

She laughs and puts her hand on my ass. "I'll take that feel after all."

Of course, she manages to squeeze right where Malibu stuck his claws in me. I wince a little and take a big step forward. At least we avoid the hourlong discussion bemoaning the fact that there are very few women race drivers. It's worth the pain.

"You think he really lived here?" she asks as she looks up at the house.

Most of the structure is either falling or fallen. Half the roof is on the ground. There can't be any more than a couple of rooms that are livable. "If he did, he had more than a few problems."

But the cat food still left in stainless steel bowls on what's left of the porch and the clothes strewn on mangled pieces of furniture tell their own story. There's no power, but cans of Chef Boyardee ravioli are in a cabinet. He must have used Sterno to heat them. Hundreds of little containers of canned heat litter the floor.

There's a bed made out of an old sofa in what looks like it used to be the kitchen. A kerosene lamp is on a table right next to a hole in the wood floor. This is the only room it might be possible to live in, and that's questionable to me. Margaret's right. Why would Phil let his brother live this way, even if he was disturbed?

"Look at this!" Ruby calls me to the side of the room. She holds up a brochure for the Dover Hotel and Casino. "I guess we're in the right place."

There's a phone number scrawled on the dirty brochure. I take out my cell phone and punch in the number. There's no answer, but the voice mail gives it away. "You've reached Phil Paxton's private line. I'm away right now, but leave a message and I'll call you back as soon as I can."

"No doubt." I put the phone back in my pocket. "It was Phil."

"So he knew his brother lived out here." Ruby brushes her hands off on her jean shorts. "You'd think he'd have put him somewhere he could be cared for instead of letting him live out here in this hovel."

"Maybe there was a reason for it."

"What possible reason could there be for it?"

I peer through a hole in what's left of the side wall. There are Brink's bags in the disintegrating room beyond where we stand. "Ten million dollars?"

"What?" She crosses the room toward me. "Are you saying you see the money?"

Before she can reach where I'm standing, the rotting floor gives way beneath her right foot. I hear her startled yelp and turn, instinctively grabbing for her hands as I see her going down. She slides into a growing hole as the rest of the old wood cracks and splinters away like ice on a pond.

The dust and soot from a few generations fly up from the hole in the floor, but after a few seconds, the rest of the floor holds steady.

I can't really see the damage until the dust clears. Ruby is holding on to me with both hands clenched on mine. I can't see her, but I can tell I'm holding all of her weight. "Ruby? Are you okay?"

She's coughing, sputtering, gasping for air, all covered in sawdust and dirt. "I think so. If you wouldn't have caught me..."

"Never mind that. Just hold on." My shoulders are already aching from the way I'm holding her. I can't see what's under her or if it's safe to let her go. I manage to pull her toward me and out of the hole with a loud grunt of determination.

She ends up pressed against me, pirouetting on about three inches of good wood. But she's safe.

"Thanks." She chokes and kisses me.

"Think nothing of it." I wrap my arms tightly around her to make sure I have a good hold on her in case she starts to fall again.

"What a lovely domestic scene." Another voice joins ours. "What the hell are you two doing here?"

NINE

"We're falling through what's left of your house." I swing Ruby away from the hole in the floor and make sure her footing is solid before I let her go. "This is quite a place you got."

I fully expect to see Phil standing there with a gun, ready to kill us. We shouldn't be here. It's not going to be good for him. Instead, his face loses its tension and he sits down on an old Coke crate near the door. I glance outside. No one is with him. That surprises me too. The man travels in packs.

Ruby crouches beside him. "It's you, Bill, isn't it?"

He looks up at her, his eyes tortured. I've seen the look on a lot of faces of criminals before they confess. I can't believe he's going to tell us the truth. Maybe he doesn't have the upper hand after all.

"It's me." He smiles at her and takes her hand. "I'm sorry I had to lie to you. When I got back, I couldn't believe everything that was going on. Then Phil died and I didn't know what to do. I panicked. The only thing I could think was that I should pretend it was me that died. I'm sure no loss to anyone. Phil's death would mean a lot."

Ruby squeezes his hand (an act I'm not too crazy about). "It's okay. Most people wouldn't know what to do in a situation like that. I'm glad you told me."

This is all well and good, but the fact of the matter is a man is dead and another man is missing. Bill may have been pretending to be Phil, but I don't appreciate his level of play-acting. "That's great. So, what happened?"

He glances up at me like he didn't see me there before. I don't really blame him. I'd rather look at Ruby too. "People say I'm kind of crazy because I don't want to live like Phil. He's offered me plenty of jobs over the years, but I don't have the right personality for them. I like living out here. I have a little garden in back. It's peaceful."

"And you have ten million dollars."

Ruby turns back to me. "Glad, we don't know that for sure."

"Yes, we do. There are Brink's bags on the other side of this wall. The house is falling down around them. Right, Bill?"

He nods. "I'm afraid so. Except there's no money in them."

"What happened to it?" Ruby asks.

"It's a long story. It wasn't my idea, but when Phil needed a place to hide the money, I let him put it in the old garage out here. He brought out some equipment and sealed up the garage. We didn't know the roof was rotting. When it fell in, I left it like that. It was hidden for good."

"And the money?" I'm not eating up this sob story like Ruby. I've heard too many to be impressed.

"Gone." Bill runs his hands over his face. "Or at least I think it's gone. I'm not sure. The casino got in some trouble and Phil stole the money. It was supposed to be a loan on the hotel and casino property. After it was stolen, he got a smaller loan to make it all look good. I think he spent all the money."

"We have to tell the police." Ruby gets to her feet and obviously comes to her senses.

Bill jumps up. "No! We can't. Don't you see? They came out here after me. I didn't tell them what I knew, even though they kicked me around. Then they killed Phil, thinking it was me. Now they have John. If we tell the police about the money now, they'll kill him too."

"That's why you needed a ride to the hotel," Ruby surmises. "You were trying to warn your brothers."

"Yes. But I was too late to save Phil. If the kidnappers find out the money is gone or that I'm not Phil, they won't hesitate to kill John."

"Come on. You expect us to believe this?" I can see from Ruby's face that she believes it. I agree it sounds almost too crazy not to be true, but I can't give in without some kind of proof. "You killed your brother because you were tired of living in this pigsty and you wanted your share for sitting on it all these years. Isn't that about right?"

"I could've had a share of it a long time ago if I'd wanted it," he argues, visibly shaking with either rage or fear. "I didn't want that life. I still don't. But I'm not going to let John die because of it."

"Of course not," Ruby assures him. "You did the right thing."

"Could I talk to you for a moment outside?" I ask my too-sympathetic wife.

She smiles at Bill and says, "Excuse us for a minute."

We step off the rickety porch together, and I can tell from the look on her face we aren't on the same page.

"How can you be so mean to him?" she asks as soon as we're out of earshot. "The man has been through a lot already. We have to help him. Don't forget, helping him means helping John."

"First we have to believe him. This is the most bull I've heard since the first day I met Bobby. There was ten million dollars but he didn't want any part of it. He comes back after being threatened and then his brother is killed, so he decides to take over his identity. That is so lame, Ruby. I can't believe you're buying it."

"Everyone says Phil tried to help his brother but Bill wouldn't let him." She shakes her head. "Doesn't everyone say that?"

"Yes, but—"

"I told you someone beat him up. Do you think he beat himself up?"

"No, but—"

"Then stop arguing and let's find some way to help save John." She marches back to the porch like a general leading troops to battle.

That's my Ruby. I love her, even though I don't always agree with her. I guess for right now we'll play this thing out Bill's way. At least until we can figure out the truth. Ruby and I are involved now. The only way out—and back to the real world—is to figure out the truth.

I walk back to where Bill is standing on the porch with her. "What's the plan? We found your brother's helmet back at the track and told the police we heard he was missing. Do they know he's been kidnapped?"

"Not yet. I got a ransom demand. Poor deluded fool thinks there's still ten million dollars left after all these years. That's what he wants. The police asked some questions, but I think I can keep them out of it for a while. The kidnapper wants the money tomorrow."

"Who beat you up?" Ruby is right on the money as usual. "It has to be the same people who kidnapped your brother."

"They wore masks. I didn't recognize their voices. They could've been anyone. There were four of them. One of them must have been the boss. He stood off to the side and didn't speak while his men worked me over."

"That's a dead end." I try to think of another approach. "Did you tell the kidnapper you'd get the money together?"

"Yes. I'm supposed to drop it off on the DuPont bridge after the speedway closes tomorrow night, and he'll pick it up there."

"What about the key we found up there?" Ruby asks him. "Was that really the wrong key?"

"I set that up to throw people off who were looking for the money." Bill manages to look contrite as he apologizes. "I'm sorry I had to give you such a bad time. I was desperate."

"You had the police trash our RV for nothing," I growl, unforgiving. "It was your goons who searched it to begin with, wasn't it?"

"No. Someone else must have been watching you."

"What were they searching for?" Ruby frowns and shifts her weight from one foot to the other.

I notice while looking at her that she has a long gash on one leg that's still bleeding. "I think we better continue this later. We need to get you home and cleaned up. That looks like a bad cut."

"Please. You don't have to do anything," Bill pleads. "But please don't say anything else about this until I can get John home."

"We won't," Ruby promises. "And we'll take good care of Malibu for you."

"I would consider it an honor if the two of you would stay at the hotel at least for tonight," he offers. "I'll have housekeeping send someone over to clean up your RV. It's the least I can do. Have dinner with me. The room is on the house, of course."

My first impulse is to say no. Then I look at Ruby. She's covered in sawdust and dirt, scratched up and bloody. She deserves a night with a big bathtub. And Bill deserves to comp us for that and take care of cleaning up the RV. "All right. Thanks."

"Great. I'll meet you back at the hotel. If you need a doctor to look at that leg," he says, "let me know and I'll send someone over."

He's crouched down beside Ruby's leg, supposedly studying the long scratch, although it looks to me like he might be looking at her butt. I find myself liking Bill less as this goes along. And why didn't his damn cat jump to him in the casino when we took him there?

I pose this question to Ruby on the drive back to Dover. Bill is behind us in his brother's Cadillac Escalade.

"I don't know. But I told you the two brothers switched places."

"Fine. The two brothers switched places. But I'm not sure if I buy this whole song and dance about him being attacked and someone else killing his brother."

"Why would Bill kill Phil?"

"Because he wanted his share of the ten million dollars."

"Then why didn't he kill us when we told him we knew about the money?" she demands. "Why tell us what I suspected was true? We could ruin everything for him."

"Except no one believes us, and Paxton has the police in his pocket."

"Stop being so cynical. Bill is a nice guy mixed up in something he can't control. It happens sometimes. He needs our help."

"Name me another person this has happened to." I'm sure she can't do it, even with her repertoire of stories from family and friends.

"There was Aunt Lida, who got mixed up in that whole post-office scam. It was *exactly* like this situation."

I zone out for a few seconds as she describes how her aunt's problem was exactly like Bill's. I don't think her aunt finding a package without the proper address on it qualifies as a murder and kidnapping, though.

"Ruby, just for once, pretend you don't have a soft spot as big as the state of Texas and let's talk some common sense."

"Oh?" She turns to me with an angry look to her luscious lips. "Are you saying I'm not making any sense?"

"I'm not saying that. All I'm saying is Bill is trading on your sympathy. I think he killed his brother."

"Fine. I'm glad you think that."

"Ruby..."

"You don't like Bill? Then *I'll* stay at the hotel and help him. *You* can stay at the RV and do whatever you want to do."

"No way that's happening. Did you see that guy looking at your ass?"

"What guy?"

"Bill! While he was pretending to look at your leg, he was checking out your ass."

"You're paranoid. I love you, Glad, but you're crazy. He doesn't think of me like that. He says I remind him of his mother."

That has to be the dumbest thing I've ever heard, and I tell her so. It's a mistake, of course, because now she accuses me of telling her she's a dummy. That's not what I mean, but the harder I try to explain exactly what I *do* mean, the bigger the hole I'm digging. My good-for-nothing father always told me to shut up when I'm ahead. I'm behind in this case, but I stop talking anyway. We ride the rest of the way in silence.

Somehow Bill has made it back to the hotel before us. He probably knows some secret back way. No doubt it's the same way they got the Brink's truck out to the old house. I don't bother telling Ruby this when I let her off at the door. Bill takes her hand and helps her out of the truck. I'm mangling the steering wheel in the way I'd like to squeeze his neck.

Ruby makes a point of not looking back. She laughs at something he says as they walk to the door. I watch them, seething, until my last chance to get out and follow them passes by. Doesn't seem like Ruby would have me right now anyway. I want to gun the engine and lay down about three inches of smelly burnt rubber on Bill's driveway, but that would mean admitting I'm upset. I take off sedately, like nothing in the world is bothering me. I make a U-turn in the parking lot and head back for the RV.

Bill must have called ahead, because the RV is cleaned up. I'm happy I left the door open. No point in locking it, since everyone is going in and out looking for things. There's a faint smell of some kind of disinfectant that I don't like. Ruby uses an herbal cleaner that smells a lot better.

I'm not going to feel sorry for myself. I grab a beer and answer the persistent pounding on the front door. It's Zeke and Louise, who are full of information about the practice I missed. They go through the list of all the drivers and what happened to them, and then Louise looks around. "Where's my Ruby?"

"She's living at the hotel with Phil Paxton." I correct myself. "No, make that Bill Paxton. He's pretending to be Phil, but that's really Phil who died on the track."

For an instant, Louise is silent. Then she purses her lips and says, "Well, at least she's with a *wealthy* Yankee this time."

"Quiet, Mama," Zeke says. "Can't you see the boy is hurting? Ruby broke his heart. He's nothing but a wasted shell of a man now. He deserves our compassion whether he's a Yankee or not."

"You're right," she admits. "The good book says we have to take care of those less fortunate than us. Come on with us, Ruby's husband, and I'll fix us some dinner."

I'm not sure if I should be angry or desperate to escape. I really don't want to be with Zeke and Louise right now. I'm afraid I'll start to believe what they're saying. But on the other hand, I don't really want to be alone. I grab another beer from the fridge on my way out. It looks like it's going to be a long night.

By the time we settle in at Zeke and Louise's RV next door, we've picked up a handful of their friends and a few of mine. Everyone knows the Furrs in the racing world. I notice two rookie drivers in the pack. At least the conversation will be about racing.

Then Whitaker joins us. Someone's wife is helping Louise make banana pudding and potato salad inside while everyone else is sitting outside helping Zeke put barbecue sauce on the mound of chicken heaped on the grill.

I never understand where all the food comes from. To be with Zeke and Louise is like a permanent buffet. I guess it doesn't matter if they're home or away. They must have a freezer stuffed in the floor of the Coachman. There's no other way to explain it.

"I heard about the Paxton boy going missing." Whitaker sits down next to me.

Can anything else go wrong with this day? "Yeah. I heard about it too." I don't offer any information, hoping he'll leave me alone.

"I also heard you and Ruby found his helmet under the grandstand." He shifts his eyes back and forth like he's looking for spies who might be listening. "What did it look like?"

"It was round. It had a number 11 on it. It was red and white. I think Paxton's name was on it." I smile at him, then take another swig of my beer. I wish I'd brought more with me. Zeke and Louise don't drink alcohol.

"That's not what I mean." Whitaker tries to explain what he means. I mostly ignore him. Finally he gets this hurt look on his face and asks, "Where's Ruby?"

"I can answer that." Bobby grabs my beer and takes a long pull off of it. "I saw her at the hotel pool with Phil Paxton. She looked like she was having a good time. I asked myself why Glad wasn't there. I didn't have an answer, so I thought I'd actually ask you."

"Because I'm here, obviously." I try to yank my beer away from him. "Get your own."

"While Ruby is swimming around in a Hawaiian bikini? That seems unlikely." He laughs and finishes my bottle of Bud. "She dumped you, didn't she? I always knew it was going to happen. You two are too different to be together. Like Chevy and Ford. Or Rusty Wallace and Jimmie Johnson."

"Blasphemy!" Zeke shouts out. "I thought I taught you better than to use those two names in the same sentence."

"Sorry, Daddy. I was trying to explain to Glad why he and Ruby aren't together anymore."

"I don't care." Zeke won't compromise. "Don't use Rusty's name like that again under this canopy."

Bobby laughs and decides to quit tormenting me when he sees two of his competitors sitting near the grill and helping his father. I'm happy to be alone in the group, now forty or more people.

Whitaker takes it on himself to console me. "We must get Ruby out of that place. She could be in mortal danger."

"I think she can handle herself." If I squeeze the empty Bud bottle any tighter, it will shatter. Ruby is swimming with Bill. In a bikini, no less. I really don't like that. I can't remember being this mad for a long time. I want to kill Bill and stuff what's left of him into an exhaust pipe. I wouldn't do anything showy with him. Just kill him, skin him, and let the buzzards have the rest.

"Leg or thigh, Glad?" Zeke asks.

"Both. And the rest of him."

I don't realize the answer isn't appropriate until I feel a few people staring at me. I stand up and open the last bottle of beer. "I'm not really hungry. Thanks anyway."

"You have to eat to keep up your strength." Louise comes out of the RV with a platter of food. "At your age, a man has to take care of himself. I know Ruby's gone. But there'll be someone else."

"I have to go." Into that I imply, *before I scream*. Everyone tries to talk me into staying, but there's no way. I can't sit here another minute not knowing what's going on with Ruby and Bill.

Whitaker gets up and walks with me. Obviously the man has no sense of self-preservation. His scrawny chicken neck looks like something I should wring if he doesn't leave me alone. "If I may, I would like to volunteer to help you rescue your wife."

"She doesn't need rescuing."

"You don't realize. Phil Paxton is like the devil. The ultimate seducer. The poor girl probably doesn't realize what's happened to her. We must storm the castle."

"I don't have to do anything. I'm sure she's fine."

"Don't ignore this important warning," he pushes me as he wraps his hand around my arm. "Your wife is in grave danger."

That's it. I snap and take his hand off my arm. "I don't need your help, Whitaker. I don't want you in my face. Understand?"

"I know you don't trust me."

"You got that right. Just because Ruby falls for that Mick Jagger accent doesn't mean I do."

"Let me prove myself to you. I can prove what happened to the Paxtons. I know where hard evidence can be found. If I take you there, will you admit your wife needs our help?"

I glance up at the hotel and casino as the lights come on. People are streaming into the buildings. Somewhere in there, Ruby is with Bill. I'd like nothing better than to drag that jerk out by his fluffy brown hair. But maybe I need a diversion. Maybe it will be better if Whitaker is right and he can prove Paxton is as evil as he says.

Ruby likes Whitaker. She'd believe him. She doesn't like me right now, but if Whitaker truly has some kind of hard evidence that can discredit Bill, I'm all for it.

We stop by my truck and I take my pistol out of the glove box. I put it in my belt at the back, under my shirt. "Okay. Let's go."

TEN

I realize before we leave the speedway that whatever Whitaker plans to show me probably isn't going to mean much. After all, he doesn't realize that Bill has taken Phil's place and Phil is dead. That puts him at a disadvantage. But I'm going with him anyway.

Of course, I don't know for sure if Bill's telling the truth. I trust Ruby's intuition on this more than I trust the cat not going to Bill. Of course, the facts seem to be on her side as well. There was the matter of Bill's beaten face and Phil's untouched one.

And that, plus the old Brink's money bags, is about it. John seems to have been kidnapped. But maybe this is another ruse to get money. Bill admitted he knew about his brother hijacking the ten million dollars, and I don't think he made a beeline for the police.

In a lot of ways, I'm sure I know more about this case than Whitaker. But he's local, and I believe he's been looking for either the finder's fee or the money itself for years. This also puts him in the position of being a suspect, as far as I'm concerned. At least for the kidnapping. Maybe he got tired of waiting and decided to take John for a ride somewhere until his brother coughed up the money.

I figure I can tag along with him and find out what he really knows. Maybe it's something that can help figure all of this out. If not, it gives me a few hours until I crawl back to Ruby and beg her forgiveness. I'm wrong. I know I'm wrong. Anything that puts me on Ruby's bad side is wrong. Especially if she plans to spend the night in the hotel without me.

Whitaker starts out at a couple of watering holes right around the track. He knows everyone in Dover, it seems, and they all know him. In a way, that's something in his favor as far as the Paxton murder is concerned. They all know he's been looking for this money and they've all heard his conspiracy theories. He wouldn't have anything to gain by killing Phil.

I get the message at the first bar that people tend to take Whitaker's obsession with the money as a joke. There's a lot of snickering and some outright laughing when we walk into the room. Whitaker fervently defends his point of view: Bill Paxton was murdered as a warning to his brother. John was kidnapped and is probably being tortured or killed at this moment for the same reason.

At the third bar, he introduces me to an ex-cop who was on the job during the disappearance of the Brink's truck. Whitaker buys the old guy a couple of beers, and we go into a dark corner of the bar to hear what he has to say.

"Yeah, I knew something was wrong," the ex-cop says. "I couldn't do nothin' about it. Those Paxtons have this town sewed up, you know what I mean?"

Whitaker's pale eyes light up. "Tell Glad what you overheard being said the night of the robbery."

"Yeah." The ex-cop takes a swig of his beer. "I was standing close by when I heard the captain tell Paxton he understood what was needed. Paxton gave him an envelope. I'm sure there was money in it."

"He?" I ask. "Is he still on the force?"

"Yeah. He was downgraded from captain to lieutenant after he got caught in another scandal. But he's the ranking officer in Burglary. Osbourne."

Whitaker nods. "I told you I could give you hard evidence."

"If this is so hard, why aren't the police looking at it?" I glance around the bar. Two guys in leather jackets have just walked in. If they aren't carrying sawed-off shotguns under there, I'll eat my shirt. There's a look and an awkward way of moving.

They order a couple of beers and stand with their backs to the bartender, scoping out the room. There might be twenty or so people sitting at the bar and in booths. There's about to be a problem, and I wish I weren't sitting here to notice it.

"You've seen how the police treat the Paxtons," Whitaker argues. "It does no good to tell them anything."

"Yeah. Somewhere there's a file with what I just told you in it," the ex-cop assures me.

"Notice anything strange about the two at the bar?" I ask him, careful not to look their way.

"Yeah. Looks like something is about to go down." He stands up. "There's a back way out. If we go now, we might not get involved."

I lean forward and stare hard into his face. "I guess I haven't been off the job long enough to look the other way yet. You two sneak out if you want. I think I can keep this from getting ugly."

Whitaker glances at the two men in leather jackets. The ex-cop nods and gets up to stroll out the back door. I take out my pistol, and Whitaker checks his revolver.

"I believe I may be of assistance in this. I'll take the one on the right."

"Good man. If we can get up there behind them before they notice us, we can move this out of here."

And that's what we do. We sneak up behind the big, old-timey wooden bar, keeping the bartender quiet and looking forward. He doesn't give us away and presses his silent alarm button as the first man pulls out his shotgun and tells everyone to hit the floor.

The look of surprise on his face is comical as Whitaker puts his snub-nosed revolver to the man's neck. "Please put the weapon on the bar. I certainly don't want this to get ugly."

The second man starts to reach for his gun, and I react in much the same way. "Throw that thing on the floor. I've had a bad day, and I don't want to make it worse by shooting you."

I look into his face. He's just a kid, a scared kid. He drops the shotgun on the floor and puts his hands behind his head. He's a scared kid with a rap sheet, I correct. He knows the drill. So does his friend. No crying. No whining. They assume the position and take what's coming. There's no sense of desperation. This is probably the first time their exploits have included weapons. They don't know it yet, but they've crossed over into the big league.

The Dover police pick that moment to break in through the back door. Weapons drawn, sheriff's deputies at their backs, they yell for the two men to freeze. Then they notice the suspects are already on the floor.

The first officer pushes his hat back and stares at me and Whitaker. "You guys did a good job. Whitaker, is that you?"

"Yes. And this is retired homicide detective Glad Wycznewski, from Chicago. It was at his instigation that we foiled the perpetrators."

"Well, I'll be." Four other officers rush forward and take over our positions with the suspects. The first officer shakes my hand. "I'm happy to meet you, sir. It's a good thing you were out tonight. Here for the race?"

"My wife and I got in yesterday. This place is hopping, huh? There was a death and kidnapping at the track, and now this."

"It's not usually this bad. But when you add 140,000 people into the mix, there's bound to be problems. I know you know what I mean."

"I haven't been off the job that long," I assure him. "I hope I won't have to testify."

"Probably not, but leave me your name and someplace I can get in touch with you. Thanks again for your help."

Whitaker leaves his name and number too, although I'm sure everyone knows how to get in touch with him. My opinion of him may have changed. I don't know a lot of men who would risk their lives for strangers if they weren't getting paid for it.

Maybe I'm wrong about the PI. I've been known to judge people too quickly, especially if they happen to have an English accent and are private investigators. That's a bad combination in my eyes, but I admit I may have been too hasty.

There's no sign of the ex-cop when we walk outside the bar. I make a decision to tell Whitaker about the switched identities in the Paxton brother's death. Besides trusting him a little more, it might be good to see what he does with the information.

His thin white eyebrows lift in surprise. "Who knew the boy had it in him, eh? Everyone has always said Bill is a little crazy, but perhaps that's not true. And perhaps Phil wanted all of us to think it was true. My word, what a change in the weather!"

I don't trust Whitaker enough to tell him about the Brink's bags buried in Bill's old house. I think this is enough for now. "Do you think Bill could have murdered Phil for the money?"

Whitaker contemplates the question. "You mean besides the right to run the casino and hotel and live a life of luxury and power?"

I have to laugh at that. "I guess that's what I mean. From what I understand, Bill has never wanted any part of it. He says he only pretended to be his brother because someone is looking for the money."

"My dear boy, many people are looking for the money. It's like a treasure hunt. People have read about its disappearance for years. Most people assume the Paxtons took it. It wouldn't surprise me if someone desperate suddenly got more aggressive in his search."

"Any ideas about who that could be? I can tell everyone knows about *you* looking for the money. Is there someone else?"

He looks affronted and slightly hurt. Either he's a damn good actor or he's genuinely upset by the question. "I do hope you aren't suggesting I might be the one responsible for this."

I shrug. "Somebody killed one of the Paxtons and kidnapped the other. Bill says it's someone who wants the money. I can't argue with that."

"Not me, I'm afraid. My quest has always been for the truth. And the finder's fee, of course. Ten percent of ten million buys a lot of tea. Besides, my wife is set on the idea of living in Florida, near her sister."

I can't tell him I completely believe he's innocent, because I don't. It's possible one of the reasons the leader of the men who attacked Bill stood off to one side and didn't speak was because he had an unmistakable accent. Or not.

"I have no way to prove it isn't me," he replies. "But I do hope you think better of me now."

"It's late." I put away my pistol. "I'm going to find Ruby and hope she isn't still mad. I'd rather leave tonight and miss the race than have that kind of argument with her again."

"Good luck. I hope to hear from you tomorrow." Whitaker shakes my hand. "She's a prize. I suggest you consider groveling. I've been married over thirty years, and it always works for me."

———————

Okay. Maybe I'm wrong about the guy. Or maybe he grows on you. I'm the first to admit Ruby has good instincts when it comes to deciding who to trust. She chose me, didn't she?

I figure the hell with the murder or anything else tonight. I'm going to bring my wife back home. I don't want to spend the night without her.

I'm smart enough to realize I'd better take a shower and change clothes first. I smell like stale beer and cigarette smoke. Not conducive to groveling. I head back to the campground and pull in between our RV and Ruby's parents' motor home.

There's a light on in my kitchen. I hit the steering wheel in frustration. I'm getting a little tired of people going in and out of my home. I don't see a police car around. Where are the cops when you need them?

I take my pistol out of the glove box again and get ready to confront whoever it is inside. I sneak up to the door and pull it open quickly, hustling up against it and staying away from the wide open space. "I don't know what you're doing in here, but you'd better get the hell out while you still can."

Ruby looks out the doorway, her mouth full of something. She's wearing her pink bunny slippers and matching short pajamas. I don't know when I've been happier to see anyone. "I got hungry. When did you go all military on me?"

I reach up, beer and tobacco smell aside, and kiss her right on the mouth. "Peanut butter. Yum."

"Make up your mind. Are you going to kiss me or shoot me? I'm not standing out here for long."

"Baby, I missed you."

"It looks like it." She sniffs and walks back into the kitchen. "I'm only gone a little while and you're out running around, getting drunk and having a good time without me."

I put the pistol away and close the door to the RV. "I've been out with your friend, Whitaker. He was showing me some of the sights in Dover. Particularly those that might prove Paxton is guilty of killing his brother."

She smiles slowly after chugging some milk from a glass. "You changed your mind, didn't you? Forsythe's a good guy, right?"

"I don't know." I reach over to hold her. "I don't care about anybody getting killed or kidnapped if I can't be with you."

"That's very sweet, but you didn't want anything to do with it anyway. I talked you into it. What else do you have?"

"I can grovel," I respond right away.

"Now *this* is what I came back for," she says with a smirk. "Can you do it in a sexy way?"

"Any way you want it, sweetie."

"Hmm. Maybe we should take this into the bedroom. I think that might be the right place for it."

I glance around. "Where's the cat?"

"I already took care of him. Now, about that groveling..."

Early Saturday morning, Ruby and I are sitting outside eating breakfast. There's a chill in the air and a threat of rain. If it gets any worse, they'll have to cancel qualifying for the Busch and Nextel Cup series. Already people are passing us, grumbling because the weather is bad and they've lost too much money at the slots. Things are sluggish, with a lot of people trying to get a few hours' more sleep before the grandstands open at nine.

"So if we trust Forsythe now, where does that leave us?" Ruby munches on a microwaved chicken biscuit. Steam from her coffee is rising up in the misty air.

"I don't know," I say. "I guess it puts us back to suspecting Bill."

"I really don't think it has anything to do with Bill, except in a peripheral kind of way. He's related to Phil, who stole the money. But otherwise, I think he's a good guy too."

After spending last night making up with her, I'm prepared to agree. It doesn't make any sense, but I don't know if I care.

"Hey, Glad!" Andy Anderson saunters up to our awning, newspaper in hand. "You're famous! The whole campground is buzzing with what you did last night. You're a hero!"

"Let me see." Ruby takes the paper from him and scans it. "This is what you were doing last night with Forsythe?"

"It happened. I'm happy we were there to help out."

She doesn't look happy about it. "Thank goodness you didn't get yourself killed! You should've let the police take care of it. Isn't that what you're always telling me?"

"This wasn't rocket science, honey. The guys were half-wits anyway. It was like taking candy from a baby."

"Anyway," Andy interrupts, "I think it's great. Just like old times for you, eh, buddy?"

"Yeah." I look at Ruby's face, wondering what she's thinking. Andy takes a couple of biscuits with him and heads toward another RV, where people might be more excited about his news. No doubt he's the one who spread the word to everyone else. I'm sure not all that many people would recognize my name without having it pointed out to them.

"There has to be someone else," Ruby says, continuing our initial conversation like Andy was never there. "Forsythe said everyone knows about the money. We have to find the person who was most eager to get there first."

I put my hand on hers. "Are you okay about last night?"

"I'm fine, I guess, since you're still alive. If you were dead, this would be a different conversation."

I see a little hint of a smile around her lips before I kiss her. "I'll try not to be in a bar that's being robbed again. That's the best I can promise."

"That's all right then." She sips her coffee. "It's kind of strange thinking about you tackling some coked-up teenager with a shotgun. I guess you *are* a hero."

"I did what I thought was right. It wasn't a big deal."

"I wonder what kind of progress the police are making with John's kidnapping." She changes the subject as quickly as she changes the color of her fingernails.

I kiss her hand. She's gonna handle it just fine. "I'm sure they'd *love* to share that information with us."

"Bill told me last night they expect him to drop the money today."

"They really think he has the money close at hand?" I grab another biscuit from the plate on the table. "It usually takes some time to get that kind of money together."

"If I saw all those Brink's bags all over someone's house, I'd think they had the money close at hand too. No point in waiting."

"Does Bill think John is still alive?"

"He does. He believes he can save him with the money."

"I hope he's right. He's a good guy. It's a tough break to get tangled up in his brothers' mess."

There's nothing more we can do about the kidnapping or the murder. At nine, we shuffle over to the grandstands to watch qualifying. Ruby is excited because she's sure Jimmie will win the pole. His car was messed up a little yesterday, but word is it's all fixed now.

Zeke and Louise join us before the cars hit the track. Both of them are in raincoats—a smart move since the sky looks like the day Noah loaded the animals on the ark. It will be a miracle if we make it through qualifying without rain.

The area is covered with television and newspaper reporters. They have tents set up everywhere to interview the drivers and crew chiefs. CNN is interviewing Mark Martin under its tent. *Sports Illustrated* has Kasey Kahne, with Jeremy Mayfield waiting in the wings.

The grandstands are full today despite the threat of rain. This is one of the main events, and a good time to show support for your driver.

I wish my driver were here. There's a certain lack of enthusiasm when I know I'm facing four hundred laps without Joe. I hope he's enjoying his vacation. Maybe he'll be at Pocono. We'll be there after this race.

We all sit up a little when the PA system calls out Team Hamilton and Bobby's car takes the track. Maybe that's who I'll pull for in this race. I'd love to see him place, anyway. No way he'll win the pole, but a nice top-twenty spot would be excellent.

Zeke is pounding the arms on his wheelchair. I've never seen the old man so excited. Bobby is doing better on the turns today, despite the humidity on the track. Louise is happy too. She actually grips my arm as Bobby pushes 140 miles per hour down the straightaway.

"He's gonna do it!" she yells as she squeezes the blood out of my arm. "Look at him! Just look at him!"

"Go, Bobby!" Ruby whoops. "This is almost as much fun as yelling for Jimmie."

"Keep your foot down, boy," Zeke advises his son from the grandstand. "You got it! Hold on to it!"

The field of cars is accelerating now. Each car is trying to take the lead and get the best position for the race tomorrow. Bobby is holding his ground, but Mark Martin is in the lead. He's a good, solid driver. Too bad he has a problem with a loose hood pin and has to head for pit road.

That puts his teammate, Carl Edwards, in line for the pole. He's usually in front in that number 50 Roush Racing Ford, but this time he's charging through the pack. The other cars are making room for him or trying to head him off.

In the meantime, Bobby has started sliding backward in the running order. He's telling Lance the car is too tight. He can't get on the gas at all. The crew chief brings him in, checks the air pressure, and makes a few track-bar adjustments. Bobby comes out of pit road screaming, but it's hard to tell if it's going to do him any good.

"I think he's gonna get a spot," Zeke predicts. "He's running hard out there. The boy deserves a spot."

At that moment, the rain starts falling. There's no warning of light mist here or there, just big glops of water all over us and the track. Nextel qualifying is over. That means the Busch qualifying will have to be postponed, as the speedway crew has to hope for the rain to stop. They can dry out the track if they get a break.

"Look at that!" Zeke is hopping up and down in his chair as they post the results. "He got in! Number fifteen. Not too bad. I knew the boy could do it!"

About that time, two men in dark suits holding the biggest umbrellas I've ever seen walk up to me and Ruby. "Mr. Paxton would like a word with you."

ELEVEN

I FOLLOW THE MEN in black back to the hotel as the rain scatters NASCAR fans like leaves on the road. Ruby walks under the umbrella with one of Bill Paxton's strong arms. I pull my hood up on my rain jacket and keep my distance behind them. I can't help it. Nothing in this feels right. Paxton and Whitaker might be as clean as Mother Mary Sebastian's habit on Sunday, but there's still the matter of a death and a kidnapping.

It's nice to finally get out of the rain when we reach the hotel. I'm happy Bobby made it into one of the top spots for the race tomorrow. Fifteen isn't too bad. If he does that well during the race, Hamilton will be doing a little jig. I know his chances aren't that good, but you never know when a miracle will happen. Every driver has to have his first win.

Of course, most of the top fifteen spots in a race like Dover are going to go to Cup regulars like Junior, Jimmie, Kurt, and Jeff. Bobby's running hard, though. He might be one of those regulars someday.

The hotel is as noisy as a campground usually is during race week. With the rain, I see a lot of familiar faces from the circuit hiding out here. Bart waves to me on his way to play the slots. Another couple stop and say hi. I'm really happy when they move on, because I can't remember their names.

That's how it is sometimes. Ruby and I know a lot of people who go to the same races we go to every year. Some of them we get to know. Others are familiar faces we wave to before moving on. I'm sure they feel the same about us.

Hoping this isn't a repeat performance of Paxton summoning us to his hotel room the last time, I stand next to Ruby in the quiet elevator. I've seen the look on Paxton's men's faces. They're hired help. Probably good pay to take care of their boss's little problems, like searching our RV and intimidating people who give him a hard time.

Ruby is thinking what I'm thinking. Not a surprise. That happens a lot. As we get out of the elevator with the hired guns behind us, she leans close and whispers, "Here we go again."

"Let's hope this time Paxton is in a friendlier mood."

Friendly isn't the word for it. He's all smiles and offers of food and drink. He's all Bill and no Phil. If I didn't know there were two of them, I'd say he had a split personality.

Ruby goes into the bathroom to dry off a little. Paxton sends his men to another room as he offers me a beer. "Sorry about the race. I wouldn't have planned it this way, but it may have worked out for the best for me and John."

"Why's that?"

"Because I need someone I can trust to deliver the money to the kidnappers."

"You probably pay those two goons enough to trust them." I take the beer and sit down on the white furniture, not caring that I might be wet and dirty. "I know you're not thinking of asking us to do it."

Paxton sits opposite me. "Those are Phil's guys, not mine. I'd be willing to pay you enough that you could have a brand-new RV. It means a lot to me."

"What does?" Ruby joins us and sits beside me.

Paxton explains his proposition. "The plan has changed. The kidnapper doesn't trust me. He wants someone else to bring the money. I don't know who else to turn to."

"Did he specifically ask for us?" Ruby is thinking like me again. Is the kidnapper someone who knows we're mixed up in this?

"No. He said someone I trust not to run away with the money. I understand how he feels. This is a lot of money."

It's on the tip of my tongue to say, *You should know.* "You got the ten million dollars together?" I find that hard to believe. Did Phil steal the money only so he could keep it around and look at it? My guess would be that it's long gone. Where does someone keep ten million in cash?

"The board of directors for the hotel and casino raised the money in the hopes of keeping this quiet," Paxton confides. "They want this under the media radar, which means keeping it away from the police. If anyone finds out about it, John will be killed."

"This isn't something we can do." I put my beer bottle on the white and gold table. "There isn't any amount of money that would make me risk Ruby's life."

"It should be perfectly safe," he continues. "After all, they're getting what they want. All you two have to do is drop off the money and then go around the block and come back to that spot. John should be waiting there when you get back. Nothing to it."

"If you got this ten million from your board of directors," Ruby asks, "what happened to the money Phil took from Brink's?"

Bill shrugs. "I don't know. Now that Phil is dead, I may never know. He controlled everything. That operation was his."

"How did he do it?" I hope to get some clue to what's really going on. I don't plan on helping him, but the information may come in handy. "I mean, it had to be tough to steal that money and get away with it. I don't think there's anyone living in Dover who doesn't think he took it."

"Phil always controlled the police," Bill speculates. "Of course, he was a master planner too. He should've been a general in the military during some great war. He could've turned the tide."

"But even if Phil told the police what to believe," Ruby says, picking up my thought, "what did he do about the insurance investigators? There had to be a mob of them here for a while. And where did he hide the money?"

Bill shakes his head, a gleam of something like admiration in his eyes for his twin brother. "He had a plan for that too. I don't know what it was. He never confided in me. But I'm sure it was brilliant. Phil knew what he was doing."

I glance at Ruby as I stand up. "I'm sorry, Paxton. We can't deliver the money for you. These people may seem like lapdogs to you, but they may have already killed once. You don't know that they won't kill again. I don't want to be there to find out."

"Glad, we have to do this." Ruby stands up next to me. "John needs us. If we don't do it, *he* could be killed. I can't live with that on my conscience."

I was dreading this part. I knew she wouldn't be able to say no. From the look on Paxton's face as he kisses her hand, he knew it too. I don't have much choice but to go with her. Unless I can talk her out of it.

We run back to the RV in the rain after Paxton tells us what we have to do. I don't try to change Ruby's mind in front of him. He's got one of those faces people feel sorry for, like those paintings of sad-eyed dogs that used to be around.

"Ruby, these guys probably killed Phil. You know that." I open the RV door and let her inside first.

"They don't have any reason to kill us, honey. We haven't done anything. All we'll be doing is dropping off the money, which they want, and picking up John, who they won't want anymore once they have the money. It seems pretty simple to me."

"More people are killed trying to do something like this without the police helping them than during bank robberies," I say to her, quoting statistics everyone should know. "It may be true they don't *want* to kill us, but if we see them, they won't have any choice."

"Well, we'll just have to look the other way. We can't say no to the chance of saving someone's life." She smiles and kisses me. "Isn't that what you told me about being in the bar during the holdup last night?"

She's got me there. How can I argue with that logic? Especially since I was the one who spelled it out so clearly for her. "All right. I'll do this. But there's no way you're going out there too."

That was the wrong thing to say. You'd think by now I'd know her better. It's like waving the green flag in front of a pack of drivers. I know I'm about to get run over.

"I'm going too. If I don't and you get into trouble, who'll watch your back?"

"I can watch my own back," I argue incoherently. "But I can't watch both of our backs."

Ruby looks in the number 48 cookie jar and takes out her little pistol. "I think we can watch each other's backs, darlin'. I'm not a helpless victim. If things get nasty, we'll take care of it. We make a good team."

There's no more time to discuss it. A horn blares outside the RV. I glance out the door. It's Paxton's goons in a black Mercedes limousine. "All right. We'll do this your way."

She kisses me and rubs off the Pink Flamingo lipstick she's wearing that transferred to my face. "We always do, honey. Don't feel bad. It's best this way."

We start out the door and meet Zeke and Louise coming back from wherever they hid to get out of the pouring rain. It's drizzling now, but not so bad. Zeke has a garbage bag tied around himself that doesn't seem to be keeping the rain off of him. Louise is soaked, but her hair is dry under the pink plastic hat she's wearing.

"Where are you two off to?" Louise asks. "We're going to have a little qualifying celebration for Bobby. Ruby, I could use your help."

"I'd like to help you, Mama, but I have something I have to do."

"What's more important than your brother qualifying for this race?" Zeke demands, his loud voice booming from his tiny body.

"I have to deliver some ransom money for John. Otherwise the kidnappers will kill him."

I look at Zeke and Louise, wondering if they're going to believe that. It seems to me like most people wouldn't. But I guess they know their daughter, and if she says she has to deliver ransom, it must be true. My old man would've slapped me in the kisser for talking back. It wouldn't have mattered how old I was.

Louise nods, water dripping from her plastic hat. "All right then. But you get on back here so you can congratulate your brother. This is a big moment in his life. He needs his family."

"Are you taking someone with you?" Zeke stares up at me. "I hope *you* plan on going with her, son. I don't like the idea of my girl out there delivering ransom by herself."

Louise tuts. "Oh, Zeke. You know Ruby can outshoot her husband. She can take care of herself. Quit picking at her."

I thought they might try to talk Ruby out of this crazy scheme she's intent on. No such luck. If it wasn't for Bobby needing to have a party, Zeke and Louise probably would've offered to go with us. Why not? The more the merrier.

We get into the limo and are heading out of town when one of the bozos in the front seat gets a call on his cell phone. He finishes talking, then looks back at us. "Change in plans. We're going out to the airport."

I'm starting to like this less and less. Whoever the kidnapper is, he doesn't have a strong grip on what's going on. That's bad for us and for John. Kidnappers who are organized and have a solid plan tend to stick to their word about not killing people. This guy probably was stupid enough to let John see his face. The chances are that John won't come home again. I hate to sound fatalistic, but I've worked too many kidnappings that ended badly.

"What's going on *now*?" I ask either of the meatheads in the front seat who feel like answering.

"We're following orders. Boss says go to the airport, we go to the airport."

The Dover Municipal Airport is only a few miles from the speedway. There are a bunch of prop jobs on the wet tarmac alongside some nice little jets. I don't even want to imagine what's coming with this. I knew it was a bad idea. I like John, I really do. I think he's had some tough breaks. But I'm not willing to lose Ruby's life or my own to save his. Call me selfish.

"Looks like we're delivering the ransom from a plane," the meathead in the passenger seat says.

"Good thing you're here, because we aren't going up in a plane in the rain." I make this statement as final as I can. I hope Ruby agrees with me this time.

She sits forward. "I wonder why they changed delivery methods."

"Who cares?" I try to cut off that line of thinking. "We can't go any further with this. I'm not going up in a plane."

"How are we going to make the delivery?" Ruby questions the driver.

"Boss says the pilot will take you up over the site and you'll drop the package from there."

"What about John? How are we going to get him back?" She checks out her lipstick as she's talking.

I'm wondering if I can do this without throwing up, and she's checking her makeup. Planes and I don't get along. That's why I have an RV. There shouldn't be anyplace we can't drive to.

"Boss says the new plan is the kidnapper will bring John home." The heavyset bozo shrugs. "It ain't my decision."

"Ruby, we have to get out of this," I urge. "It was bad enough the other way. This is worse."

"Why? You were worried about the kidnapper killing us," she reminds me. "This way, we're out of range unless he wants to shoot

139

down the plane. I feel safer. Besides, you know how much I like to fly."

I don't want to think about it. Last year for our anniversary, we went skydiving over the Infineon Raceway in Sonoma. I came close to throwing up and embarrassing myself in front of the other sky-divers. It wasn't a pretty picture. Ruby loved it. She said it was like being a bird. I guess except for race cars, I'm conservative with how many times I come close to losing my life.

I'm about to argue my point further when it occurs to me that this might be for the best. Our anniversary is coming up again. Maybe if she goes up today, it will be enough of a thrill to keep her from want-ing to skydive again.

"You're right." I laugh at her open mouth and push her chin up with my finger. "Relax, sweetie. I'm in this with you. Whatever it takes."

Of course it sounds suspicious. It doesn't matter. Some thoughts I manage to have without her thinking the same thing. This is one of them.

While I'm congratulating myself, we get out of the limo and run to the plane, which is already warming up on the tarmac. Our escorts see us onboard and then hand me two suitcases that look like they came from Goodwill. I guess Bill didn't want to drag out the Gucci for the event. The board's money doesn't have to travel in style.

The plane is red, white, and blue. I'm sure I saw it yesterday flying over the speedway with a big banner advertising Shrimpfest, "All You Can Eat for $12.99." The pilot shakes my hand. The en-gine is too loud to hear much. I suppose he knows the plan.

I'm surprised our escorts don't join us. After all, we could persuade the pilot to fly us somewhere else with this money. I'm sure he'd do it for a million, leaving us with the other nine. Bill must trust us more than I'd trust most of the people in my family.

With that thought in mind, I start to open one of the suitcases as the two bozos close the door to the plane and it starts moving down the runway.

"What are you doing?" Ruby watches me.

"I was thinking Bill might have pulled a switch and kept the money. It doesn't make any sense that he would trust two people he just met with ten million dollars."

Ruby smiles and shakes her head, calmly closing the suitcase. "There's something to be said for trusting your fellow human. Don't forget, Bill and I spent time talking in the RV before any of this happened."

I'd worry about that statement, except I know Ruby was driving and her mother was with her. Louise won't even let *us* fool around in front of her, and we're married. No way she'd sit there and watch Bill flirt with Ruby. Although she was quick enough to write me off when she thought Ruby had left me for Bill.

We're sitting in our seats as the plane takes off. The sky is cloudy, with a light rain falling across Dover, but no storms like Thursday night. I'm assuming this would have been called off if that happened. I'm happy I don't have to find out.

"I think the pilot is going to signal us when we're supposed to drop the suitcases," Ruby yells over the noise from the plane. "Don't worry. I'll do it. You stay here. I think it would be better if you don't hurl all over whoever is waiting down there for the money."

I look around the passenger area. Evidently, not many people fly in the plane on a regular basis. There are two seats, a lot of boxes, and a few parachutes I hope won't be necessary during this trip. I wonder if Paxton owns the plane or if the pilot is a friend. Does he know we're dropping ransom money? Maybe that's how Paxton means to keep us honest.

"I wonder how far out this is?"

"You're not sick already, are you?" She looks at me with a worried frown.

I kiss that place where her brows come together when she frowns. "I'm fine so far. I just want to get this over with."

"We'll all be happier when John is home again. We can do this, Glad. It's a piece of cake."

I hug her and hope she's right. The plane is weaving back and forth like a race car looking for an opening in the back of the pack. The engine sputters a few times but continues on. There's a little window near where we're sitting, but I avoid looking at it. I don't think anyone should have their feet this far off the ground.

Ruby is in her glory. She takes off her seat belt and dances through the empty body of the plane. Her arms up in the air, she yells, "Look! I'm a bird!"

"Come and sit down before you fall and get hurt. They put these seats and seat belts in for a reason."

"You sound like my mother." She laughs at me and takes it back. "I'm wrong. My mother isn't afraid of flying. My father isn't either. I don't think my granny is afraid either."

"Okay. You made your point. No one in the world is afraid to fly except me."

"I'm sorry." She sits down beside me again. "I shouldn't make fun of you. You can't help how you feel."

There's a buzzing sound and the pilot's voice joins us. "We're approaching the target area. You should open the door and get ready for my mark. When I say drop, drop the suitcases."

I take off my seat belt and move the suitcases close to the door for Ruby. "I hope these are old Samsonites. That's the only way they won't shatter and leave this money flying all over a few acres down there. Remember those old commercials when they dropped the suitcase and it stayed in one piece?"

Ruby positions herself close to the door. "I don't remember those. I must've missed them."

That's when I realize she probably was a baby when those commercials were on TV. I try not to let those kinds of things bother me. We're a few years apart, but I know Ruby loves me. We might be from different generations, but our souls are in the same time zone.

"Be careful," I warn as she pushes open the door in the side of the plane. "Don't sit too close."

"I'll be fine," she yells back. "Stop fussing."

The pilot tells us we're over the mark. Trees and roads form between cloud banks below us. I don't see anything. It must be coordinates on a map. I push the first suitcase close to the opening so it will be easy for Ruby to get it out the door.

She grabs the handle and slings it out of the plane. It drops like a rock through the misty clouds between us and the ground.

I push the next one toward her and she grabs the handle. As she struggles to get the suitcase into the air, the plane takes a sudden dip and turn. Before I can move to hold her back, Ruby falls out of the plane, still holding the handle of the suitcase.

TWELVE

RUBY DOESN'T SCREAM. SHE falls silently. Her gaze meets mine for a split second. Time stands still.

Then the suitcase flies out of her hand. Suddenly, everything is frighteningly real and the full impact of what's happened crashes down on me.

It takes less than a second for me to realize what I have to do. It's funny how unafraid I suddenly am when faced with seeing her fall. All I can think about is doing something, anything, that will keep her from dying.

Inside, I'm a screaming madman. Outside, I calmly grab two parachutes and strap one of them to my back. In the next breath, I jump out of the plane.

The last time I did this, I was terrified. This time, I'm calculating what I need to do to catch up with Ruby. I know she's falling faster than me, accelerating because of gravity. I remember that much from the experience last year. I have to reach her with the extra parachute before she falls too far.

I maneuver myself like the instructor told us to over Sonoma. I need to get a visual on her. If I had a moment to stop and realize what I'm doing, I might question how much I really remember and how much is wishful thinking. I don't have that time, so I'm amazed I remember anything. I didn't realize I'd paid such close attention until now.

She's about a hundred feet below me. I remember they told us something about streamlining your body. It was a no-no to go head-first straight down, because it causes you to fall faster. That's not good when you're skydiving. You're supposed to spread yourself out so the wind pushes up on your body until your parachute opens. The other way, the wind can't grab you and you're like a bullet sliding through the air.

I'm not sure, but it seems to me I have to reach Ruby before my parachute opens. Once I have that drag, I'll never get her. I can't let myself think about it. I'm going to find a way to reach her and help her put on the spare parachute before it's too late. Anything else is ridiculous. I won't lose her to a stupid mistake.

I point myself straight down toward her, holding my legs together and keeping my arms at my sides. I feel like a missile flying at her. The instructor was right. I drop like a stone in a few seconds, but I have a hard time finding her. The clouds are so thick in places, it's like looking through cotton candy.

There's a break in the clouds and I see her. We're side by side, almost close enough to touch. I can't believe she still isn't screaming. Hell, I can't believe *I'm* not screaming.

A shift in the wind currents propels me away from her as I reach my hand out to grab her arm. I'll never forget the look in her eyes. She's not panicked or thrashing around, but her blue eyes are filled with terror.

It's that look that spurs me to push against the strong current of air. I'm passing within inches of her, but moving my arm toward her is like trying to lift an old Dodge. There's so much pressure against me, I'm not sure I can do anything. I grit my teeth and force my arm out another six inches. The effort causes my head to pound and sweat to break out on my forehead. Still, it's not enough.

"Ruby! Give me your hand! I can't reach you. I need your help."

At first, she doesn't move. She seems too scared to respond. I keep pushing against the wind current trying to tear us apart. I yell at her again, trying to get through to her. I've seen people look like this when standing at the edge of a burning building or not moving as a truck comes toward them in the street. I don't know what else I can do. I feel like someone has kicked me in the gut. This can't really be happening.

"Honey! You have to focus. Look at me! Try to reach me. It's the only way."

She blinks and stares at me. It can't end this way. There has to be some way to get through to her.

"Baby, if you don't try hard to reach me, somebody is gonna get all your Jimmie Johnson collectables. I know you don't want that to happen."

"Glad!" She finally snaps out of it and yells back. "What are you doing? It's stupid for both of us to die. Get back on that plane!"

"It's stupid for either of us to die," I holler back. "I have a parachute. And I don't think this ride goes up."

"Put your parachute on. Save yourself."

"I have mine on already, and I have a parachute for *you* too." I hold it up to show her. The wind almost rips it out of my hands. "I can't reach you. Hold out your arm or try to move this way. Remember what the skydiving instructor told us last year. You have to move with the wind."

Ruby has the same problem I'm having. She lifts her arm toward me, but can't quite reach. She tries to change position, but by now, she's falling too fast and can't figure out how to do it. "It's no use. I can't reach you."

"No! Try again. Don't give up." I push my arm another inch or so when it occurs to me: I can change position and reach her with my legs. I reach her side again and lock my legs around her. We start falling faster, but at least we're together.

"Thank you. Thank you. Thank you." Ruby holds on to me like a baby monkey as she kisses me over and over.

"We're not out of the woods yet, sweetie. We have to put this parachute on you. Help me."

Together we begin putting the second parachute on her. I'm not sure how long we've been falling or how close I am to where my parachute needs to be opened. The ground is coming up out of the haze pretty quickly. I start to make out people and houses in the fields below us.

Somehow we manage to get the parachute on her. We move away from each other and nod as we both pull our ripcords. I don't know what to expect at this point. I hope we're still high enough to survive the fall. I can hear the noisy racket of the plane high above us, but I can't see it. I wonder if the pilot has reported this new glitch to Paxton.

I pull on the left cord to angle the parachute that way. I can see what looks like a cornfield below us. Ruby is headed that way too. Better to have a bunch of plants to break your fall than the trees to the right.

There's a farmer with a tractor who looks like he's starting into the field for the day. He's pulling a lethal-looking piece of machinery behind him. Sharp spears are pointing up right at me. It's not enough I jumped out of a plane after almost having a heart attack watching my wife fall into the sky, there has to be some weird killing machine on the ground waiting for me. Sometimes it doesn't pay to get out of bed.

At least Ruby is safely away from the murderous farm equipment. I pull and pull on the left cord, but I'm not moving. I hope the farmer will see my dilemma and move away from the spot. But he seems so amazed to see people falling from the sky on top of him that all he can do is sit and stare.

At the last instant, a gust of wet wind blows me away from the machinery tines and I drop to earth in the cornfield beside the tractor. I fall flat and realize I probably should have rolled or stuck my feet out (I can't remember which at this point). The huge parachute drapes across the tractor and the farmer, catching in the sharp edges of the farm equipment.

For a moment, I lie on the wet ground, not moving. I take a deep breath. The air smells like summer rain and corn. My ankles hurt, but otherwise I seem to be in one piece. I can't believe it. I feel lucky enough to play the slots or check out a horse race. Then I realize I may have used up all my luck for this year.

"Glad!" Ruby runs through the crackly corn stalks, shouting my name. "Glad, where are you?"

I push myself up and look into the farmer's face. It's deeply tanned from long hours in the fields. Brown eyes are alive with questions beneath a wide straw hat. "Sorry about your corn."

"That's okay." He laughs. "I wasn't expecting visitors. Lucky thing Margaret has some fried chicken left over for lunch."

It's not as easy to get disentangled from the farm equipment. The farmer, whose name is Joe (a lucky sign for sure), helps me and Ruby cut the lines to the parachute. Ruby hardly waits for me to get clear of the nylon before she jumps and wraps her legs around me. We both fall to the ground. There's no time or breath to talk as she kisses me over and over while we lie between the crushed cornstalks on the muddy ground.

"I can't believe you saved me. Not that I didn't think you would if you could. But I can't believe you saved me. I thought I was dead. Mama would've been furious if I'd died that way. It was stupid. This whole thing is stupid. I don't know why we're even involved." She glances around us. "Where do you think those suitcases went?"

"Is that what fell before you two?" Joe untangles the last of the parachute from the farm equipment.

"Yeah," Ruby answers. "There were two of them. Did you see them?"

He points toward the other side of the cornfield, which seems to go on for miles. "Those two young fellers pulled up when they fell and put them in their Jeep. Paid good money to wipe out some of my corn too."

"Do you know who they are?" I guess I should probably offer him something for the corn we crushed as well.

"Nope. Never saw them before."

"What did they look like?" Ruby pursues the subject.

"Tall. Big. Dressed in black suits with some kind of decal on the pocket. They looked like nightclub bouncers or FBI agents." Joe scratches his head. "You two need a ride back to the city?"

"Did they contact you before today to tell you they'd pick up the suitcases?" I begin to feel like I fell out of a plane and hit the ground too hard.

"Sure. They came by yesterday and told me it was a prank. They said they'd pay for the damages and pick up the things that fell from the plane. Will they come back for you?"

"I don't think so. Is there anything else you noticed about them that may be helpful?" I'm beginning to get a bad feeling about this.

"Now that you mention it, both of them were wearing a pin of some kind. It was small, gold with red and green lettering."

Ruby pulls a business card from the pocket of her jeans. "Did it look like this?"

He nods. "Like that in pin form. It matched the emblem on their blazers. You two want some lunch?"

———————

After a hearty lunch of probably the best fried chicken and dumplings I've ever had (I'm not saying that to Ruby, since Louise's fried chicken and dumplings have won medals at the North Carolina State Fair), we climb in Joe's old truck and head back to Dover.

Ruby's eyes are full of unspoken anger and questions. We can't really talk in front of Joe, but we both know what it means that the two men who retrieved the suitcases could be identified with the hotel and casino. They were probably two other men who work for Paxton.

Beyond that, I don't know what it means at this point. Paxton dropped ten million dollars in a cornfield and had his men pick it up. I don't know how this will impact John's kidnappers. It looks to me like Bill may be *pretending* to be Phil, but the twins obviously think alike.

I know Ruby is thinking the same thing. That's why she's mad. Bill tricked us and probably planned to keep the money from the beginning. He had us drop it out of the plane, not knowing we would be dropping out after it. Otherwise we would've gone back to Dover and never known the difference. The last-minute drop swap makes sense now.

The pilot knows what happened. It makes me wonder what kind of reception we'll get when we get back to Dover. Bill has to know we know what happened by now. He also has to know Ruby well enough to know she won't keep her mouth shut.

Maybe we shouldn't go back to Dover at all. Joe's not racing anyway. I've had about enough of this quest for the ten million dollars.

But anger and the distinct feeling of being used sends us back. I know Ruby feels the same. It would be nice to forget about it. Except we were almost killed and John is still missing.

We slam into the hotel after thanking Joe for the ride and offering him some money, which he doesn't accept. We don't wait to be escorted up to Bill's private suite. Instead, we take the elevator up and pound on the door.

It's a letdown when the door swings open. Furniture and clothes are strewn everywhere in the gold and white sitting room. Ruby and I both take out our guns and glance at each other.

"Isn't there some kind of hand signal you're supposed to do when you might be walking into a trap?" she whispers.

"If there is, neither one of us would know what it meant. Stay behind me and we'll look through the suite."

She nods and heads for the door on the opposite wall. What was there about what I said to make her think she should wander off by herself? I hiss and try to get her attention. She ignores me. I don't want her to encounter anything else by herself today. I follow her into the next room.

It looks the same as the sitting room. Pieces of paper are torn up, glasses smashed. Everything in the room seems to be in more than one piece.

"It looks like the RV," she says. "What do you think happened?"

"I don't know." I see a jagged line of what looks like blood splattered on the wall beside a chair. The chair is soaked in it. "I think we'd better call the police."

"You know they don't like us."

"I know. But we may be standing in a crime scene. There could be tapes of us being here. I would rather call and make them angry than pretend we didn't see this and leave."

"Do you think Bill is dead? Maybe the casino men who got the suitcases weren't with him. Maybe they took the money and whoever kidnapped John came in and killed Bill."

I take out my cell phone as the door to the suite is kicked in, breaking off its hinges. Someone yells, "Dover police! Don't move!"

"This is a mistake," Ruby tells them. "We just got here and Bill was already gone."

"Drop the weapons and kick them toward us. Then get down on the floor with your hands behind your heads."

"We were about to call you," Ruby tries again. "You got here just in time."

I put my pistol on the floor and use my foot to slide it toward the officers. "You can't reason with them right now, sweetie. Just do what the nice officer tells you. We'll have a chance to tell our side in a little while."

"But Glad—"

"Drop the weapon." The officers take aim. "Don't make us tell you again."

Ruby sighs and drops her pistol. "I'm really getting tired of this. Is everything in this place screwed up? Where I come from, police officers listen to what citizens are telling them."

"Let's just lie on the floor and argue later." I put my arm around her and we both sink down. "Let's not make the officers nervous or anything."

Ruby huffs and puffs but finally lies down with her hands over her head. The officers rush forward and pat us both down. Then they cuff us and are in the process of helping us to our feet when Ann joins us.

"You two again?" She takes a deep breath and looks around the room. "Any sign of Mr. Paxton?"

Two of the officers shake their heads. "No ma'am. Just this mess. It looks like someone was taken by force."

"Let them go," Ann tells them. "They have a knack for being at the wrong place at the wrong time, and this is the civilian who stopped the robbery at Paddy's last night. I don't think the media would like to see him in handcuffs."

"But they were here in the room, weapons drawn," one young officer argues with her.

"Glad Wycznewski may be a lot of things, including forgetful and unavailable, but he's not a killer or a kidnapper. Let them go."

When our hands are free, Ruby and I walk out into the hall with Ann. We tell her everything we know from the beginning, and I hope it makes sense.

She nods and sticks a piece of gum in her mouth. "This is getting too confusing. We got an anonymous tip that something was wrong up here. I had a feeling Paxton knew more than he was telling us about his brother's disappearance."

"I think he may know more than you realize about a number of things," I tell her.

"It would seem so." She shrugs. "Think you can tell me how to get to this place in the woods you're talking about?"

"Not a problem. We'll take you there."

———

We spend the next hour going back over everything we've done and every place we've been since we got to Dover. I can't really tell if it's helped when we're finally in the police van and heading back to the speedway. The money is still gone. Both brothers are still missing. This is the worst race weekend I've ever been to.

"You're sure about all of this?" Ann asks us after talking on the phone.

"We're sure." I glance at Ruby and she nods. "Why?"

"Because the officers I left behind at the old farmhouse tell me the Brink's bags we saw there aren't real. Someone made them up to look like the real thing, but it must've been for show."

"The question is," Ruby drawls, "whose show was it for?"

Ann shakes her head. "I don't understand."

"Well, Bill said the boys threatened him out there. He thought they were the kidnappers. Glad and I saw the bags and thought they were real. We pointed you that way. Who was supposed to see them?"

"I don't know." Ann looks at her notebook, pencil in hand. "We won't know until tomorrow at the earliest whose blood was on that chair in Paxton's suite. I hope we have something to go by that will tell us which brother it was. Otherwise we may never know the truth about this whole mess."

"I have an idea about that," Ruby admits. "I've taken it on face value, so to speak, that Bill was the twin in the casino. I saw him with those marks on his face, so I knew it had to be him."

"I understand that now," Ann replies. "What are you getting at?"

"The thing that's been bothering me, and I know it's been bothering Glad too, is why Malibu wouldn't go to Bill at the casino. When he was in the RV, I could tell the cat was his familiar. He would've gone to him no matter what."

Ann rolls her eyes. "I'm not completely up on my witchcraft, but I seem to remember a familiar being a witch's sidekick. Is that right?"

"I don't think she means like that," I say, jumping in to defend Ruby. "I think she means the cat and the man had a close relationship."

Ruby shrugs. "Call it what you like. When a cat chooses a person, they stick with them for life. Malibu may like me or Glad, but he'll never be close to us like he was to Bill."

"Maybe you could come to the point?" Ann rests her head on her hand. "It's been a long day."

"My point is that it's possible the Paxton who sent us out with the ransom wasn't Bill after all. He could've been Phil."

"But what about his face and the bruises?" Ann asks.

"Well, what if Phil wanted us to think he was Bill? What if this whole thing was a setup that all hinged on us thinking Phil was Bill?"

Ann appears to be in pain. "Please, for the love of God, come to the point."

"Makeup." Ruby says it quickly and then smiles at me. "You can do anything with the right makeup. Do you still have the dead body from the track?"

"I'm sure we do. I doubt if there's been time for an autopsy yet." Ann thinks about it for a moment and then picks up her cell phone. "I'm getting a headache thinking that the dead man we identified as Bill, who you said was Phil because Bill told you so, may really be Bill. I think I need a drink before we go to the morgue."

"Amen," I add. "Could we stop for a pizza on the way too?"

THIRTEEN

THE KENT COUNTY MORGUE is a sterile environment, like every other morgue in the world. Ann introduces us to the assistant medical examiner, who is very firm about rules governing handling of evidence, which prevent Ruby and me from stepping into the lab. He's pleasant but not budging, which is fine with me. You've seen one autopsy, you've seen them all. They can glam it up on TV if they like, but I know better.

He shows us a window where we can watch him. Ruby is disappointed, but I've been present at plenty of autopsies. They may look disgusting, but the smell is far worse.

"Dr. Lightner isn't ready to do the full autopsy yet," Ann tells me and Ruby, deciding to stay outside the room with us. "He's willing to indulge my curiosity about which twin he has. In the meantime, I have an APB out for whichever twin is missing. I hope we can get some kind of handle on which is which. This case is driving me crazy."

"I'm surprised to see you actively involved in this," I say. I don't mind razzing her a little. "I don't know if any Paxton would approve."

"I know." She shrugs. "Sometimes you have to go out on a limb. With Phil Paxton missing, I have to take some initiative. Don't act so superior anyway. I know there were some untouchables when you worked for Chicago PD. It's the same in every town. There are always rich, powerful people who are well connected who can't be touched."

I agree. "At least not until the time is right."

"We've both been there, Glad. What I did was handed down from the top brass."

I'm willing to compromise. "You're right. I know you do a good job. I've talked to a few ex-cops who speak very highly of you."

"Shh!" Ruby silences us, her nose pushed up against the glass like a kid at a candy store. "He's getting ready to start."

But I have another question while Dr. Lightner is putting on his gloves. "Ann, what about this Forsythe Whitaker character? He knows everyone and seems like he's a joke for chasing after this money the Paxtons supposedly took from the Brink's truck. I'd like to know the truth about him."

"I can only tell you what I know. You're right. He knows everyone and everyone knows him. I think the whole Brink's job is an urban myth. Investigators from the feds on down to insurance agents looked into it when it happened. They didn't find anything. There's no doubt the truck and ten million dollars disappeared. The insurance company reimbursed the Paxtons. But if they had anything to do with it, I think someone would've found some clue.

The investigators had to have known everything about them, including what they eat for breakfast. It was that thorough."

"That's what I thought." I glance at the doctor as he removes Paxton's body from a drawer. "Do you think Whitaker could be involved in this new scam? I like him for all three: the robbery, murder, and kidnapping."

"Your guess is as good as mine. Whitaker used to be a detective at Scotland Yard—according to him, anyway. There was some kind of scandal and he came here with his family. That was right before the first heist. He's been like a dog on a bone since then. It probably has something to do with him being the security inspector for that shipment. He was fired. I think he took it personally."

"That's some interesting information." I turn my head to look through the window as the doctor displays the upper part of Paxton's body. So Whitaker *could* have been involved with the first missing ten million dollars. Obviously he doesn't have the money. I don't think he'd be there nipping at Paxton's heels for it if he did. But he could've helped plan the theft.

On the other hand, why were there fake Brink's bags at Bill's house? That doesn't make any sense. Why would someone (Bill, I suppose) want someone to think he had the money? This whole thing is too weird.

"Look!" Ruby points. "I was right. He's wearing makeup. Someone wanted us to think it wasn't Bill who fell from the bridge. That's why the cat wouldn't go to the fake Bill."

Ann looks in on the bruises beginning to show on the dead man's face. "So our dead man is really Bill after all. He was beaten at his house, according to what the woman at the rest area said and what you were told. Then Phil pretended, at least with the two of you, to be Bill."

"But you can see he had information about his brother and what happened at his house," Ruby debates. "Phil said he hadn't seen his brother for months. But he knew what happened to him. Why would he pretend to be Bill?"

"To get us to take the ransom for John," I conclude. "He needed a couple of sappy race fans like us to do him a favor."

Ann frowns, her dark brows knitting together. "At this point, I can't tell if Phil had anything to do with Bill's death, but he seems to be involved with the new missing ten million dollars. We have to find him."

"And John," Ruby reminds her. "It's been a while and there's been no sign of him, right? You left an officer at the hotel in case he was dropped off there."

"You're right," Ann agrees. "I'll check in with Officer Douglas, but I'm sure he would've called if either Paxton showed up."

I offer my humble opinion. "It makes me wonder if the kidnapping was real at all. Maybe this whole thing was a setup to get the money."

"Maybe." Ann pulls out her cell phone. "But where is John Paxton?"

"I hope his brother didn't hurt him," Ruby frets. "Phil may have murdered Bill. If so, he probably wouldn't hesitate to kill John too."

"In the meantime"—I glance at my watch—"we're less than twenty minutes until the start of the NBS StonebridgeRacing.com 200. I think it'll be dry enough to run the race. I missed everything else today. Any chance you can get us back to the track before then?"

Ann smiles. "My pleasure. I appreciate your help on this, and I'm sorry you got caught in the bad end of it. I was only following orders. I hope you understand."

I shrug. If she can get us back for the 200, who am I to split hairs?

One of the big problems in any race is wrecks. Dover is big enough to get up some speed but has those high banked turns that make it feel like a short track, which can mean some bad wrecks for unwary drivers. You'd think the multiple grooves in the concrete would help with handling, but even a good driver—or several good drivers—can get caught up in someone else's wreck.

Good spotting can go a long way to keeping a driver out of a situation. I'm envious of the spotters up on the grandstands with their high-powered binoculars and radio contact with the driver and crew chief. It would be great to see things from that vantage point.

The track is dry despite the bad weather earlier in the day. They were able to run the Busch qualifying without a wreck, but the 200 is a different story.

Under the green, the field of forty-three cars races along for several minutes with no mishaps. Todd Bodine had a few problems getting his car to stay on the track. Jimmie Johnson's number 48 car is able to move into the lucky-dog position of being the first car one lap down for nearly thirty laps in the middle of the race.

Ruby is ecstatic. She jumps up and down with her headphones on while I listen in to Jeff Gordon and his crew chief, Robbie Loomis, with Zeke and Louise. They had to find another driver to pull for after their longtime favorite, Rusty Wallace, retired. They picked Gordon because Louise said he seemed so nice at the drivers' autograph session. Zeke agrees and adds that he isn't a flash in the pan like some of the newer drivers.

I'm surprised they didn't pick Junior, since they're tight with the Earnhardt family. But it's hard to say why someone picks their driver. It's not always about winning or what the person looks like. I think I like Front Row Joe because he reminds me of myself. He works hard and he does the right things. Besides, he's a great guy.

On lap 157, so close to the end of the race, Jeff Burton's number 31 car suddenly hits the side of the track and spins out of control. Drivers who have enough time and really good spotters in the stands are able to avoid the wreck that follows.

Burton's car takes out three others, including Kasey Kahne's. The race is under the yellow caution flag to clean up the track and hopefully get the drivers back into the race.

You can see the looks of exhaustion on the drivers' faces (with binoculars or a battery-powered TV during the interviews). Burton is out for the race, as are two of the rookie drivers. Kasey Kahne's number 9 car isn't damaged too badly. He'll race again.

"Jimmie and Chad saw that one coming," Ruby says. "It's like they have ESP. Extra Special Driving Powers."

"Wouldn't that be ESDP?" I don't want to put a damper on her moment of victory, but lots of other drivers managed to get around the wreck as well.

"You're mad because Joe isn't here." She leans close and kisses me. "Cheer up. He'll be at Pocono."

A lot of good that does me here.

The race finally gets started again. Mark Martin takes the lead away from Jimmie Johnson with only a few laps to go. People are on their feet yelling. It doesn't get better than this. Whether you're pulling for Jimmie or Mark, to have it come down to a neck-and-neck finish is always exciting.

Martin holds his lead into lap 198, where he has to pit during the final caution of the race for another wreck, involving Carl Edwards. Jimmie has to pit too, so it's still hard to say which one will take the race. Both men have to be wound up tighter than a lug nut.

Jeff Gordon is right behind them when they come out of pit road. The crowd is going wild—stomping, whistling, and throwing whatever comes to hand. The fence prevents anything from getting on the track. The throwing is followed by spurts of Gatorade in various flavors and Cheetos that seem to come from heaven.

It's finally over, with Martin taking the checkered flag. No one can be too upset about it, even if their driver didn't win. It was one hell of a race.

"I can't believe it!" Ruby throws her headphones down on the seat. "He was right there. Jimmie deserved to win."

"Martin took him," I console her. "Jimmie can't win all the time."

"Jeff did a good job," Zeke says. "Too bad we can't pull for him tomorrow. But with Bobby racing in the 400, he gets my support."

"I love Bobby." Ruby retrieves her headphones. "But I have to pull for Jimmie. Imagine how upset he is after this race. He has to win tomorrow."

"Good luck to him." Zeke laughs. "But he'll have to get through my son to do it."

We all laugh at that, but who's to say this isn't the beginning of a great driver's career? Everybody starts out this way: driving on the short tracks, racing up and down the road. Some of them can harness that energy and go on to have a career like the Allisons, Pettys, and Earnhardts. It's possible.

Ruby has already signed us up for the charity fun walk on the track right after the race. Zeke and Louise leave us to it so they can go back and get ready for Bobby's party. I'd rather help them than walk around the track. I know it's for a good cause, although I can't tell you what that is. Ruby says it's important, and I guess that's enough for me.

The sponsors and supporters of the walk give us these little half hats Ruby says are sun visors. She puts hers on and flips her hair up in the back, big curls spilling down her neck.

I don't have any hair to put in mine, so I decide not to wear it. The visors are a pretty shade of blue, and all the women are trying to decide exactly what color blue it is. Is it peacock blue or lapis blue? Is it the color of Debbie's eyes or the color of Cindy's T-shirt?

It could be the color of meatloaf as far as I'm concerned. I'm not rude about it, but I stick the visor in the pocket of my jeans. If there's another man out here, I don't see him. It seems like I'm the only man walking with a group of a hundred women.

Normally, I wouldn't mind these odds. What man would? Not that I plan to do anything with any of them. Ruby is the only woman for me, and most of the time, she's more than I can handle. But a man likes to stand out in a crowd. I imagine that's what I'm doing right now.

We've walked the track almost completely around, and I'm thinking I might puke if I hear one more story about Oprah, when a male voice hails me. Even though it's Whitaker, I'll take whatever male company I can get. At least he's not wearing one of these blue sun visors.

"I've been looking for you everywhere," he starts breathlessly. "I think I may have a lead on where to find John Paxton."

I'm not sure what to think at this moment. I'm pretty sure Whitaker is okay after last night. But with today's revelations, I'm rethinking everything. If he's a con artist, he's a good one. But I've met some damn sharp cons before.

"What kind of lead?" I ask as I keep walking.

"A man saw him being taken out of a car only a few miles from here." He falls in line beside me.

Ruby, who's been getting a recipe for lemon chicken, comes back and starts walking with us. "Hey there, Forsythe! Where have you been?"

The question brings a spate of conversation about everything he's done in the past few hours. "I believe I'm on top of this situation now. In fact, I believe Glad and I are close to cracking this case wide open."

"Really?" Ruby glances at me, no doubt wondering why I haven't shared my abundant information with her. "What have you discovered?"

"A friend," he says, "an informant, actually, told me he saw John Paxton being taken out of a car, blindfolded. He told me where I could go to retrieve him. I came for backup. I'm hoping Glad will go with me."

"And will he?" She asks him but looks at me.

"I didn't answer yet. I wanted to know more about the situation," I explain, making elaborate facial distortions and rolling my eyes behind Whitaker's head. I hope it will show her how I feel without saying it.

"I say, dear boy," Whitaker addresses my weird behavior, which he's caught out of the corner of his eye. "Are you quite all right?"

"He's fine," Ruby answers for me. "He's had a little too much sun. He's allergic, you know."

He stares at me. "I didn't know. What a dreadful thing. Is there nothing that can be done?"

"Beer helps," I answer, naming the only cure I can imagine for everything. "Otherwise I have to stay inside until nightfall."

"I suppose we should *all* go check this place out," Ruby says. "But we'd better wait until it gets dark."

"My thoughts exactly, lovely lady." Whitaker does everything but kiss her hand.

"We're having a big party at my parents' RV for Bobby tonight," she says, despite my even stranger facial distortions. "You should come."

"I'd love to." He smiles and nods his head like a tall scarecrow. "We'll leave from the party, then. Perhaps Bobby would like to join us, since he and John are such good friends."

"I think we should leave Bobby out of this," I disagree. "He's got his mind on other things tonight. We need to be sharp."

"Indeed we do," he agrees. "Good thinking."

Ruby tells him to meet us at Zeke and Louise's around seven. The fun walk is starting to break up for most people on the second or third lap. All the little blue visors are drifting apart while the smell of steak sizzling on the grill starts drifting through the campground to the track.

It reminds me that I never got that pizza. I didn't really want to see the dead guy again, but I wanted that pizza. When Whitaker finally takes his leave of us (his words, not mine), Ruby and I start back for our RV.

"I think I need a snack," I tell her. "I think we missed lunch."

"There's not much time before dinner," she reminds me. "Maybe you could just have something to drink so you'll still be hungry for the barbecue. It won't be as good as Gene's BBQ back home, but it will be better than any you'll find around here."

"You're a barbecue snob."

"I am not. They barbecue *beef* here, Glad." She shudders. "There's something wrong with that."

I laugh and veer toward one of the concession stands that advertise Italian and Polish sausage. "I think I need a sausage to make it through."

"All right. I'll have a Coke and some fries since you're eating."

"You don't have to force yourself to eat because I'm eating." I kiss her nose and flick my finger against her sun visor.

"I'm hungry. Can't a person be hungry?"

She smiles, and I think about how much I love her and how wonderful it is to share my life with her. It makes up for finding my ex-wife cheating and for all of the crap I put up with for too many years on the street. They tell you being a detective is a step up, but it still isn't worth the pay grade.

We sit at a makeshift picnic table with a yellow umbrella above us while I eat two Polish and Ruby takes out some fries. Thousands of people are crammed into a very small space. Most of them are milling around eating or looking at display tables from various businesses. The atmosphere is friendly, with music playing and people dancing. Kids are jumping on one of those blowup castles, yelling and calling to each other. Everyone is excited about the race today and hoping tomorrow's race will be more of the same.

"So, what do you think about Whitaker knowing where they're keeping John?" I ask between bites. Not bad Polish for someone outside the city.

"I don't know." She dunks her fries in ketchup. "I like him, but it sounds suspicious to me. Why didn't he go to the police?"

I shrug. "They wouldn't listen? He wants the glory? It's anybody's guess. But I agree after today that it may be he's the one who kidnapped John."

"I suppose he could be the one who was the leader of that group who beat up Bill at his house. The one who stood off to himself."

"My thoughts from the beginning."

"Yeah, but you didn't like him from the beginning."

"But I was starting to like him."

"After your barhopping, robbery-thwarting adventures with him?"

I shake my head. "Laugh if you want, but a man can tell another man's mettle by how he reacts to that kind of situation."

"Unless the other man is trying to throw off the suspicions of the first man by pretending to have mettle."

"I don't even want to know what you're talking about."

"It's obvious." She dusts salt from her hands. "He knew you didn't trust him. He set up a scene to win you over. He succeeded."

I stare at her to see if she's joking. There's no way to tell.

About that time, Bobby rolls up and jumps out of his car. He runs over to us, the expression on his face almost comical. I can only wonder what emergency has come up now. The Furrs have a flair for the dramatic.

"Glad! Ruby! You have to come with me right now!"

"Where are we going, Bobby?" Ruby asks with an impatient sigh. "You know Mama and Daddy have gone to a lot of trouble to get this party together for you. If you disappoint them, I'm liable to run over your foot with the RV. It might be hard to drive fast with a cast on your toes."

"No," he argues, "you don't understand. I think I saw John. We have to go and save him. You two have to come with me."

Ruby and I stare at each other. Maybe Whitaker was on the level.

"I think we should call the police," Ruby tells her brother.

"You'll come, right, Glad?" He looks at me with eyes so like hers.

"I'm driving, right?" I glance at the Mustang.

"Sure. I guess."

"You're on."

FOURTEEN

Bobby directs me into one of the old neighborhoods in Dover. That's saying a lot. This place gets pretty old. I think these houses may have been standing when Delaware ratified the Constitution. They aren't slummy looking, just really old and kind of leaning, like a strong wind might blow them over.

"That's it!" Bobby points to a green two-story that needs a paint job. The neighborhood seems quiet. There are children playing in yards, running under sprinklers. Old men are sitting out on porches with straw hats and tall glasses of iced tea. Not the kind of neighborhood you'd expect to find a kidnap victim in.

"It needs paint." Ruby wrinkles up her nose. "That's the worst color I've ever seen. What is that? A cross between army green and puke yellow?"

Not wanting to get into another color debate like the one with the sun visors, I ignore her remark. "You're sure about this?" I ask Bobby instead.

"That's what my source told me." He looks at the palm of his hand, where the address is written.

"And who is your source?" Ruby asks him.

"I can't say. It would be better if you didn't know."

She hits him with the palm of her hand on the back of his head. "What do you mean you can't say? You drag us all the way over here with some stupid idea that we can rescue John and then you can't say who told you about it?"

He shrugs. "He didn't tell me who he was. I got the call when I walked past the pay phone near the garage. He started blurting out information. I asked him who he was. He wouldn't say. Then he hung up."

"So whoever it was knew someone at the garage would answer the phone and probably send the police after John." I consider the possibilities. "That's probably what we should've done."

"Duh!" Ruby sits back on the seat behind me. I can almost feel the yearning she has to slap me on the back of the head too. "You were so hot to drive Bobby's car, you wouldn't listen to reason."

"It's not too late." I take out my cell phone.

"We're already here now." Ruby pushes out of the car and looks at us like we're slugs as she pulls out her pocket-sized pistol. "We might as well go in."

"I'm not going anywhere with you holding a gun," Bobby declares with a passion he usually reserves only for driving. "Or at least, you have to go first. I don't trust you behind me with that thing."

"That's fine. I don't mind being first." She turns on her heel and starts toward the house.

"Hold on!" I jump out of the car. I probably won't get to drive it back. Too bad. It handles like a dream. "I'll go first."

"You're either crazy or insane," Bobby assures me. "Whichever it is, I hope you have me in your will. I could use that big old RV."

"Never mind that. This was your idea. Quit screwing around and get out here." I take my pistol from my belt and catch up with Ruby.

Bobby's right. That's not something I think very often. But in this case, it's justified. I'm crazy *and* insane, as he so aptly stated. This should be some Dover police rescue squad with sharpshooters, not an ex-cop, a fledgling driver, and a gun-toting ex-beautician. How do I let myself get into these situations? And why don't I realize they are "these situations" until I'm already in them? If I'd been this stupid as a rookie cop, I'd be dead by now.

My only excuse seems to be that love has destroyed my brain. I'm thinking this as we sneak up to the ugly green house, me in the front, followed by Ruby with Bobby behind her. I have no common sense anymore. My old Irish sergeant would shake his head and cross himself if he saw me here.

I stop as we reach the doorway. Like the Three Stooges, Ruby runs into me and gives a little cry of surprise. Bobby runs into her and stubs his toe on the brick walkway. He howls before he thinks to close his mouth. Good God! Can this get any worse? No wonder people who aren't into NASCAR think race fans are stupid. They've probably met us.

The doorway area is shaded by a huge old tree. It looks sinister, and I think for the first time (believe it or not) that this could be a trap.

Then I realize no one would believe the three of us would come after John. The chances are it isn't set up as a trap, since they would've been expecting the police to storm the house.

Oh well. We're here now. I can't walk away without looking like a pathetic loser. I might be a *dead* pathetic loser after I open the door, but at least I'll go out looking good. I grip my pistol a little tighter and then advance to the door.

I raise my leg to kick it open. Common sense weighs in at that point. Better late than never. The door looks pretty solid. I'll probably break my leg before I knock it out of the way.

Lucky for me, I don't have to. The door is slightly open, and I push it carefully the rest of the way until I can see into the room behind it.

It's a small living area: sofa, chairs, TV set. The room is in the shade of the old oak too. It's dark and shadowed, not easy to see into the corners like I wish I could. I caution Bobby and Ruby to hang back with a hand gesture. Ruby frowns. I know what she's thinking. We had that discussion about hand gestures.

I take one step into the room. The wood floor under my foot creaks like the door hinge on a '57 Chevy that's been rusting in someone's yard. Ruby and Bobby both shush me, and they're almost louder than the noise from the floor. If there *is* someone in here waiting for us, we might as well call out and tell them we're here.

"Help me," a voice croaks from an unseen room. "Please help me."

"It's John!" Bobby races past me into the house. "Hang on, buddy! I'm coming for you!"

Ruby puts away her pistol. "Well, I guess they know we're here now."

"It looks like he's here alone. Maybe we were wrong about Phil getting the money. Maybe the kidnappers set it up to look that

173

way, but they got the money and took off." As theories go, this one won't win any prizes, but it's all I can come up with.

"He's back here!" Bobby's disembodied voice floats back to us from a room down a long, dark hall. "Call an ambulance, Glad. He may be hurt."

"Why do anything that *should* be done?" I put away my pistol too.

Ruby takes out her cell phone. "Good thing it lights up. Is there electricity in here? Or do we have to stumble around in the dark?"

I walk to the wall and feel around until I find a light switch. The electricity works, though I can't say the light from the ceiling improves my feelings about the ugliness of this house.

"That's better." Ruby smiles as she speed-dials 911 on her phone. "What? Why are you looking at me like that? I thought it would be a good idea to have an emergency number I could get to fast."

"Because actually pushing three buttons would be so much harder than pushing one?"

"Never mind." She nudges me hard. "You do things your way. I'll do things the right way."

Actually, she may be right. Our lives were fairly placid until recently. Now we seem to need various emergency services quite a bit. Maybe I'll put 911 on my speed dial.

"Hey!" Bobby yells. "Hey, you two! Come on back here. You aren't gonna believe this."

We run down the long, now brightly lit hallway toward the sound of Bobby's voice. We find him in a small bedroom with a man tied hand and foot to a thick wooden chair. His face is a mass of bruises and cuts, like he's been beaten, but he's clearly not John.

"Phil?" Ruby moves into the room, her voice reaching dolphin levels as she can't believe her eyes. "What are you doing here?"

"I don't know. I was leaving the hotel and someone hit me in the head. Have you heard from the kidnappers? Is John safe?"

"Now why would we believe anything you tell us?" Ruby asks. She can get hardcore. It's rare, but this is one of those times. She stands over Phil in his chair like a drill sergeant. "You lied to us. You told us you were Bill. You wanted us to feel sorry for you so we'd deliver that stupid money, which you stole for yourself. We're on to you. We're not going to believe anything you say."

"I don't care if you believe me or not," he snivels. "I pretended to be Bill. I'm sorry. You seemed to like him so much. I needed someone to deliver that money to save John. I used you, yes. But only to save my brother."

"You could've used us just as well by telling us the truth," Ruby blurts out.

"I think what my wife means is that we would've dropped the ransom for John whether we thought you were Bill or not. There was no reason to lie to us."

"None of that really matters now," Phil insists. "Cut me loose. Take me to see John."

Bobby spins the old chair around so that Phil faces him. "You know we didn't find John. We thought he'd be here. Instead, here you are, probably pretending to be hurt so everyone will feel sorry for you."

"I don't know what you're talking about." He struggles with his ropes. "Let me out of here. I want to see my brother."

"That would be nice," I say as I hear the sound of approaching sirens. "But John is still missing. And unfortunately for you, your two goons were identified by old Joe out there in the cornfield. The police have a few questions for you. If you really stole that ten million the first time, you must've done it a whole lot smarter."

Officer Franks of the Dover PD is the first one in. I've been coming to this race for five years and I never even met a police officer before this year. Now I know one by name. "What are you two doing here?" He's looking at me and Ruby, so I'm assuming he's talking to us.

"It was my idea." Bobby steps up. He tells Franks about what happened while the paramedics are taking care of Phil.

Franks calls the other responding officers to let them know John could be on the premises as well. He thanks Bobby, gives me and Ruby a weird kind of look that says he hopes he doesn't see us again, and turns to Phil. "Mr. Paxton, Captain Barker has instructed me to place you under arrest, sir."

"What do you mean?" Phil demands. "Look at me! Do I look like I did something wrong? I'm telling you, the same people who killed my brother kidnapped me and beat me up to try to find the missing money!"

Franks looks like a man who's driving down the highway without much gas and knows a station is a hundred miles away. He's not going to make it, and he's uncomfortable as hell about it. But there's nothing he can do. "I'm sorry, sir. I have my orders. One of my officers will accompany you to the hospital."

"What are you arresting me for?"

"We're arresting you for fraud and embezzlement at this time," Franks tells him. "You have the right to remain silent. You have the right to an attorney."

I draw Ruby and Bobby out of the ugly green house. All the people out on their porches when we got here are now standing in the front yard, looking to see what happened. Police are searching the house and yard. A K-9 unit is rolling up with a German sheppard who looks like he could eat a small child.

"We still didn't find John," Bobby laments. "I wonder why whoever called didn't say Phil was here instead of John."

"Maybe he knew no one would come after Phil," Ruby says. "I don't think John was ever here. And who are these people who keep beating up the Paxtons?"

"Who can say?" I make a move to get behind the wheel of the Mustang and drive back to the speedway. Before I can reach that golden destination, Officer Franks calls me back to the house. Bobby grins and hops in the driver's seat.

I walk back to Franks, hoping he's not going to accuse me of beating Phil. "What can I do for you?"

"It looks like John Paxton might have been here too. We found evidence of another person being held in another bedroom. It could've been him. We'll know more after the crime scene team finishes."

I'm not sure how to respond to this new spirit of cooperation. I don't know what he's looking for from me. "I hope forensics will confirm that," I say.

"Maybe. I think the captain is making a mistake authorizing Phil Paxton's arrest. Her job could be on the line because of this."

I nod. Where's he going with this? It's like we're suddenly old buddies telling war stories over beer at the local bar. "Could be. Does she like him for killing his brother?"

"I don't know yet, but I think there must be something more than the fraud and embezzlement, you know?"

"Yeah." I can feel myself planting my feet wide apart and assuming the traditional position law enforcement officers seem to learn on the first day at the academy. I switch stances really quick. That's not me anymore, even though it may seem like it is.

Franks draws in a deep breath. "I heard you and the captain had a thing once."

"That was a long time ago."

"But you probably know her pretty well."

"Not really." *What the hell does he want?*

"I was wondering," he continues, "maybe you could put in a good word for me. I'm taking the sergeant's test this month. I need a good recommendation to go with it."

I almost laugh out loud. A thousand thoughts were going through my brain as I wondered what he was leading up to. He wants me to talk sweet to Ann about his promotion. The man must have scrambled brains even worse than I do.

"She's not too friendly toward me." I smile. "I was supposed to call, you know?"

"Oh. Okay. I get it."

"No. It's been a long time, and I've been married twice."

"She talks about you."

"Really?" I glance back at Ruby, who's waiting impatiently in the Mustang with Bobby. "What does she say?"

"Not much. But it's enough. You know what I'm saying?"

I see Ruby get out of the car and head our way. I have to wrap this up before I get into more trouble than any of this is worth. "If I have a chance to talk to Ann, I'll put in a good word for you, Franks."

He shakes my hand. "Thanks, man."

We're wrapping up our male-bonding session by the time Ruby's lips form the words, "What's keeping you, Glad?"

"Nothing, sweetie." I put my arm around her waist and nod at Franks. "I'm ready to go."

The ride back is an endless session of questions, with Ruby trying to figure out what I was saying to Franks. I'm flattered he thinks Ann still has a thing for me. It's not true, but an old war horse like me enjoys hearing it anyway.

"Can we stop talking about Glad and the cop for a minute and try to think how we can find John?" Bobby asks. "He's been gone more than twenty-four hours. He could be dead or crippled and not ever able to drive again."

I can tell from the sound of his voice that the first alternative would be preferable over the last to him. "He's got a good point, Ruby. We need to think how we can find John."

"What about Forsythe?" she suggests. "He said he knew someone who might know something. That could be a place to start."

"And you said my pay-phone call was lame." Bobby laughs at her. "This English dude knows someone who *might* know something. Now that's lame."

Ruby hits him in the head, and he jerks the car slightly off the edge of the road. He recovers fast (good reflexes), but I really don't want a repeat performance.

"You're lame," she tells him.

"No, you're lame," he taunts her.

"Okay, you guys!" I warn. "Bobby, don't make me have to drive this car."

"You wish!" He laughs at me and turns on the radio. "The best way to ignore your sister is not to listen to her."

He's a decent driver, but the boy has some vacant space in his head. Lucky for him he's young, good looking, and knows how to put his foot down on the gas. I'm sure he'll be fine. It's not rocket science.

"Well." Ruby turns back to me. "I think it would be a good idea to find Forsythe when we get back and see what he knows."

"All right. Let's try to get this wrapped up by tomorrow. I'm not missing the 400. I don't care who's dead, beaten, or kidnapped."

She smiles. "That's saying we make it back to the speedway."

Apparently, not listening to your sister isn't always the answer. I can see from the annoyed look on Bobby's face that he heard what she said, and she didn't even yell.

We get back to the speedway and find Bobby's good-luck party in full swing. I never knew there were enough pigs to make that much barbecue. It's a good thing, though, because half of the 140,000 race fans are here drinking a swimming pool of iced tea and eating a mountain of barbecue.

Zeke and Louise see Bobby as we pull up, and the crowd actually lifts him out of the Mustang and passes him up to the RV to be with his parents. It's like a reverse rock concert. I notice a few of the girls who help pass him are a little liberal with where they touch him, but I don't see him complaining.

"What a crowd!" Ruby says in a loud voice over the louder music.

"We'll never make it up to get a plate. We might have to eat it in our hands."

The face Ruby turns toward me tells me what she thinks of that idea. "I'll make it through. You wait right here."

I don't really have much choice anyway, because it only takes a minute to get partially sucked into the crowd. There's a lot more liquid here than tea. I can smell Jack Daniels on at least half of the people standing around me. The other half smell like beer.

"Glad!" Andy and June Anderson squeeze in beside me. "Where's Ruby?"

"Up there somewhere between the plates and her brother." I shake Andy's hand and smile at June. "What have you guys been up to?"

"We won some money at the slots," June says. "Then we lost it on a horse race."

"Easy come, easy go," I remind her.

"But we had a good time doing it," Andy tells me. "We had lunch at the Festival Buffet in the hotel. It was great! You and Ruby should try it."

Bobby has finally reached the front of the crowd. Zeke is trying to quiet the noise, and it passes back to us. "I want to thank you all for coming." Zeke's steady voice booms out over the silent partygoers. "I want to say a thank-you to the Lord for getting us here tonight and providing us with all this food. My boy is gonna win that race tomorrow. It's gonna be that kind of day."

Bobby hangs his head. "Aww, Daddy. Ain't no way I'm gonna win tomorrow. But I hope to give those boys, Junior and the rest, a damn good fight."

Zeke yells out, "That's my boy! You all have plenty to eat and help us pull for Bobby tomorrow!"

The crowd whoops loud enough to be heard over a car revving its engine. There's applause and laughter. Television cameras are headed our way as the media hunts for noticeable happenings the night before the race.

Ruby pops up at my side with a paper plate. "Hungry?"

"You know it." I kiss her. "Thanks."

I start to walk over to the barbecue when a dark shadow on top of our RV catches my attention. It's the damn cat. Someone else has been in our home.

FIFTEEN

AFTER MORE THAN HALF an hour of chasing Malibu through the campground, we finally catch him eating sausages waiting to be put on a grill ten RVs down from ours. Ruby picks him up and strokes him, tells him he's fine, while I pay the man for his sausages. It's okay, though, because it turns out he pulls for Joe too. We commiserate for a few minutes and I tell him about Bobby. He promises to pull for him at tomorrow's race. We're both looking forward to seeing Joe at Pocono.

Ruby and I take the cat back through the RV forest. "Do you think we should call the police and tell them we had another break-in?"

"Hell, it probably *is* the police. I don't see much point in calling them. Maybe we should see if there's enough barbecue for them at the party."

Still, we approach the RV with caution. Ruby has the cat and we don't want to go through chasing him again, so we decide I should go in first. "Be careful," she warns. "No telling who might be in there this time."

"I know. I might as well install a revolving door."

The door is still open slightly. I ease it open the rest of the way and look inside. It's dark, of course. Someone could be waiting in there with an Uzi and I wouldn't know it. I have to get to the switch to turn on a light. I think we'll get the Clapper next time we go to Wal-Mart. That way at least I'll be able to see who wants to kill me.

I'm dreading seeing the inside again. I hope this time whoever got in here cleaned up before they left.

I ease up the stairs and reach the light switch. Light from the kitchen floods the front of the RV. Nothing wrong so far. I creep to the back and check out the bedroom. Nothing there either. If someone was here, I can't tell. Maybe someone walked by and accidentally opened the locked door. I think we need an alarm system.

I go back and give Ruby the okay to come in. She brings Malibu in and closes the door behind her before she puts him down. "What's up?"

"Nothing, as far as I can tell. If someone was in here, they left us a clean house. If not, maybe the cat just wanted to get out."

We're both a little tense while walking through the RV to check the closets and the bathroom. Ruby looks in all the cabinets. I sit in the driver's seat and look around up there.

"Anything?" she calls from the kitchen.

"Nope. You?"

"Nope." She flops in one of the living room chairs. "It's weird."

"But what about this race hasn't been?"

We're starting to feel less anxious. I grab a beer from the fridge. Ruby flips on the TV. She likes to watch that tech stuff: computers and other gadgets. She's really good with them. She doesn't seem like the type, but that's one of the holes in profiling. Just when you think everyone can be buttoned into a certain pattern, along comes a sexy, gorgeous blond beautician who can probably hack into the Pentagon.

"What do you think they wanted this time?" she asks as I sit down with her.

"I don't know." I yawn. "It's been a really long day that I'd like to put behind me. I'm sore in places I didn't know you could be sore. I want to go to bed and get up for the race tomorrow."

Somehow, don't ask me how, she kind of slides from her chair into mine. She drapes herself across me and kisses me. "I can get into the whole bed thing."

"I mean sleeping," I tell her with another yawn. "I'm exhausted."

She kisses me again and moves down to my neck and shoulder. "Are you sure?"

"Now that you mention it, I think I can make an exception for a while." I push the strap on her tank top down and kiss her shoulder, then look into her big blue eyes and feel a rush of emotion. "You know, I almost lost you today. I don't ever want that to happen again."

"How do you think I felt when I saw you come after me?"

"What did you think I'd do? Just stand there and watch you fall?"

She hugs me, and my arms tighten around her. "I love you. Thank you for saving me."

I know it's not right. I should be more of a man about it, but I can't speak for a moment or two. It's all I can do not to blubber like a baby. "I love you too, sweetie. Let's not let something like that happen again."

"You got it, baby." She starts kissing me again and I'm thinking we should head into the bedroom when she hears someone talking about some gadget on the tech show. "Oh, look, Glad! There's that thing I was telling you we need."

By this time, I really don't want to see anything except Ruby without her clothes. Reluctantly, knowing this isn't going to happen until I look at the damn gadget, I take a peek. "Wow. Cool. What does it do?"

"Stores information. You know how you always have me save the track and race information? This would let me take it off the computer and put it on my keychain. That way if there's a fire or someone breaks into our RV, we're covered."

A couple of weeks ago, even a couple of days ago, I would've laughed at the idea. But maybe she has a point. I'm hoping to put all the information we've saved about the tracks, drivers, and races into a book. I don't know what I'll do with it after that. Maybe I could sell it and make a million dollars. We could get a new RV, one of those top-of-the-line models.

"Sounds good. Where do we pick one up?"

Before she can answer, there's a knock at the door. I think we should ignore it. The party next door at Zeke and Louise's is still going full blast from the sound of it. There are going to be plenty of hangovers in the morning and lots of Tums tonight.

But Ruby is already at the door. The mood is gone. I might as well drink my beer and go to bed.

"Forsythe!" Ruby says in surprise. "It's nice to see you. Would you like to come in?"

"Thank you, my dear. Your brother's party is the highlight of the event. I hope he fares well tomorrow."

"Thanks. I hope so too. He's been racing since he could reach a gas pedal. I think he'll be okay." She glances back at me. "Glad, we have company."

Like I couldn't figure that out in the small space we live in. "Hello, Whitaker. How's it going?"

"Tolerably well, thank you." He comes in and sits across from me. He reminds me of a stork in a polo shirt and khaki pants. "I heard about your excursion into old Dover today."

"Yeah? I suppose the police scanners picked it up."

"Would you like a beer or some sweet tea, Forsythe?" Ruby asks.

"A beer would be lovely." He turns back to me. "I heard you found Phil Paxton instead of his brother. Is that right?"

"That's about it." I tell him about Phil's condition and his denying being involved with the missing money.

"It's happening again." He shakes his head and tells Ruby thank you as she gives him the Bud. "He's going to get away with stealing another ten million dollars. It's unbelievable."

I agree. "The police have him this time. Sending his goons out for the money wasn't very smart."

"It's arrogance. Paxton doesn't believe he can be caught." He sips his beer and mourns the loss of the money. "We'll never find any of it."

"There's still John to consider," Ruby reminds us. "That money doesn't mean anything compared to his life. If Bill was killed for it and Phil staged this whole thing to get his hands on another ten million, what's to stop him from killing John so he doesn't tell anyone?"

I ask her, "Why kill him?"

"Perhaps John knows his brother is responsible for this. The way Bill knew Phil took the money the first time," Whitaker offers as he lifts Malibu onto his lap. The cat purrs and hunches down on him, green eyes staring hard at me like he's trying to tell me something.

"Let's think about that for a minute." Ruby sits down and turns off the TV. "Let's say Bill knew where the money is and kept the secret all these years for Phil. He really was threatened by someone who beat him up looking for the money. Maybe he came back here and told Phil he couldn't keep the secret anymore. That's when they got into the fight. Then Phil pushed him off the bridge. He knew that key was up there."

"But that was all part of the props for trying to get this new money," I remind her.

"Oh yeah."

"My theory suggests that Bill got tired of waiting for his share of the money and threatened to expose his brother," Whitaker tells us. "He was helping Phil set up this new scam by planting the key on the bridge when Phil took advantage of the situation and killed Bill so he wouldn't have to share."

I shake my head. "I can't believe there's still ten million dollars hidden somewhere. Why wouldn't they have spent it a long time ago?"

"Maybe they were scared they'd get caught," Ruby suggests.

"Or what seems more likely to me with this new scam," Whitaker says, "is that they spent the money and managed to conceal it. After all, everyone knows the Paxtons have money. We expect them to lead extravagant lifestyles. But they ran out of cash and thought of a way to get more."

It sounds plausible to me. Even the part about Phil being arrogant enough to send his own men to pick up the money in Joe's cornfield. People get cocky. Some of the most notorious criminals have been brought down because they were so sure they couldn't get caught.

"But why would Phil set all that up in that old house?" Ruby asks. "I'd take the money and run."

"There's nowhere he could hide," Whitaker tells her. "Especially since this is his second strike. The insurance companies would find some way to bring him back. They are more relentless when they lose money than the CIA and Scotland Yard combined."

"He can't possibly think he's going to get away with this." Ruby balls up her fist. "If he hurt John . . ."

Whitaker's cell phone goes off. He's messing around with Malibu's collar, which is caught on his watch. The cat meows and tries to jump down while Whitaker tries to disentangle himself.

He answers the phone with his other hand, and Ruby tries to keep Malibu on his lap while she separates the watch and the collar. Finally she takes off the cat's collar and puts it on the cabinet. Malibu jumps down, and Whitaker excuses himself to step outside and talk on the cell phone.

"We have to find John." Ruby's words are absolute. "We can't let him become a victim in all this."

"I don't think Paxton means to kill his brother. He didn't finance his racing career, but that doesn't mean he'd hurt him. Just because he killed Bill for getting greedy doesn't mean he'd kill John." I hope I'm right about that. One thing's for sure, I don't know where else to look for him. He could be anywhere.

"If Phil was using John to get the money," Ruby says, "then he might still have him stashed somewhere. He can't get to him to do his miraculous reappearance, because he's in jail."

"If that's the case, let's hope he put John somewhere he can survive on his own."

Whitaker comes back in, closing his cell phone. "I believe I may have found John. If you'll recall, I told you I had an informant who thought he knew where Paxton left the boy. At the time, my informant didn't realize it was indeed the older brother trying to reap another ill-gotten gain. But now, it seems assured."

"Where is he?" Ruby asks. "Let's go get him."

"Whoa!" I hold her back as she makes for the door. "Remember falling out of the airplane? Let's think about this."

Ruby looks at Whitaker. "Is he in an airplane?"

"No. Did someone tell you he was?"

"All right," she says to me. "Let's go."

"I'm not marching out there in the middle of the night on a wild goose chase because someone told someone John might be somewhere. You can forget it. Let's call the police and let them do their job for once."

Forsythe sniffs indignantly. "Lead on, Ruby. I'm right behind you."

————————

Of course, I go with them. But in my own defense, I have my cell phone on hold for a police detective. Robbery, homicide, I don't care which one. But I'm not letting Ruby go by herself. Let me amend that: I'm not letting Ruby go with Whitaker. I'd rather she go by herself.

I can't explain exactly what it is that bothers me about the man. He seems okay on the surface and he helped me out at the bar. Maybe I don't like how Ruby acts as though every word he says is the Gospel According to Saint Whitaker. Or maybe I'm a little cheesed to be dragged out of my home on another fool's errand. Especially when Ruby and I were about to cuddle up for the night.

"So where are we meeting your informant, Forsythe?" Ruby ignores me as I hunch in the back seat and try to get someone from the police department on the line. Don't these people work on Saturday night?

"We are meeting him at one of the prestigious historic sites in Dover," Whitaker explains in his usual long-winded fashion. "And a very apt one it is, if I do say so myself. Did you know Delaware delegates met in secret on December 7th, 1787, and ratified the Constitution at the Golden Fleece Tavern? That made Delaware the first state."

"Nice history lesson," I interject. "But what kind of place is this? I've seen a few historic places I wouldn't want to take Ruby in at night."

"Oh, Glad!" Ruby shakes her head as she follows Whitaker's instructions into the old part of the city. "You make me sound like I'm two years old."

"It's not that kind of place at all," he assures me. "In fact, it's not a *place* at all."

"What the hell does that mean?" I know I sound a little irritable. Okay, a *lot* irritable. "Are we meeting this guy at a tavern or not?"

"We're meeting the gentleman at the place where the tavern *used* to be. All that is left is the sign." Whitaker looks back at me and smiles.

At that moment, the detective on duty picks up the phone. I tell him who I am and where I'm going. "We believe we have a lead on finding John Paxton. Could you send someone out?"

"Who did you say this is?" the detective asks in a supercilious manner.

"Does it matter who it is?" I ask back in a way that's bound to raise someone's hackles. I know better, but I can't stop myself. "We're about to meet an informant who knows the whereabouts of John Paxton."

"Who is this informant?"

"I don't know. He's a friend of Forsythe Whitaker's."

"Well, you and Mr. Whitaker better come in to the station and tell us what you know. We'll handle it from there."

"Look, most informants don't hang around waiting until the police say it's okay."

"We don't go out on civilian calls, Mr. Wycznewski," the detective tells me. "You come in. Bring your friend, and we'll decide what to do."

I push End on my cell phone and put it in my pocket. This is not my night.

"Pull over there, Ruby." Whitaker points to a parking space on the infamous village green in historic Dover.

I can see the sign for the Golden Fleece from here. The area isn't well lit, and not a lot of people are hanging out here. I look around, gauging where someone could be hiding. I might as well forget it. The question is, where *couldn't* they be hiding?

Last time we were in Dover, Ruby and I went on a ghost walk in this area. There must be a hundred ghosts in about one block. I don't really believe in dead people walking around holding lanterns or their heads. On the other hand, I believe in some places being bad luck. This could be one of them.

Ruby and Whitaker hop out of the truck. I follow close beside them, feeling like some kind of damn bodyguard. They're talking and laughing like this is Sunday afternoon in the park instead of a dark, quiet street where anything could happen.

"What's this man's name?" Ruby asks Whitaker.

"Oh, he's a contact I made some years ago. He has had valuable information from time to time. I don't even know his name." Whitaker chuckles. The two of them laugh, the sound echoing off the dark houses around us.

"Okay. That's it. Kindergarten cookie time is over, kiddies." I step between them. Both of them stop and look at me. "If we're gonna do this, we're gonna do it my way."

"And why is that?" Ruby challenges me.

"Because my way is the safe way, and the two of you sound like you're sharing one brain cell tonight. So here's how it's going to go."

I outline my plan for them. "Ruby goes back and locks herself in the truck. Whitaker and I meet with his informant. We bring the information back to Ruby and leave as quickly as possible in case this whole thing is a setup."

"What sort of setup are you referring to, Glad?" Whitaker asks me.

"The kind where someone takes advantage of you because they know how desperate you are to find the first Paxton millions."

Whitaker's astonishment is almost comical on his long face. "I would *never* endanger Ruby's life that way. I've known this snitch for years. I don't understand why you would think he is dangerous."

"Because he's paranoid," Ruby explains. She pulls on Whitaker's jacket. "Let's just get over there and get the info so we can find John."

"Ruby, I'm half-tempted to let you do this without me," I warn.

"Maybe *you* should wait in the truck." She continues walking.

I only have one other card to play. I don't want to play it. I've tried to work around it. But I don't have any choice. She could be walking into a life-threatening situation.

"What was that?" I look out into the darkness around us.

"What?" Ruby responds, trying to follow my line of vision.

"Did you see that?" I ask, frowning.

"What?" She looks at me. "What did you see?"

There's only one thing I've ever found that gets to Ruby. She was raised by a family who believes they see ghosts almost everywhere. Ruby's dead great-grandmother was a regular visitor in her grandmother's kitchen. Her mother saw a spectral train running through the farm at least once a month. There were Confederate battles in the woods fought by long-dead soldiers. I won't say she's afraid of ghosts, but Ruby is wary of them.

"I'm sure I saw the ghost of that woman we heard about last year," I tell her in a no-nonsense voice. "I saw her come across the green and disappear into one of those buildings."

"Was she holding a lantern?" Whitaker asks in a breathy voice. "If she was, it could be the ghost of Rebecca Bartlett. A tragic story. She was brutally murdered right here on this spot a hundred years ago. They say she appears to people who are about to die."

I don't know if Whitaker really believes this stuff or is trying to scare Ruby too. He's definitely helping my cause, whether he knows it or not. My only question is: is my wife buying it?

"Maybe we *should* go back to the truck." Ruby's voice is squeaky as she moves closer to me. "We can fight the living, but we can't fight the dead."

"She's right." Whitaker moves closer to me as well. I can't believe I hit something he's afraid of too.

"That's okay." I slap him on the back and take a step away from him. "Why don't you take Ruby back to the truck and I'll meet with your snitch."

"Oh no!" Ruby clutches my arm. "You can't stand out here by yourself. What about Rebecca Bartlett? She might be looking for you."

"I can handle it, sweetie." Maybe it's better this way. If Whitaker and Ruby are both back at the truck, neither one of them can get hurt.

"Okay, honey." She looks around. "But be careful."

As Ruby and Whitaker scuttle back to the truck, I forge ahead to the lighted sign of the Golden Fleece. It's so quiet here I can hear my footsteps as I cross the street. I know I won't be mistaken for Whitaker, so I hope I can convince the snitch I'm working with the man.

There are two narrow passageways between the old houses that sit on the street by the sign. Both are too dark to see anything. I stand under the old tavern sign and wait to make contact. In the meantime, I hear another set of footsteps coming close. I can't see anyone, but I'm not a cat and I don't see in the dark.

The footsteps stop right behind me. A rough voice says, "Who the hell are you?" as the barrel of a gun lodges in my back.

SIXTEEN

I FEEL KIND OF stupid. I could've had Ruby and Whitaker out here with me, but I had to play the hero. I *never* do that. I don't know what's wrong with me. So now I'm stuck on a dark street with a gun in my back and no one to call for help. Good thing I was a cop and know so much about what I'm doing. Yeah, right.

"I'm Glad Wycznewski." I try to BS my way out of it. "I'm here in place of Whitaker."

There's no reply, but the gun is still stuck in my back. Not a good beginning.

"We're trying to find John Paxton. Whitaker said you had a tip."

Still no reply.

I consider whether I have a snowball's chance in hell of twisting away, avoiding the inevitable shot, and grabbing the gun. Or if that would only piss him off.

It sounds like a lot to do, but I've done it before. Five years ago, but I don't think I should let a little thing like that stop me. After all, he could just shoot me and I could bleed to death in the street before Ruby and Whitaker get out of the truck.

I start to make my move, lightning fast and almost invisible to the naked eye. At least I hope so. Too bad he doesn't see it the same way. He pokes the gun harder against me and gruffly tells me to cut it out or I'm dead.

I'm starting to get a little pissed. I might not be twenty-five anymore but I'll be damned if I'm going to roll over and play dead.

With a snarl for courage, I push back and whip around in time to land him on the cold cement. I kick the gun out of his hand and hear a distinctly female, Southern "Ouch!"

Breathing hard, I sit on my victim. "What the hell were you trying to pull?"

"I got you!" She laughs up at me. "I scared the crap out of you, which is what you deserve for trying to get rid of me."

"Ruby, honey, I could've *killed* you. Don't *ever* try that again."

"Then don't ever send *me* back to the truck like some bad child. Do you think I couldn't see through that whole ghost routine? Come on, Glad. That was really lame."

"Yeah, right. You got your nerve back after you got to the truck," I accuse her. "Your knees were knocking out here."

"I knew right away." She pushes up against me. "*You* didn't know it was me holding my finger in your back. That's for sure."

"You weren't holding your finger back there." I continue straddling her. "Tell the truth. You stuck your gun in my back."

"No way. I'm not that stupid. Get off of me. You weigh a ton."

"Say please," I tease her.

"No," she grunts. "Okay. *Please*."

"Pretty please," I urge, laughing. "Did Whitaker stay in the truck?"

"Yes. You really did scare *him*."

"Excuse me?" A strange voice comes from the general direction of the dark walkway. "Are either of you Forsythe Whitaker?"

I get up quickly and help Ruby to her feet. She slaps my hand away and pushes the hair out of her eyes.

"I'm here to see Forsythe. I have some information for him."

"Forsythe couldn't be here. I'm Ruby, and this is Glad. We're helping Forsythe look for John. So anything you can tell us would be good."

I can't see him, but I can feel him staring at us, wondering if he should tell us anything. He probably thinks we escaped from the loony bin. "If it makes you feel any better," I say, "I used to be a cop."

"Why would that make me feel any better?"

"Some people feel safe around the police. At least you know we won't try to kill you."

"I never thought of it that way." There's a lull in the conversation where I guess he's thinking it over. Finally he says, "All right. Someone has to help that poor boy. I'll tell you where to find him."

He hands Ruby a piece of paper. "This is a map. John is being held on a fishing boat on North Bowers Beach. The name of the boat is *Tomorrow's Dream*. You'll find him there. But you better be careful. He's heavily guarded and they're armed."

I hear a faint rustling sound and then say, "How do you know all this? Why didn't you go to the police?"

There's no reply. I hear the rustling sound again, kind of like a cross between fall leaves left in the trees and one of those old-time starchy petticoats my sister used to wear when we were kids. The noise is followed by a strange scent. It's like perfume, yet with an odd moldy smell, like the refrigerator when it needs to be cleaned out.

"You smell that?" I ask Ruby.

"Yeah. What could it be? Oh, I bet it's a ghost. Oh, Glad, I'm so scared." She snorts. "Cut it out."

"No, really. I think he's gone, but I don't know what that noise and smell are."

"Okay. That's enough. We've got the map. Let's go find John."

"Did you pick up your gun?"

"How am I supposed to find it in the dark?" she demands. "I think you bruised my hand too. You either didn't know it was me or I'm really angry at you."

This opens the way for a strategic retreat from my original stance on whether or not I knew the gun in my back belonged to Ruby. "All right. You got me. I didn't know it was you. I'm sorry I hurt your hand. Don't stick a gun in my back again."

She sniffs. "Now my Kel-Tec is gone. It's the one Uncle Ed gave me for my twelfth birthday. It has my initials on the handle. I learned to shoot with that gun. Uncle Ed died right after that."

"Probably from hearing one of your impossible stories." I say it an instant before I kiss her. "Fine." I take out my souvenir LED flashlight I got from Daytona last year. It's shaped like a race car and attached to my key chain. I shine it around on the sidewalk until I catch the gleam of her pistol.

"Thanks." She follows the beam and picks up the gun. "You *really* hurt my hand. I think you're going to have to make it up to me."

"It all depends on what you have in mind, sweetie."

We walk back to the truck. I hear that strange rustling sound again, followed by something like material dragging on the street. The scent of perfume (lilac, I think) is very strong. From the corner of my eye, I see something white and wispy moving slowly across the green.

The whole thing is raising the hairs on the back of my neck. "Ruby, have you really seen a ghost?"

"I have. They aren't all that scary. Kind of more sad and pitiful."

I look at the green again, but nothing is there. Whatever was drifting by is gone. There's no more rustling sound either, though the scent of lilacs still fills the air.

No way, I decide as we reach the truck. There's no such thing as ghosts, despite what Ruby's family believes. I sure don't believe in anything I can't touch.

Whitaker jumps about ten feet and his head hits the roof of the cab as I open the door. "I say, did you see anything out there? I thought I saw something a moment ago. I hope it wasn't Rebecca. I'm not ready to die yet."

"We didn't see anything except your snitch," Ruby says as she climbs in the cab. "He gave me this map and told us John is being held at a beach on a fishing boat. Are you sure you trust him?"

"Implicitly. Let me see the map."

I switch on the overhead light and Ruby hands him the map, which is drawn on a Jack in the Box napkin. I'm happy they're looking at it, because it seems useless to me with all those chocolate milkshake stains on it.

"Oh yes," Whitaker proclaims. "I see exactly what he's talking about. I know that area. It's quite secluded from the rest of the marina. It won't be easy getting in there."

"He said there are guards," Ruby explains. "Maybe this would be a good time to call the police."

I click my seat belt in place and start the engine. "I don't think it will do much good. I tried talking to them earlier. It's a little too much like the boy who cried wolf."

"We'll have to take care of it, then." Ruby puts on her seat belt like she's girding herself for war. "How many of them can there be anyway?"

"I count six," Ruby says. "How about you two?"

"I'm pretty sure I saw eight guards." My finger is itching to dial 911 and take my chances. I can tell the police something is going on out here and maybe they'll come out and take a look for the hell of it. Maybe they'll come out and arrest me so I don't bug them with phone calls anymore, if nothing else.

"I can't really tell from here," Whitaker says. "I'm afraid I need a new prescription. These old eyes aren't what they were."

We're sitting near a dock at a small marina close to the Bowers Maritime Museum. There are a few lights on some of the restaurants that are still open. A few more lights are highlighting large and small boats up and down the marina.

It would be a peaceful setting except for the men with guns bulging under their dark suit coats and the other men with rifles. Occasionally we see one talking into a radio, but mostly they seem to be milling around, guarding something. It's hard to tell if they're trying to keep someone in or out.

"I think we could get the police to come out on this," I tell Ruby and Whitaker. "That's the only way we're going to get close to that boat." The name *Tomorrow's Dream* is set at an angle so that the light from the pier shines on it. If I had a boat (not that I've ever wanted one), I'd name it something fast, like *Thunder* or *Lightning*. Something exciting.

"Not necessarily." Ruby smiles. "It's a nice warm night. I could use a swim."

"If there are armed men out here," I remind her, "it's probable a few more are on the boat with John—*if* he's here."

"Brilliant plan!" Whitaker enthuses. I have the feeling he's not talking about me calling the police.

"We could climb in the water over there, where it's dark." Ruby's plan continues to emerge. "Then we could swim to the boat, grab John, and swim away. No one will even know we were there."

"Except for the men onboard who shoot us," I suggest.

"I'm afraid I'll have to let you go this one alone," Whitaker says sadly. "I never learned to swim. My father had a fear of witches, you know."

I glance at him. "Witches?"

"They float, you see. He believed when a person could swim, it was because the devil was helping him."

I look at Ruby, who's taking off her shoes. "Is there any way I can talk you out of this?"

"None that I can think of." She smiles back at me. "Come on, darlin', where's your sense of adventure?"

"I lost it with my lunch this morning when you fell out of the plane and I jumped out after you. I don't expect to ever have one again."

She kisses me. "That's okay. I can do this alone. How hard can it be?"

That question keeps coming back to me as we sneak barefoot the few hundred yards from the truck to the dark spot Ruby points out on the beach. To begin with, it's one thing for her to leave her shoes in the truck. She can walk on pine cones and glass shards without flinching. It's another for me. I have a hard time with shag carpeting.

I think they must've piled every sharp-edged oyster shell on the East Coast right here on this beach. I'm sure the bottoms of my feet are going to be ragged and bloody by the time I reach the water. I follow Ruby, who's kind of gliding across the ground while I walk like Igor following Dr. Frankenstein.

We finally reach the water and start to wade in. But this isn't Florida, and the water is like a Slushee. It only takes a moment or two before my painful feet are numb. I believe I heard once that you only have a few minutes in water this cold before you die. Go ahead. Bring it on.

"What's the matter?" Ruby is up to her neck while I'm still battling with the ice water around my knees.

"It's freezing," I chatter. "How can you stand it?"

"It's not even cold. Don't be such a baby. We swam in colder water every time we took a bath when I was a kid. We didn't have inside plumbing, and sometimes we had to scrape the ice off the water in the horse trough to climb in."

"That's the worst story I ever heard. No way Louise ever lived without indoor plumbing."

"Suit yourself." She shrugs. "But get out here. We can't hang around here all night trying to find John."

I eventually get used to the water as we start swimming around where the boats are moored. Either that or I can't feel anything.

I'm not sure which. Ruby is a strong swimmer. We're pretty evenly matched.

"How are we going to know which boat it is from out here?" Ruby asks as we tread water for a moment.

I glance at the side of the fishing boat nearest to us. She's got a point. It's too dark on this side to see the names on the boats. I wish she'd thought of that before we swam out here. "I can't help you. I left my flashlight in the truck. Maybe we should head back to shore."

"We're this close." She pushes the wet strands of hair out of her face. "There has to be some way."

"If there is, I don't know what it is."

Then I notice a flag fluttering in the breeze on a boat a hundred yards and three other boats away. It's distinctive even in the dim light: blue and white background, like clouds, with a castle on it. I saw one of the armed men standing under the same flag.

"I guess you're right," Ruby says. "We'll have to go back."

"I think I have something." I point toward the flag. "At least there's some light up there. I'm sure that's the flag on the boat."

We're between two big boats that are totally blocking out the light, and I can't really see Ruby anymore. I don't have to. She scoots in close and wraps her arms around me and kisses me. "You are the best, honey," she whispers. "That's why I married you."

"Really? I thought it was for my RV." I put my arms around her.

"Nah," she teases. "I knew a man with a much bigger RV who wanted to marry me. He just didn't have anything else to go along with it."

By this time, we're starting to swallow water as my feet and legs get tangled up with hers. It might look like fun on a hot, sunny day in clear blue water, but out here, I think it might be safer to get this over with. Maybe if we can find John, we can get back to what we came here to do: racing.

We strike out again slowly and carefully, mindful of the nets and fishing equipment hanging off the charter boats. The shadows stay with us until we reach the side of *Tomorrow's Dream*. I can see a couple of the men we noticed from the road as they prowl the shore and topside of the boat.

"How the hell are we going to get past these guys?" I ask her as she treads water beside me. "There's no way they won't see us, even if there's some way to get up on the boat."

"I think I have an answer for getting up on the boat. It's got one of those big nets hanging off."

I look where she's pointing. "And?"

"Remember when we climbed up that rock wall in Texas? It's the same thing."

"I wasn't crazy about that when we did it the first time."

"Maybe not, but you were good at it. I'll go first and you follow. I'm sure we can do it quietly enough that we can sneak onto the boat from this side, where it's dark. No one will see us."

"I hope that includes no one shooting us." I help push her out of the water as she grabs the net and starts climbing. There's not much point in arguing about it right now. We're here, and if John is on this boat, we're going to rescue him. I hope.

I look up to see how she's doing. Not surprisingly, she's already halfway up. I'd swear she trained for the Olympics.

I start up after her, hand over hand, gaining footholds in the net. Lucky for us, this net is meant to hold a lot more than we weigh. It smells like fish and seaweed. I get a whiff of diesel from the engine as well.

"Come on, Glad," she whispers down to me.

I look up to answer and she's gone. I'm hoping she reached the top and climbed over. I didn't hear a splash, so I have to assume she's up there. I thought I was prepared for anything. I'm not. I guess I need a waterproof flashlight, goggles, and a wetsuit. I never thought I'd need that equipment for the Monster Mile, but I guess you never know. My old man always told me to be prepared.

"Ruby?" I whisper up to her.

No response. It's so dark I can't see my hands working the net. I can only feel the rope as I climb.

I don't try calling her again. If she's in trouble, I might be a surprise that can help. If not... well, I'm going up this way no matter what.

I reach the top of the deck and look back at the dark space where the water is below me. I can't see it, but at least I'm out of it for now. Hopefully, if they don't shoot us, they'll throw us off the boat on dry land.

I wish I could tell which way Ruby went, because as usual, she didn't wait for me. We're going to have to come up with some kind of plan for this type of thing. Tie ourselves together or something.

I walk toward the back of the boat, away from the light. I can hear the men talking close by, but they can't see me. A radio beeps and a man answers that everything is clear. I crouch down low as I pass a lifeboat to the left. A cold, wet hand drops out of it onto my shoulder.

I won't say I almost scream, but I say a few choice words from my youth. Then I grab the hand and feel the familiar wedding ring. Ruby is hiding in the lifeboat.

"Shh! Get up here. They'll see you."

I throw my leg over the side of the lifeboat and kind of fall inside of it. For an instant, we huddle together, silently waiting to see if anyone hears us.

Nothing happens. No running footsteps on the deck or sounds of radio static as they try to communicate the possible threat we've become.

"Geez Louise!" Ruby mutters. "I can't believe they didn't hear you."

"I wasn't that loud."

"Whatever. Look, we have to circle around to the front of the boat."

"You mean where all of the armed men are standing?"

"There's no other way. That's the only entrance to the cabins. We have to get down there and try to figure out some way to get John off the boat."

"He can climb back down the net with us. Then we can all swim away and live happily ever after."

She hits me in the shoulder. "Be serious. This is a matter of life and death."

"I'm not even going there." I lay my head back against the bottom of the fiberglass lifeboat. "So what's your plan?" I ask.

"What makes you think I have one?"

"Because you're you. You always have a plan."

"Thanks, honey. That's a nice thing to say." She cuddles close, wet and cold, putting her freezing lips on mine.

"Don't mention it."

"Well, I do have a plan. You're not going to like it."

"What else is new?"

SEVENTEEN

RUBY IS RIGHT. I definitely don't like this idea.

Squirming around in the lifeboat, she tears a few holes in her T-shirt and then ties it up under her breasts. She starts to strip off her jean shorts, but I put a stop to that.

"Whoa! You didn't say anything about stripping to get their attention." I can barely see her in the light shining through the nylon covering above us.

"If I don't make it good, honey, they won't be looking at me. That means they'll see *you* trying to sneak off the boat with John. I'm sure neither of us wants that."

"I think you'll get their attention like you are." I kiss her and run my fingers through her wet hair. "Are you sure you're okay with this?"

"Don't worry about it. Did I ever tell you about Streaker Day at Central Cabarrus High School? I tried my hand at that right before graduation. I think I was pretty good at it. I never got caught."

I go along with the plan, although I'd rather all the goons out there beat the crap out of me than have Ruby do this. Not that I think them pounding on me would help get John out of here. *If* he's here, which we haven't established yet. Whitaker and his friend had better be right.

"Okay." Ruby is ready to go. "I'm going to jump back in the water. Wait until you hear them talking to me and helping me out of the water."

"Yeah, I got it. What do you plan to do to get away from the goons after they save you?"

"I won't have to do that." She kisses my cheek. "You'll grab their attention when you take John. They'll forget all about me and go after you."

"I think I missed this part of the plan."

"Don't worry. You'll have a head start and they won't be able to catch you. I'll run off the boat and meet you back at the truck. Easy as pie."

I don't know about that, but I don't have a better plan. Ruby climbs over the top of me (I like this part of the plan), and a few seconds later I hear a splash.

"Help! Help! I can't swim!"

I feel the movement on the boat as all the goons run to the right side. I'm assuming Ruby is bobbing up and down in enough light to show some cleavage. I'm not sure if rescuing John is worth all this. But now we're committed. In order for the second part of Ruby's flawless plan to work, I have to let the first part happen.

I hear footsteps and laughter from the goons as they admire Ruby's attributes and joke about her being too drunk to swim. They're standing right next to the lifeboat. I can't move without getting caught. I feel a knot develop in the pit of my stomach that may become the ulcer everyone always said I'd get one day.

Finally, the goons decide to help out the little lady. The two voices I heard disappear as their footsteps fade away toward the dock. I can only assume they're going to watch, even if they don't help. I might only have a few moments to make it into the cabins below.

I look out from under the nylon tarp. No sign of anyone else around. I drop out of the lifeboat and crouch down for an instant, watching to see where everyone is. When I'm sure it's clear, I move quickly toward the back of the boat.

All of the goons on shore and on the boat seem to be gathered around Ruby as they help her out of the water. One of them even gives her his suit coat. That's class. I have to hand it to Ruby for coming up with another one of her plans. This one might work.

"Hey!" A large dark form approaches me, looming up out of the underbelly of the boat. "Who the hell are you?"

Before he can form another syllable that might ruin the plan, I pop him one in the jaw. It stings like hell. I forgot that part. But I'm lucky and Paul Bunyan's twin topples down the stairs. Glass jaw, I guess. I'm not exactly the heavyweight champion of the world.

I run across him, sprinting into the short hall that separates what looks like four cabins, two on each side. I take my chances and open the first door. It's empty. I push open the second and third doors, still hearing the goons outside laughing and talking to Ruby. There's nothing in either one of those cabins.

Finally, I look at the floor and notice there's only one cabin with light coming from under the door. Of course, it's the last one.

I push open the door and John jumps to his feet. His face is bruised and battered, but otherwise he seems okay. "Glad! I can't believe you're here. How did you get down here?"

"No time to talk," I tell him, gratified that he's actually on the boat. "We have to get off this boat. Follow my lead. You can swim, can't you? No witch fears in your family?"

"No, I can swim. What do you have in mind?"

We make our way across the man on the stairs and creep across the deck to the netting beside the lifeboat. I have him go down first, giving him a bare explanation of what we're doing. I wait until I think he's had time to get away from the side of the boat and start toward the far end of the marina.

Ruby is still keeping the goons in stitches by the dock. But nothing has happened that will take their attention away from her. I have to create the next diversion.

Just as I'm ready to get started, the big goon from the stairway decides to put in another appearance. He charges up the stairs and yells when he sees me. All of the goons on the dock hear him and come running.

I'm not worried about the guys who aren't on the boat. I have time to get away from them. It's the big palooka who's coming right at me that's getting my attention.

I feel the side of the lifeboat move behind me and push it toward him. He runs right into it and falls back on the deck. God, I love dumb crooks.

Without another thought, I jump off the side of the boat and hope nothing large or metal is in my way. It's like diving into the night, not sure if you'll find daylight again. I turn my head as I'm going over the edge and see Ruby running for the truck, those long

212

legs eating up the distance between her and safety. The sight brings a smile to my lips as I hit the water.

I swim underwater as far as I can. Then I realize those loud noises and popping sounds I'm hearing are guns shooting at me and bullets hitting the water. Where did it say anything about getting shot at in the plan?

I swim around the back of *Tomorrow's Dream* as I hear the sound of her engines start up. I can't see anything and have to hope I actually rescued John and he's out here somewhere.

The boat is big and unwieldy, like an old Chrysler Imperial trying to maneuver in a compact-car parking spot. I'm two boats away before the cursing, shooting goons can even figure out how to back out of the slip.

I hear a splashing sound in the water. It's John swimming for all he's worth. I can't see him, but how many other fools would be out here swimming in the dark with fishing boats going in and out around them?

"Not too far now," I tell him. "You holding up?"

"Yeah. I'm okay. I don't know how I'll ever thank you for this."

"You can ride me around on the track a few times," I sputter as some wake hits me in the face. "None of this wimpy 130 miles per hour either. I want full throttle."

"You got it, buddy. Ruby too."

Two more boats to swim around. *Tomorrow's Dream* has finally come about, and the goons are shining spotlights on the water. I hear something coming our way. It only takes a second before I realize what that welcome sound is: sirens.

John starts having a hard time as we get into the last dozen yards. I tow him back. Ruby and Whitaker are on shore urging us forward.

Exhausted, I finally feel the land come up out of the water to meet us. Ruby is in the water with her arms around me. Whitaker helps John to shore. Together we collapse into a heap just out of the reach of the water.

"You did it!" Ruby kisses my face and hugs me at the same time.

See, that's what I like best about following through on one of her plans. It doesn't matter if I'm painting the kitchen or risking my life jumping off a boat as men are shooting at me. My Ruby makes everything better. "You called the police," I gasp, not realizing how out of shape I am. Geez, I can't even swim for a while without wheezing.

"Indeed!" Whitaker is even more breathless than me. "I reported shots fired. That brought them running, by George!"

"We should get out of here," I say. It's what I want to do, but my legs feel like jelly.

"No," John protests. "I want them to get those bastards who did this. I'm not running away. I want to see them in prison."

"I don't know if you heard," Ruby tells him, "but they arrested Phil for keeping the money he was supposed to give to your kidnappers."

"No way. Not Phil," John says, defending his brother. "He'd never hurt me or Bill. I don't believe it."

There isn't much to say to that. You can't argue with a brother's love for even the blackest sheep.

It's just as well he doesn't want to run away. A group of police officers is waiting at the truck by the time we get there. Officer Franks shakes his head when he sees us. He calls something in on his radio and looks back at us. "Well, well. What a surprise. You know, it's always dull around here when the race isn't in town. When you're gone this summer, Wycznewski, it's going to be like a graveyard. What the hell happened this time?"

"Out of your jurisdiction, aren't you, Franks?" I'm surprised to see him here with the other officers.

"Yeah. We both got lucky tonight. I was down here as part of an intercity task force. We had a road block not two miles away. But what about you, Wycznewski?"

We all explain what happened and who did what. The police nab *Tomorrow's Dream* and escort the goons away in handcuffs. I'm surprised not to see the FBI with a high-profile kidnapping like this. If they're here, they're keeping their heads down.

When Franks has filled up his notebook with our statements, he reads through what he has and asks us if it sounds right. We all agree, and he laughs. "You people are the craziest racing fans I ever saw, and I've seen some weird people. I hope you move on quickly after the race tomorrow, before one of you ends up in the morgue."

"Thanks," I tell him. "Mind if we go now?"

Franks glances at the man in charge from the State Police. The other man nods, and Franks waves us toward the truck. "Yeah. Go on. Get out of here. I know you're not going anywhere until after the 400 tomorrow."

The ambulance takes John away. He seems to be in decent shape, but I'm not a doctor. Whitaker, Ruby, and I get in the truck, feeling pleased with what we've done.

"Perhaps it was one of those men who killed Bill," Whitaker suggests. "It's possible we may have misjudged Phil. He may not be involved in this at all."

"Except for the matter of his men picking up the ransom intended for John, I agree with you. It seems more reasonable to me that Phil is behind all of this."

Ruby slides a glance at me. "Why would his men still continue to hold John even after Phil was caught?"

"Maybe he couldn't communicate with them that it was all over." I shrug. "He *has* been in jail."

"Or perhaps he didn't want his brother found until he could extricate himself from the charges against him," Whitaker says. "It is possible John could prove the final witness against Phil. We didn't have enough time to speak with him. He may have known Phil was involved."

"I don't think so," I say. "He told me Phil wouldn't hurt him or Bill. The important thing is that we found John before the race tomorrow."

"You mean today." Ruby taps her watch.

We drop Whitaker off at his car and finally get home at a little after two a.m. The party next door at Zeke and Louise's is finally winding down. I don't see Bobby anywhere, so I'm sure he's in before his curfew. He wants to drive in the 400 worse than anything else.

"Looks like we're in luck," I tell Ruby as we approach the door to our RV. "I don't think anyone was in here tonight. What a change!"

"Yeah. Maybe whoever it was found something else to do."

"Or was in jail and didn't have the chance to break in again."

I open the door and switch on the light. Once again, everything we own is scattered throughout the RV. The door may have been closed and locked this time, but apparently it was only to cover up the act. "I don't understand what the hell is going on."

"And if Phil is the one responsible, why is this still happening?" Ruby sighs as she starts picking up kitchen utensils from the floor.

"There's something going on we're not getting." I wade through the piles of clothes thrown into the hallway that separates the bedroom from the rest of the RV. "Someone, probably not Phil, is looking for something they feel sure we have."

"I'm too tired to deal with this tonight." Ruby stacks a few cups on the counter. "Let's do it in the morning. The race isn't until two. I'd be willing to miss some pre-race activities not to have to clean this up right now."

"Sounds good to me." I check the RV to be sure we're alone and no one stayed behind. "We can throw everything off the bed again and crash."

Ruby glances around. "Where's Malibu? I hope they didn't let him out again."

We look everywhere for the cat and finally find him in a pile of clothes in the bedroom. He barely looks up at Ruby when she calls his name.

"Something's wrong with him, Glad." She picks up his limp body. He faintly meows but doesn't move. "Look at him. They must have poisoned him or something. We have to find a vet."

I'm not overly fond of the little beast, but she's right. When he can't even reach out to claw me, something's definitely wrong. What kind of sicko poisons a cat in someone else's RV?

It's not easy to find an all-night vet when you're not familiar with a town. Both of us are on our cell phones dialing numbers from the Internet, hoping to find someone who can look at the cat.

Ruby finally finds someone in Leipsic, the next town over, who's willing to take care of Malibu. She wraps the cat in one of her old sweaters and cradles him against her as we go back to the truck. I don't know if this night is ever going to be over, and I don't mean that in a good way.

"Drive faster, Glad," she urges, crying and telling Malibu it will be okay. "I think he's dying. We have to get him there. There has to be something they can do for him."

The cat looks like he's about to give up one of his lives. It makes me mad thinking about it. Maybe I've wanted to kick him across the room a few times, but I wouldn't. And maybe that's why someone poisoned him. Maybe he got in the way trying to protect our home. I put my foot down harder on the gas. The bastards better not have killed our cat.

Luckily, we don't attract any police attention. The roads are full of race fans looking for late-night entertainment and snacks. Almost everything is open. That's one thing towns love about having a race nearby. We drop plenty of money during weekend races. For some places, they depend on it like Jamaica does cruise ships. An influx of a few hundred thousand people every year can make a big difference to a town's bottom line.

We finally see the sign for Leipsic. Now we only have to follow the map Ruby printed from Mapquest to find Dr. Simons's office.

"Glad, I don't think he's breathing." Ruby's voice is flat and thick with tears. "I think we should pull over and be outside with him. I hate for him to die in the truck."

"I think if he's going to die, he's probably happiest right where he is." I see the lighted All-Night Vet sign on the left and make a quick turn into the parking lot. "We're here, anyway. Let's not give up on him yet."

I turn off the engine and go around to Ruby's side to get the door for her. She gets out, holding Malibu tightly to her, tears streaming down her face. I put my arm around her as we walk into the vet's office. There's not really much comfort I can offer at this point. I hope the little guy makes it.

Dr. Simons is a small man with thinning blond hair. It matches the rest of his demeanor. He doesn't really look at us as he asks us what seems to be wrong with Malibu and Ruby explains. He nods and has Ruby put the cat on an examination table.

Ruby stands close to me while the vet looks at Malibu. If the cat is breathing, it's hard to tell. I tighten my arm around her as I realize it could've been her these idiots hurt.

After a minute or two, Dr. Simons fiddles with something in the pocket of his white lab coat and adjusts his glasses. "I think this cat has been drugged. He'll probably be fine. I'd like to draw some blood to find out what was used on him. Did this happen at a groomer?"

"No. Someone broke into our home." Ruby launches into the whole story as she moves forward to stroke Malibu while the vet draws blood. "Why would anyone want to hurt a cat? I don't understand why they'd drug him."

"Maybe he tried to scratch them or jump on them," the vet suggests. "It's a common practice for groomers with difficult animals. That's why I asked."

Don't ask me why, but seeing Whitaker mess around with Malibu's collar and the resulting scratch when the cat wasn't happy with it suddenly comes to me. Maybe they've been after the cat the whole time. That could be why Malibu was outside after they ransacked the RV last time.

"Ruby, where's Malibu's collar?"

"I don't know." She rubs her eyes and thinks about it. "I took it off of him when Forsythe got his hand tangled in it and I was afraid Malibu would do some serious damage to him. I put it down on the counter. Why?"

"Was his shot record attached to it?" the vet asks. "I'll need to know if he's been vaccinated."

"It was on there." Ruby looks up at me. "Is that why you asked?"

"Not exactly. We'll talk about it later."

The vet examines the blood sample and confirms his diagnosis. "Malibu was definitely drugged. It was almost an overdose. But he should be fine now. I'd rather keep him overnight if that's all right with you. I'll call you in the morning when I see how he is, but I expect him to be on his feet tomorrow. Cats are resilient little animals. I feel sure he'll be fine. You might want to consider laying off some of his snack food, though. He's a little hefty for his size."

"I'm so happy he'll be okay." Ruby sniffles as she hugs the cat on the table.

"We'll leave him tonight and call in the morning," I say. I think it might be best for the cat not to be with us at the RV right now anyway. At least he'll be safe here, where no one can find him.

We exchange phone numbers with the vet. Ruby gives him my cell phone number as well as hers, Bobby's, *and* Zeke and Louise's. One thing's for sure: he'll find somebody to call when it's time to pick up the cat.

I look back at Malibu as we start to walk out the door. He opens his eyes and meows a little. It gets to me. I go back and scratch his ears. "It's okay, little guy. You're tough. You'll be back tomorrow scratching my hands without any problem, okay?"

I look up at the watery smile on Ruby's face and gruffly clear my throat. "I just wanted to let him know everything is all right."

She hugs me and cries all over me. "I knew you'd come to love him too. He grows on you."

That's about all I want to say about the cat. It's not that I'm afraid to cry. It's just that there's no point. The cat is going to be fine. It's silly to cry about it. It's different for Ruby. She can get away with a lot of things I can't do.

When we finally leave the clinic after a discourse from Dr. Simons about the long and noble history of cats, I turn to Ruby in the truck and tell her about my suspicions concerning Malibu's collar.

"You mean you think someone has been after his collar all this time?"

"I don't know. It's hard for me to believe they'd be after the cat, although I guess that's possible."

"What could possibly be in his collar that would have any value?"

"We'll have to find it to answer that question. But it makes sense when you think about it. Maybe that's why Bill left the cat with you in the first place."

Ruby considers the idea as we leave sleeping Leipsic behind us and reach the outskirts of Dover. "I don't know, but if I ever find out who did this to Malibu, I'm going to hurt him or her bigtime."

EIGHTEEN

The Internet and the *Dover News-Journal* have the whole story about John in the morning. I read the paper while Ruby reads about everything online.

We're lounging in bed with free doughnuts and coffee, supplied by a local tire store. We snuck out earlier despite the gloomy drizzle, grabbed what we could, and snuck back.

Ruby gets off the cell phone when she's done talking to Dr. Simons. "He says Malibu is fine and we can come get him anytime after ten."

"Maybe we should leave him there." I'm distracted by what I'm reading and don't realize what I've said until Ruby hits me with a doughnut. "Hey!"

"I thought you liked Malibu now," she accuses. "You were just trying to get rid of him."

"I wasn't, really. I meant maybe we should leave him there until after the race."

"But he'll miss us."

"Maybe." I finally look up at her. "I think we have to realize this might not be over yet. We don't know what it's all about. Did you find the collar?"

She jumps out of bed, doughnuts flying everywhere. "I totally forgot about that. I'll go check the kitchen where I left it."

I put down the newspaper and start cleaning up the mess in the bedroom left behind by last night's break-in. The way it looks, we'll be lucky to have it done by two o'clock, when the race starts. I don't think there are any clothes left in the closet or the dressers. They even ransacked Ruby's jewelry box with the little musical ballerina in it.

Putting her earrings and a few necklaces back in it makes me think about how little she has. No diamonds. Even her wedding ring is a sapphire. Most of what she has isn't even real. Plastic beads and glass baubles don't make much of a treasure chest.

"Are you playing with it or picking it up?" she asks from the doorway, collar in hand.

"I guess I was thinking what a lousy husband I am." I close the jewelry box and put it on her dresser. "You don't even have any real jewelry. I guess I should've bought you something nice for your birthday last year instead of that Jimmie Johnson talking coffee mug."

"Don't be stupid. I love that mug."

I look at my watch and realize we're running late. We pick up the ice chest and Ruby grabs her sun hat before we scramble to the track. We've already missed some of the opening ceremonies and the introduction of some of the drivers. But at least no one has taken our seats. Zeke and Louise are probably protecting them with their lives.

"It's about time," Louise scolds Ruby. "Where have you been?"

"I don't have time to explain right now." Ruby puts on her headphones. "But I can tell you what ten million dollars *doesn't* look like."

Once the race gets started, there's no time or breath to talk. The drivers are hitting 160 miles per hour and more as they take on the Monster Mile to get points for the Chase.

I'm still kind of down, I guess, because the race can't hold my attention. It doesn't help that Joe isn't here. I'm keeping an eye on Bobby. I have my headphones set to listen to him and his crew chief, like Zeke and Louise do. I know Ruby is focused on Jimmie.

Matt Kenseth is on the pole and makes a good start, but Elliott Sadler is coming right up behind him. Brian Vickers moves up five spots to number sixteen, right behind Bobby.

I hear Lance Maxfield, Bobby's crew chief, telling him to watch his tires. "Take care of those tires, Bobby," he says. "Don't abuse them."

Zeke yells at his son, "Go for it, boy! Don't let him push you out of there."

You can see there's some bump-drafting going on with Vickers on Bobby's bumper. The kid is doing a good job keeping Vickers from getting around him. I think if I had him on the radio, I'd be telling him to watch the wall. He's getting too close, and it doesn't take much to get into trouble. This is a narrow, fast track and there's not a lot of room to maneuver. I know he needs to show everyone what he's made of, but if he loses his car, he won't be showing them anything.

Kevin Harvick starts making a move forward from the number thirty-one spot, but he loses control and brushes the outside wall. It causes him to spin on the front stretch and hit Reed Sorenson. Bobby Labonte takes advantage of the situation and moves forward from his twenty-four spot. It takes good spotting from his team to get him around that mess.

The caution flag goes up because of the Harvick wreck. Greg Biffle and Kurt Busch both make pit stops. All the cars slow down. Bobby has made it forward two spots to number thirteen.

The green flag comes up after everything is sorted out, and Jeff Gordon comes screaming out, eating up five spots to make it to number four behind Ryan Newman, Carl Edwards, and Matt Kenseth. The field is wide open. Anything could happen at this point.

Maxfield calls Bobby and tells him a spotter notices his car is leaking oil on the track. "You'll have to come in."

"Oh, man." Bobby spouts off a few expletives. "I can't believe this."

"Better watch it," Maxfield warns. "Just come on in."

Zeke and Louise both groan at the news. "Things were going so good," Zeke mourns. "What a mess."

While Team Hamilton makes an assessment on Bobby's car in the garage, I look up at the DuPont Monster Bridge. All fifty-five theater-style seats with personal scanners and flat-screen TVs appear to be taken. That's the way to watch the race.

Down on the field, David Stremme pulls side by side with Jeff Burton. He's a good rookie driver who is working his way up through the ranks. He's doing fine until his right front tire blows and he hits the wall. Burton manages to get out of the way and starts nipping at Kenseth's bumper. In the meantime, Junior, trying to maneuver into third place, is passing Jimmie Johnson, who is right behind Carl Edwards.

Bobby comes back on the track on lap 223. He's way behind, but his mechanic feels sure the rear-end cooler-mount problem they experienced is fixed. Now all he has to do is catch up with everyone else. It's probably impossible, but then what were the odds he'd ever make it this far?

Stremme is limping off the field. It looks like there's a fire under his hood. Sure enough, when he pulls into pit road, his crew rushes out with fire extinguishers. He might not be back for the rest of the race. This guy has some rotten luck.

I hear Ruby yell and then swear a few times before her mother nudges her. Jimmie's tire got away from him, and he has to restart at the end of the longest line.

Kasey Kahne spins out heading into turn four and runs into Tony Stewart, who already has a lot of damage to the nose of his car. Robby Gordon changes his engine after it blows up and then comes back in lap 340 and hits the wall.

"It's a mess out there," Zeke yells. "Doesn't anyone teach these boys to drive anymore?"

Probably no one besides me actually hears him. The older generation of racing fans are always complaining that things aren't like they used to be. I don't see how he could want a more thrilling race. If any of the cars manage to stay together long enough, the race is still up for grabs.

Bobby is only a lap down and well on his way to picking up a few more spots. He sounds determined and calm on the radio. I almost wouldn't recognize him from his usual joking, careless self. He scoots by Martin Truex Jr. and takes the number seventeen spot. Kenseth seems to remind everyone else they have to pit as Elliott Sadler, Greg Biffle, Mark Martin, and Reed Sorenson follow him to pit road.

Sterling Martin, Ryan Newman, and Carl Edwards stay on the track, hoping to take a few spots while some of the other drivers are out of the way. David Ragan spins but somehow doesn't hit anything. Edwards drops from the lead to twenty-third as he misses his pit and has to come back. Stremme makes it back on the track only to get high out of turn four and back into the wall.

Bobby advises Maxfield that there is smoke coming from his engine. "I think we blew it."

"Come on in," Maxfield tells him.

Zeke takes off his headphones and throws them on the grandstand. "That's the stupidest damn move I've ever seen. What's a little smoke? I've seen drivers go a whole race with their engine smoking. What's the big deal?"

With less than six laps left, Jimmie Johnson and Jeff Burton are in the lead. Junior is bump-drafting Burton, trying to get around him so he can challenge Jimmie. But Burton is cool and in control. He holds Junior off, even though it means letting Jimmie take the race.

Jimmie spins through the infield as he finds his way back to victory lane again at Dover. He's a good driver and picks up a lot of points for the Chase. The field is rounded out with Jeff Burton coming in second and Junior in third place. Behind them are Carl Edwards, Jeff Gordon, Greg Biffle, and Kurt Busch.

"What a race!" It comes out before I have a chance to take it back. The Furr family isn't appreciative.

"You mean what a damn stupid mess of a race." Zeke starts trying to get through the crowd as people begin moving out of the grandstands.

"It was a good race, Daddy." Ruby rubs his shoulders. "You're so tense. You have to lighten up."

"This from the girl whose man just won the race," Louise reminds her. "You should be grieving. Your brother, your own flesh and blood, was cheated out of his first win."

"It's not like he ever had a chance to win, Mama. He's just getting started. It was a big deal for him to be in the race at all." Ruby adjusts her sun hat. "We have to go and get Malibu from the vet."

"Well, I'm ready to go home." Zeke almost runs into a young couple who aren't moving fast enough for him. "I've had about all of this race I want to have. I figure we can pack up now and be back home tomorrow."

"You'll just have to wait," she tells her father. She takes Malibu's collar out of her bag and gets a strange look on her face. "Look what I found! It was on Malibu's collar the whole time."

"Well, I can go home if I want to," Zeke persists.

I move closer to Ruby to see what she's talking about. Whatever she's looking at is almost making her jump up and down. It looks like a piece of plastic to me.

"Look at this! Guess what it is." She's holding the collar in one hand and the blue plastic thing in the other.

"I give up. What is it?"

"It's what they've been looking for." She does a little dance in her heart-stamped shorts. "It's the key to everything."

Zeke eyeballs what she's holding as we head into the campground. "It don't look like the key to my RV, and that's all I'm interested in."

"Hush!" Louise says to him. "This must be something important."

It doesn't look like the key to anything to me. I look at what Ruby's holding again. It's a little blue piece of plastic about the size of my fingernail. Maybe it's a child's toy. "I don't know what that is."

"Glad, you haven't been paying attention! I've been asking for something like this for my cell phone. It's a micro SD card. It's the *key*, get it?"

Well, that makes all the difference. "I still don't know what that is. Maybe if you pretend I'm totally challenged by any technology and tell me in easy-to-understand English what it does, we could be on the same page."

She rolls her eyes. "Never mind. Let me get my adapter and I'll plug it into the laptop. Maybe then you'll understand."

"We're going," Zeke says again as he veers his wheelchair toward his RV. "You all do what you want. We're going home."

Louise shakes her head as she walks behind her husband. "Don't pay him any mind. You two take care of that micro whatever it is. We'll be here."

I follow Ruby into our RV and watch her plug the blue plastic thing into the computer. She taps a few keys, excited by whatever it is. I should've paid more attention in computer training. It's embarrassing sometimes when she does this. How does she know all this stuff?

"See? I was right. This is what they were looking for."

I look over her shoulder. It's a map. There are driving directions with it. "Do you think this is what I think it is?"

"The way to ten million dollars?" She laughs. "Yes, I do. See that image over there? That's the trademark Brink's uses on the stock exchange. I think this is what those men wanted from Bill. He kept the secret all these years. He knew where the money was hidden.

Phil must've thought Bill had it on the bridge with him when he died."

"And it was all in the cat's collar?"

"All on this little chip." She kisses me and squeals. "I do believe I feel a new RV in our future, sir. Let's go find that money."

"Shouldn't we finish cleaning the house first?"

"No! We can always clean up as we're moving out."

"Ruby, honey, I don't want to burst your bubble, but it's been a while since the Paxtons stole that money. I don't think you should count on much of it being left."

"But you don't know that." She laughs again and does a little dance. "We have to call Forsythe, of course. It wouldn't be fair to find the money without him. We'll have to share it. How much does an insurance company usually give for a reward on something like this?"

I shrug, not wanting to rain on her parade. "Probably ten percent. Maybe more."

"That's one million! Even if we split half with Forsythe, that's five hundred thousand dollars. We could have one of those really nice RVs like we saw at the RV show in Daytona. The kind with the slide-out, pop-up everything. That would be great."

I'd like to be more enthusiastic, but I don't think we're going to find all that money. The Paxtons didn't steal it to bury it somewhere and leave it alone. I'm sure it was absorbed and laundered to become part of their profit from the casino and the hotel.

I'm kind of depressed she wants something I can't give her. Maybe it's not jewelry, but it's still out of my league. We do all right thanks to my uncle's investments on my behalf, but the kind of RV she's talking about doesn't come cheap.

She throws on a Miles the Monster T-shirt for good luck. "I'll call Forsythe while you get your lucky Dover ball cap."

I wade through the pile of clothes that used to be our bedroom and find my lucky Front Row Joe shirt. I pull on tennis shoes and slap the Dover ball cap on my head. I'm ready to go.

Maybe I'm wrong. Maybe there will be money out there. I guess there's no way to know without checking.

Forsythe is still dressing when we pick him up at his place. I can see the eager excitement in his eyes as Ruby explains everything for the tenth time. "By God, I think you've found it. I insist in you sharing some of the prize."

Ruby laughs. "Good thing. Otherwise I'd have to leave you out here and go find it alone." She holds out her hand to him after he scrambles into the back seat. "Fifty-fifty?"

He hesitates. He's looked for this money for a long time. I'm sure he wishes he could have found it without us. Five hundred thousand dollars is a lot of tea and crumpets. But one million is a yacht where you drink your tea.

He finally takes Ruby's hand. "Done. I've been waiting for this moment for a very long time. It's nice to share it with people like you."

"All right!" Ruby beeps the horn. "Let's go, Glad!"

The map she printed out from the SD card shows the money is buried outside the little town of Milford. We take Highway 1 out of Dover, Ruby and Forsythe talking nonstop about what it will be like to find the money.

Out of the city, everything turns to old barns, big farmhouses, and lots of green growing fields. There's no address on the map. It's kind of like X marks the spot, X being where the two roads meet.

Ruby calls out names from the map as we pass the places. "Are you going the speed limit?" she asks at least ten times.

"We're behind a tractor," I answer at least three of those times. "I'm going as fast as I can."

We finally arrive in the quaint little town of Milford. All the houses look like they've been here since way before anyone thought to have wider streets. We pass the Parson Thorne Museum and the Milford Museum. There are plenty of people out walking despite the drizzle. Traffic here is almost as slow as it was behind the tractor.

Ruby and Forsythe have no time or interest for admiring the old churches or the picturesque scenery. I feel like I'm taking two kids out shopping. The only thing missing are the cries of, "Are we there yet?" And that's only because Ruby knows where we're going and I'm just the big, dumb Polish driver.

"There!" She points her finger and I come to a stop on the side of the road a few miles outside Milford. "Look at that. I think it might be where we're going."

I look at the map she's holding. I'm not sure how she's making that decision, but then I didn't know what an SD card was either, so I guess this is her show.

"See the two old roads?" She looks out of the window. "I think this might be where they meet."

"There is an old structure of some sort." Forsythe points off in the field. "Perhaps the money is buried there."

"That's a lot of field to dig up without even one shovel," I tell them. "We're going to have to get better directions. Maybe something about this would be familiar to John."

There are several boos from the back seat and hisses from the front seat, followed by distinct declarations. "A three-way split is unacceptable!" Whitaker protests.

"He's right," Ruby agrees. "That wouldn't be enough for a new RV. Besides, the police will probably weasel the information out of Phil and be out here taking our money before we can get in touch with John. I'm with Forsythe. We can find this by ourselves."

NINETEEN

Two hours later, we're walking around in circles after exploring a barn that has mostly collapsed. I think the Paxtons have a thing for buildings that are falling down. I look at my watch. It's time to call a halt to the treasure hunt. "I think we need some help."

Ruby sits on the ground and sighs. "All right. We don't have any choice. We'll be too old to spend it at this rate."

"I'm afraid I'll have to insist we don't call John Paxton."

I look up, surprised to see a revolver in Whitaker's hand. It seems out of place here in the middle of this big field of grass. "What's your problem? I thought we were in this together."

"We are." He smiles at Ruby. "I wouldn't do this if I wasn't desperate. You have no idea how little money private detectives make. My wife is threatening to leave me if I don't get a real job. I *need* this money."

"So you never meant to share with us in the first place," Ruby accuses. "Glad was right about you from the beginning. I shouldn't have told you we found it."

Whitaker glances at me. "What did you say about me?"

"He said never trust a man with an accent who is also a private detective," she recites, as though he isn't standing there holding a gun on us.

"Thanks," I add to her remarks. "He could kill me now just for saying that."

"I don't think he plans to kill anyone." She smiles at Whitaker. "Do you, Forsythe?"

"I'd rather not. But I do mean to have that money. I've waited a long time for this. I hope you understand."

"I don't understand," she pouts. "I trusted you. I thought you were our friend. I can't believe you'd turn on us this way."

"I truly regret it, Ruby. You are such a dear girl. And I will be happy to share with you. Maybe not half, but a large percentage."

I'm listening to them, gauging what it will take to grab the weapon from Whitaker. It doesn't look like that big a job to me. But maybe this would be a good time to get some straight answers. He has nothing to hide. He may be wrangling with Ruby over the money, but the chances are he doesn't plan to hurt us. He hasn't worked this hard for the ten million to go to jail for it.

"Is that what happened to Bill?" I goad him. "You got tired of waiting and took him out of the picture when he wouldn't give you the information you needed?"

"Not at all." His eyes narrow. "I did not hurt Bill."

"Then you set John up to get the money from Phil."

"I haven't set anyone up," he denies. "I only want the money."

"But you just said you'd do anything for it," I remind him. "What's a murder and a kidnapping compared to twenty million dollars?"

"I certainly do not plan to keep the money." His voice is full of high dignity over the accusation. "I plan to give back every penny and collect the reward. It has been my plan from the beginning."

"That was before we found out where it was hidden, right?" Ruby demands. "Because you'll have to kill us if you plan to go through with this. We're not keeping quiet about it. Right, Glad?"

A little less drama would be nice. Personally, I'd at least promise not to say anything even if I had every intention of turning him over to the police. He doesn't have to know that. But Ruby is a big believer in putting all her cards on the table, even though this isn't the best time for it.

"I don't want to hurt anyone," he says again. "Especially the two of you. We wouldn't be this close if you hadn't found the information on the cat. I certainly owe you a debt of gratitude."

Ruby gets up off the ground. "You have a funny way of showing it."

Whitaker looks uncomfortable but doesn't offer to give up the gun. "If you will let me see those directions, maybe I can make some sense of them."

He holds out his hand to Ruby and she shakes her head, putting the information behind her back. "I'm not giving you anything but a kick in the ass if you get too close."

"Please give me the information," he almost begs her. "I don't want it to be this way."

He's focused on her, and I decide to take my shot. I reach over, clamp my hand on his revolver so it moves away from Ruby, and push him on the ground. It's not too hard after all.

He looks up at me with amazement on his face.

"Didn't anyone ever tell you not to point a weapon without using it?" I ask him. "Someone will take it away and use it on you."

"It's about time," Ruby sasses as she looks at him on the ground. "What took you?"

"If you were so impatient, why didn't *you* take it away from him?"

"I didn't want to hurt him." She smiles at me. "Or make you look bad."

"What are you planning to do with me?" Whitaker asks.

"I don't know right now. Once we get back to Dover, I'll probably hand you over to the police."

"You can't do that," Ruby argues. "He didn't hurt anyone."

"He held this revolver on us. That tells me he had intent."

"But I wouldn't have used it," Whitaker adds. "It's not even loaded. Check it yourself if you don't believe me."

Ruby takes the weapon from me and checks it. "See? He was just acting crazy. It happens sometimes. That doesn't mean he's a bad guy. Let's put this behind us and walk up that hill a ways and see what's on the other side."

"I'm not really comfortable with that idea." I can't imagine why she doesn't feel the same way. "He might start acting crazy again and shoot us next time."

"Not with this gun." She tosses it back to Whitaker.

"Great! Now he can hit me in the head with it. Ruby, you take the cake."

She kisses my cheek. "Thanks, darlin'. If we don't see anything in the next few minutes, we'll head back."

That's the first sensible thing she's said in the last few minutes. She helps Whitaker off the ground and brushes the dirt off of his clothes.

"Okay. But he's walking first," I say, giving in as gracefully as I can. "I don't want him going crazy behind me."

Whitaker starts crying and thanking Ruby. The two of them walk in front of me toward the small hill. This isn't what I had in mind. It's crazier than Whitaker could ever get. But here we are, and I guess we're going to look in this last place before we leave. I keep a sharp eye on the PI and transfer my own pistol from the back of my jeans to the front pocket, where I can pull it out fast if I need to. Another motto of mine is: Don't trust a man who's pulled a gun on you.

"Look, Glad!" Ruby gets excited and points to the other side of some trees. "There's an old shack. Maybe the money is hidden there."

"That would be Paxton's style." I watch Whitaker take the news, looking for any "crazy" moves from him. "Let's check it out."

There's not really much to check out. It looks like somebody's old one-room cabin. Or at least what's left of it. Most of the roof is gone. You can see into it from the hillside. There seems to be a floor, just wooden slats with grass growing through them.

"Well, I wouldn't think to look here," Whitaker remarks as we come closer to the cabin. "I suppose it would make a good hiding place."

"It seems kind of far away from the casino." I glance around us at the rapidly clearing sky. With any luck, we'll have torn down this shack and gone on our way in the next few minutes.

"That makes sense to me," Ruby weighs in on the subject. "Everyone was looking for it. They had to put it somewhere no one would think to look. They set it up to make it seem like it was out there with Bill, but it was out here all this time."

"Considering how many people were looking for the money," Whitaker adds, "it truly does make sense. Right after the rumors spread that the Paxtons had stolen the money, hundreds of bounty hunters tried their luck. The casino and the hotel were broken into repeatedly. They even had trouble with people looking around the track for the money."

"All right. Let's get this over with." I pull on a pair of gloves. What's left of the shack isn't going to come down by itself.

The three of us put ourselves into a frenzy of destruction. Ruby isn't even watching her nails, which is unusual. But I suppose the idea of a new RV can do that to you. Whitaker is kicking down what's left of the walls. There are sticks of furniture left inside, along with an old kerosene lantern that looks like it's been here for a hundred years.

I start inside, throwing the wood we've taken down into the field around us. Ruby's right about one thing: it would be tough to find this place. It's protected by the hill and the tall grass. We were lucky we saw it at all. Or we will be if we find the cash. I'm not overly optimistic on that subject. Even if it is hidden out here, I'll bet the Paxtons found a way to come out and dip into the well more than a few times.

I stomp hard on the wooden slats left in the floor. A few give way, and I pull out the crowbar we brought from the truck. The wood is so old and weather-beaten it splinters when I touch it. The smell of mold and something else flies up in my face.

"Ruby? Have you still got the flashlight?"

"Sure." She brings it to the corner where I'm working. "Did you find something?"

"Maybe." I kneel at the edge of what looks like a hole dug down under the shack. It's been carved out of the rock beneath it. Something old, molded from damp and years in the ground, shows up in the flashlight's beam.

"What is that?" Whitaker asks as he joins us.

I put my hand into the hole and pull up a dirty white cloth bag that doesn't seem to have much in it. "I think it might be what we're looking for."

Together, moving so fast you can probably only see our hands blurring as they go up and down through the hole in the floor, we take out about twenty white bags that look exactly the same.

"Who wants to open the first one?" Ruby asks excitedly.

I'm sure ten million dollars isn't hidden in these lightweight bags. She and Whitaker can open them with my blessing. I hate for her to be disappointed. Apparently the great Paxton treasure has either all been spent or was never here.

Ruby tears open the bag she's holding. A few moldy one-dollar bills flutter to the ground. But it's enough to inspire her and Whitaker to rip the rest of the white bags to shreds. Each bag is about the same. There's a little money but not a fortune. You might be able to buy lunch at the hotel. That's about it.

"You were right, Glad." Ruby drops down on what's left of the wood floor next to me. "They spent all the money."

"There wasn't any money here, sweetheart." I rub my hand down her back. "Millions of dollars don't come packaged in one-dollar bills. This is some kind of hoax."

240

Whitaker shakes his head. "No. This is it. I saw the map. This is merely to throw off those who are not persistent enough to find the real treasure. The money is here somewhere. I can feel it in my bones."

"Let's go, Forsythe. There's nothing else out here." Ruby dusts off her shoes.

"I'm not ready to leave yet. We haven't even begun to dig through the rest of the floor. We have no tools. With a shovel and an axe, we could really get to the bottom of this." He looks at her hopefully.

She tells him, "I guess there's no such thing as real buried treasure. Please come back with us."

"No. I'm going to stay out here. I'm sure I can find something."

"Okay." She hugs him. "Do you have your cell phone?"

"Yes. I'll be perfectly fine. You two go on." He smiles, but there's more frustration and sorrow in his face than joy.

"Good luck," she tells him.

He doesn't reply. Ruby and I start back for the truck. "I'm sorry, honey. I wish it would've been there. I know how much you wanted to find it."

"It's okay. It would've been nice, but it's not the end of the world." She smiles at me and takes my hand. "I've got all I need."

Seeing her this way makes me want to go out and get a loan for a new RV, even though I don't know how we'd make the payments and still stay on the road. I wish there was something else I could do.

"Let's talk about something else. Like how I'm ever gonna get my hands back in shape." She holds them out for me to see. Most of her nails are broken, and nearly all the pink nail polish is gone.

The ride back to the track is melancholy, with me thinking about letting Ruby down and her probably thinking about the lost treasure.

We no sooner get back to the track than Ruby's cell phone rings. She looks at the screen and squeals. "It's Forsythe! Maybe he found the treasure after all!"

She answers it, but after saying hello twenty times gives up. "The line went dead. Something happened to Forsythe."

"Good. Excuse me for not sounding sympathetic, but the man held a gun on us. I hope he can figure out what to do about it."

"Glad, if I got that mad every time someone pulled a gun on me when I was growing up, I wouldn't have made it to the cheerleader squad. Sometimes it seems like the best way. Besides, Forsythe felt bad about what happened. He was sorry."

"Are you two getting out of that truck and breaking down my RV or what?" Zeke demands from outside my door.

Ruby ignores her father. "We have to go back for him."

"If I knew what the hell the two of you were talking about," Zeke says, Louise joining him, "I might be able to render an opinion. Do you want to tell us what's going on?"

Ruby runs through the events that have happened since Thursday in text-message brevity. I can almost see the abbreviations. "So then we left Forsythe out there to find the treasure, if one is still there."

"Damn, girl!" Zeke says. "Didn't I raise you better than that?"

I think he's agreeing with me about trusting Whitaker, but of course, I find out it's something completely different.

"You shouldn't have left that man out there on his own knowing there was that kind of money involved! I can't believe you came back here without the money."

Ruby flicks a glance at me. "Glad said there was no treasure."

"So it's all *my* fault?" I don't care if Zeke and Louise *are* listening. I try not to argue around them, since I know nothing would please them better than Ruby and me breaking up. "You wanted to come back too."

"There's no point in us arguing about it," Ruby says. "We have to go out there and see if Forsythe is okay. He's not answering his cell phone."

"I'm not going out there. You can call the police out there. Maybe they'll check on him."

"I can drive out there without you too," she threatens. "You don't have to go."

"That's fine. I'll stay here and catch a few drivers on their way out."

"Hey!" John Paxton yells from behind us. He's limping and he looks tired, but he seems to be in good spirits for a man who missed a race. "There's my two favorite fans. You two want to go to dinner with me, Junior, and Jimmie?"

Ruby looks like her eyes are going to pop out. Her mouth moves but no sound comes out.

I push her chin up until her lips meet. "We'd love to. Thanks, John."

"No problem. You two probably saved my life. I wish there was some other way I could say thank you."

"I ... I can't." Ruby is almost in tears. "I wish I could. But a friend of ours might be in trouble. I have to find him."

"Is it that private detective who's always hanging around?" John asks. "I thought I saw him right before the race started. You'd think he'd give up on that Brink's money after all these years."

243

"It's hard to give up on ten million dollars," I tell him.

"I don't think there was ever that much, *if* it really happened." John smiles. "What kind of trouble is Whitaker in now?"

Ruby tells John about her concern for Forsythe. "He called, but his cell phone died. I can't get in touch with him now."

"Not a problem," John answers. "We'll take my brother's Hummer out where you saw him last. I'll get a few of his security men to go out with us. We'll find out what happened and then come back for dinner with Jimmie and Junior."

It sounds a little too good to be true to me. Zeke and Louise excuse themselves and head back to their RV. Zeke prefaces his exit with, "I guess we're not leaving tonight, so we might as well go home."

John is already on the phone having someone bring the Hummer around. I really don't want to do this. Going out with the goon squad doesn't make me feel any better. I'm definitely not letting Ruby go without me.

So I give in gracefully. "Great! That takes care of the beer and conversation."

She glares at me. "Just hush and let's get this over with. We still have to go get Malibu."

John finishes his phone conversation. "Yeah. That poor cat. How's he doing?"

Ruby launches into Malibu's condition as I see the black full-size Hummer coming toward us. I think she's right and we might as well get done with this. Tomorrow we'll be on our way back to North Carolina and all of this insanity will be behind us.

We get in the back of the Hummer. Two goons are in the front, and two are in the back behind us. The bulge in their hotel jackets tells me they're all packing.

The door closes behind John and we get started. The windows are heavily tinted. There's a perfume-like scent that must be one of those car air fresheners. It makes me want to sneeze.

That's when I start feeling really uncomfortable. My stomach is rolling around, and all the hair on the back of my neck stands up. My mouth is dry, and my hands are cold and clammy. The Hummer is already at the edge of Dover. I feel like I'm getting the flu.

Ruby is chatting and laughing with John. The goons look out the windows and don't say a word.

But something is wrong. My gut tells me we're in danger. I'm not worried about Whitaker. He can take care of himself. But I don't like Ruby and me being in this situation, whatever it is.

The whole trip goes by with me not being sure I don't have to stop and puke. We reach Milford, and I suddenly get it. It's late, maybe too late. But at least I know what's wrong.

How did John know about Malibu? Even saying we mentioned having the cat at some point in the past few days (I don't recall discussing that with him, but let's say we did), how does he know something is wrong with the cat? I know we haven't seen him or talked to him since we found Malibu drugged in the RV. That's what's wrong. That's what my gut is trying to tell me.

I have a short-lived surge of victory. Then our position hits me like a sledgehammer. The only way John could know about Malibu is if he's responsible for what happened to him.

I look at Ruby, her pretty face, as she laughs and sweet-talks John. I have to think of a way out of this without telling her what the problem is. We're out in the middle of nowhere. I don't even know who we can call for help. But I have to get us out of this vehicle. I hope this is one of those times when Ruby and I are on the same wavelength.

But if she's upset at all or notices anything strange, I can't tell. She looks like she's having the time of her life.

Finally, I can't take it anymore. "Can we pull over at the next gas station? I think I'm feeling the effects of too much beer and not enough food."

I guess I must look the part, because John takes one glance at me and taps the driver goon on the shoulder, telling him to pull over.

"Thanks." I play it up for all it's worth.

"No, thank you." He laughs. "Better out there than in here."

"Good!" Ruby jokes. "I could use a Coke and some peanuts. There's something about a race that always makes me hungry."

"Please don't talk about food," I groan.

The goons kind of chuckle as we pull over into the parking lot of a small gas station. There are one or two other cars. No police, unfortunately. That would be too easy. I figure I'll go in the men's room and call for help. I don't know how long I can hide out in there, but maybe it will be long enough.

Ruby and I get out first. John gets out and stretches his long, lean body. Two of the goons get out with him. I wish I'd seen their faces before we got in the Hummer. Both of them were his captors on the boat.

TWENTY

I WALK CALMLY INTO the gas station like I have all the time in the world and I'm not worried about anything. In real life, my heart is pounding and I feel like I'm going to be sick.

I hope Ruby follows me. I can't get close enough to her to tell her what's going on without giving it away. She said she was going inside for a snack, but she's standing around talking to John and laughing at something one of the goons say to her. *Come on, Ruby! Notice his face! He's one of them. John is the bad guy.*

I don't waste any time getting into the men's room. Lucky for me, it's empty. I start to close the door when Ruby scoots in with me. "What are you doing?" I ask, still holding the door open.

"Close that door and get on the cell phone." She walks around the little room looking at the filthy sink and worse toilet. "Those boys with John are the same ones who kidnapped him. I can't believe he doesn't recognize them."

I smile and hug her close to me. "I think he's one of them."

"I can't believe it! I thought he was abused by his family. I thought he needed help. He set us up and he hurt Malibu."

"I agree. We have to call the police and hope they show up before John breaks down the door."

We both try our cell phones. Neither one of them have enough signal way out here even to call the cashier in the next room.

"We have to do something." Ruby paces as much as the little room lets her. "We can't walk out there and let them kill us."

"Why would they kill us?"

"Because they know we know about the money. Ten million dollars makes for bad blood. I wish we had different cell phones. Maybe if you had Sprint and I had Verizon, one of us could get through."

"All right. Let's not panic." She could be right. I thought about John wanting us to take him where the map said the money was buried. I didn't think about him being angry because there's no money. "I'll sneak out and use the cashier's phone."

"That sounds good. I'll try to keep the boys busy."

I stop her before she goes out the door. "Be careful. Don't keep them *too* busy."

She hugs me. "Don't worry. You know me."

Which causes me to worry even more. I watch her walk around the store, pick up a few things, pay for them, and then walk out again. None of the goons or John are in the store. The coast is clear for me to use the phone.

I creep out of the bathroom, one eye watching the group by the Hummer. The cashier is eyeing me suspiciously. "Can I use your phone?" I ask in a loud whisper.

"What for?"

I hustle up to the counter and he shrinks back a little. "I need to make a call. My cell phone is out of range." I look at him, meaningfully hoping something in my face tells him how distressed I am.

It works, I guess. He empties the cash register on the counter and lies down flat on the floor. "Don't hurt me. Take the money."

"I don't want the damn money." John is looking inside the store while talking to Ruby. He's getting suspicious. "Just let me have the phone."

The clerk points to it but won't get up off the floor. I walk behind the counter and grab the grubby phone and dial 911. John and one of the goons are walking toward the store.

The 911 operator answers. "Please state your emergency."

"I'm a former homicide detective from Chicago. Five men with guns are holding me and my wife hostage in a black Hummer going south on Highway 113. We're outside Milford at Kenny's Kwik-Mart."

"What's the license number on that vehicle, sir?"

"I don't know. I can't see it from here. Send help." I put down the phone and grab a 7-Up from a fake polar bear display full of ice.

"Hey, man!" John enters the store and looks at the clerk on the floor. "What's wrong with him? Are you shaking him down for money?"

I'm assuming the clerk thinks I'm trying to rob him. I wish I could get on the floor too and it would be that simple. "I'm really sick." I leave a dollar on the counter and wish I could make myself throw up without putting something down my throat. "Sorry."

"Not a problem," John says. "Are you good to go now?"

"I think so."

John and the goon walk out of the store behind me, laughing as John tells the goon about the clerk on the floor. There's nothing I can do but go along with them.

Inside the Hummer again, I smile at Ruby, hoping she'll know I talked to 911. Whether or not they can get someone out here fast enough to help us is another story. Too bad we don't have our guns. Tracks frown on that kind of thing at a race, but they sure would come in handy right now.

The only other thing I can think to do is try to fake them out when we get to the field where the shack is. Because it's down the hill, we might be able to get them to think nothing is there. John would have no reason to make a move against us. Between the tall grass and the hill, he won't be able to see the shack. Maybe we'll be safe.

"Hey! I know this place!" John says as we come to the field. "My dad used to have a hunting shack out here. I wonder if it's still here. I guess it would be a good place for Phil to hide that money."

So much for Plan A. Plan B goes something like the police get here before John goes down to the shack and realizes the money is gone. I hope that plan goes better than Plan A. I really want to see Joe race at least one more time.

I'm hoping they park the Hummer on the side of the road, but John tells the driving goon to take the vehicle in. "We were all over this field in ATVs when we were kids. There's nothing out here except the hunting shack. Even if there was, this baby could tackle it."

That may be the end of Plan B. If the police can't see the vehicle from the road, how will they know we're down here?

That takes me to Plan C. I'm not sure at this point what that plan consists of. I suppose it will be something like doing whatever we have to do to fight them off when the time comes. Maybe we can pick up a few pieces of wood and hit the goons with them while they shoot us.

The hill and the hunting shack come up way too fast. John claps his hands when he sees the spot. "Just like I remember." He grins at Ruby. "Well, almost anyway. I think it was in better shape back then. I remember spending the night out here."

"That must've been fun," Ruby says, trying to make conversation. "How old were you then?"

"I was part of the second family," he explains. "My dad had Phil and Bill with his first wife. He married my mom when they were about ten. I guess I was about five or six when we used to come out here. I really looked up to Phil and Bill. They were great older brothers."

The Hummer stops next to the shack. There's no sign of Whitaker. I don't know what happened to him or even if it happened out here. He may have hitched a ride back to Dover.

"Looks like this thing was hit by a tornado." John jumps out and stalks toward the shack. Immediately, two of the goons follow him. That leaves the two in front with Ruby and me in the vehicle.

Ruby looks at me and I know what she's thinking. It's not telepathy or anything weird like that. But sometimes we think a lot alike.

In this case, she's thinking we might not have a better chance to escape. I tend to agree with her. I scan the floor and the back seat, but there is a decided lack of tools in the vehicle. I can't imagine not having a handy wrench or something in the back seat.

Ruby improvises and hits the goon on the driver's side with her two-liter bottle of Diet Pepsi Jazz. It kind of bounces off his head.

Not exactly the intent she was looking for. I follow her move with a quick right to his big square jaw. Surprisingly, he falls out of the Hummer.

Goon number two isn't so easy. He grabs Ruby by the hair and hauls back his hand to hit her. I figure I'm not going to get lucky a second time like I did with goon number one, so I push myself back on the seat for leverage and kick him hard in the face. He looks at me like I must be joking, and I kick him again. He slumps against the door.

"I'll push him out." Ruby moves to the front seat. "You drive."

"I'll push him out," I argue. "He must weigh two tons, and you drive faster than me when you're scared."

It seems to be going well. Ruby starts the engine and I kick goon number two out of the vehicle and slam the door closed. "Let's go! I said you drive fast."

I glance at her, and she's holding her hands in the air. Goon number one came up faster than I hoped. He's holding a gun to her chest.

"Is there a problem?" John sprints back toward us. He takes one look at the situation and shakes his head. "I was hoping this wouldn't have to get ugly. I like the two of you. I would've been happy to share some of the money with you when we found it."

"There's nothing here," I tell him. "I don't know if there ever was."

"You've already been out here." He looks toward the shed. "Too bad. But you were looking in the wrong place."

"You said yourself there's nothing else out here," Ruby reminds him. "And we found some empty bags. The money was here. I think Phil and Bill spent it all."

"Funny. Bill was willing to die rather than give up the location."

"You killed your own brother?" Ruby stares at him.

"He was stupid and obnoxious, just like Phil. They always knew what was best. Especially when it came to telling *me* what to do. They never shared. It was like I should find my own sponsors while they hoarded all the money they took."

"Except for that last ten million, right?" I figure I might as well let him talk. It might buy us some time.

"You're catching on." He offers his hand to Ruby and helps her out of the vehicle. "It worked the first time. Why not the second time? Once Bill was dead and I was kidnapped, Phil would've done anything to save what was left of his family. It wasn't too hard to set the whole thing up to make it look like he'd stolen the money again without regard for the safety of his poor little brother."

"You were the one who beat him up," Ruby accuses him. "Why did you bother? You had ten million."

"Because twenty million is much better. I thought I could get him to tell me where the money was hidden. I think now that he didn't know. He made Bill his accountant, so to speak. He didn't know where it was. When he needed money, he called Bill. It was their way of keeping each other honest."

"Well, they must've made a lot of withdrawals." A goon holds his gun on me, gesturing for me to get out of the vehicle. "I'm telling you, there's no money out here."

"You looked in the shack, right?" John grins. "I knew it as soon as I saw where you were taking me. I should've thought of this years ago. Of course they'd stash it out here. But not in the shack. In the meat locker."

"The meat locker?" Ruby echoes.

"Yeah. My dad dug it out of the rock bed. It's cool down there and animals can't get into it. If I were going to hide some money bags—or a couple of dead bodies, for instance—that's where I'd put them."

This doesn't sound good for us. I guess it's going to be Plan C. I'm already looking around for a good-sized piece of wood.

"It's right this way." John nods at his goons to escort us in that direction. "I'll give you a personal tour."

I look at Ruby, who smiles and winks at me. I hope that means she has a plan that's better than mine, because the closer we get to the Paxton meat cellar, the more uncomfortable I get with this situation. Where's a damn cop when you need one?

We walk a few yards from the shack and John starts stomping around on the ground, trying to locate the hidden meat locker. "It's here somewhere. I'm sure we'll find it." He looks back and smiles at me and Ruby.

I think when he finds it, I'll rush up and kick him into it. Then as the goons come to help him, that will give us a chance to kick their asses … or die trying.

"Here it is!" John leans down to open the door to the meat cellar. The goons crowd in close behind me and Ruby, but aren't holding on to either one of us. I guess this is it.

At that moment, the double doors leading to the meat cellar burst open. John is flung back on the ground. Whitaker pops out an instant later and yells, "Duck!"

Ruby and I hit the ground. Whitaker comes up throwing chunks of wood wildly but it's enough to hit two of the four goons. The other two rush him with their weapons. Whitaker drops back into the cellar and it slams shut. As the men pound the sturdy oak doors, Ruby and I get the guns from the fallen goons.

"Hey!" Ruby yells at the two still assailing the meat cellar. "You better turn around and drop your guns unless you want us to shoot you in the ass."

The two goons turn around, ready to fire when they see what the situation looks like. They don't drop their weapons, but they run back to the Hummer and take off.

Ruby sighs. "It's so hard to get good help these days. You can't even find someone to take a bullet for you."

I rush over and hug her, then kiss her until neither one of us can breathe.

Whitaker clears his throat as he pops up out of the meat cellar and observes the situation. "Where did everyone go? I was getting my second wind."

"Lucky for us, they decided to run instead of fight." I laugh as I shake his hand. "I never thought I'd say this, but I'm happy to see you."

"I was terrified, but I knew I had to make it work, you see. Watching out for the young ones, you know." He shakes my hand until I think it might fall off. "You'll never guess what I found in there."

"Money?" Ruby guesses. "The lost Brink's/Paxton treasure?"

"Exactly. I can't tell how much of it is gone, but there's a considerable amount left." He kisses her hand. "Enough for us to share, I'm certain."

We hear Paxton groan as he gets to his feet. It's accompanied by the sound of sirens on the road, which we can't see from here.

"I guess they finally got the message," I tell Ruby. "I'm happy we're still here to know about it."

"This is my money," John tells us. "I've been looking for it all of my life. Leave now and I'll forget this happened."

"Good for you." Ruby saunters up to him. "But my memory isn't that short. I don't care if we have to drive up here a hundred times to see you go to prison, you disgusting piece of trash."

"We can share," John offers. "Don't forget, I know where the other ten million is hidden. We'll all be rich. There's no reason it can't happen."

Whitaker walks up to him and pops him in the jaw. "I have twenty good reasons why it can't happen. I'm sure a court will want to hear all of them."

The sirens sound like they've stopped at the road. But a helicopter flies low over the field, obviously looking for us. I wave to it and the pilot waves back. I imagine it won't be long before the police swarm down here.

John starts running away from the road. There's a large group of trees in that direction. If he gets in there, it could be hard to find him. I hand Ruby my borrowed weapon. "I'll be right back."

"You want me to go, honey?" she asks, knowing what I'm going to do.

"No, that's okay. You stay here and wait for the police." I kiss her and then run after John.

It doesn't take long to catch him (good thing). He's not much of a fighter, and by the time the police reach the shack, I'm headed back with him. Whitaker is explaining the process of getting the money from the insurance company to Ruby. I'm not sure at this point what our cut will be, but whatever it is, we're buying a new RV. We'll work out the details later.

"Thanks," the deputy sheriff says when I hand John over. "I think there might be a reward in this for all of you."

Ruby grins. "We know. We found the Brink's money Bill and Phil Paxton stole."

The deputy shakes his head. "I'm talking about the millions we found stashed in the back of the Hummer. It's probably insured. You'll get a percentage of it since you alerted us to the crime."

Ruby starts jumping, laughing, and hugging me all at the same time. "We can buy Malibu a new collar—a gold collar, if we want to. All this and Jimmie winning the 400. What a weekend!"

———————

Malibu is in rare form when we pick him up at the vet the next day. He scratches me and leaps to Ruby, who pets him and holds him like a big black teddy bear. Dr. Simons assures us he's fine. I could tell that without a degree in veterinary medicine.

On the way back to the RV, Ruby speculates on how much money we'll get for our part of the reward. "They said in the paper this morning that there was still 2 million left in the meat locker where Phil stashed it. He'll have to face charges on that. With the 10 million in the back of the Hummer John took, that makes 1.2 million for us to split with Forsythe."

"Unless he decides he doesn't want to split his share."

"He'd be a fool not to, since my part is so much bigger."

"*Your* part? Which part is *my* part?"

"I'm just teasing you, honey. And the RV we buy with that money will be for both of us. And Malibu, since it looks like he doesn't have a home with both of the living Paxton brothers going to jail."

I'm already figuring ways we can save some of that money and invest it. After we get the new RV, of course. "I guess the only good Paxton is a dead Paxton."

"Very funny." She looks out at the street. "It's very quiet when a race is over. I bet they have the same problem Lowe's has, with tons of trash to pick up."

"And lots of happy merchants who made plenty of money on race fans."

I'm surprised when Ann stops her car and gets out. I'm not sure what to think at this point. I'm hoping it's just a pat on the back and "See you later."

"Glad." Ann smiles at me, ignoring Ruby. "That was some fancy footwork you did. You always were good at BS-ing yourself out of a jam."

"Thanks. In this case, it was some pretty profitable BS." I wrap one arm around Ruby's waist. I don't want there to be any repeat of Ann's kiss for both our sakes.

"Good luck with it." Ann glances at Ruby. "I know he must be a handful."

Ruby smiles graciously. "You don't know the half of it."

"I'm sure it's better that I don't." Ann turns back toward her car. "Take it easy, Glad. I guess it was good to run into you again, but I hope I won't be seeing you when you're up for the next race."

We watch her drive away. I know how many questions are fighting to get out of Ruby's mouth. I know I'll have to answer them at some point. At least most of them. But not right now.

There are still a few cars and a bus or two in the casino parking lot. But the area around the speedway is quiet and almost empty. There is only one other RV besides ours out here. Even Zeke and

Louise left for home this morning. Louise's cousin, Janet, offered to drive their RV home since she was going for a visit anyway.

I don't mind. I have a surprise for Ruby when we get to Pocono. It has to do with a certain RV she had her eye on in Daytona. With a little Internet finagling, I was able to get things set up so we can be in our dream home before the next big race.

Bobby pulls up in his Mustang as we get back to the RV and start getting ready to leave. "Looks like I'm not racing at Pocono. Mr. Hamilton thinks I need time on some short tracks to build up confidence."

"That's not a bad idea." I'm half-listening as I hook up the Ranger to the back of the RV. "Lots of famous drivers started there."

"Yeah, but I was racing short tracks when I was sixteen. I don't need practice. I need a good car. You know how it is when you aren't the lead driver for a team, Glad. You get the hand-me-downs."

A big black limousine pulls up next to Bobby, and a tinted window slides down. "You still here, boy?" Abe Hamilton laughs, his big belly shaking. "If you drove my car on the track the way you drive that Mustang, I'd get you another car for Pocono."

Bobby's eyes get big. "I can do that, sir. If you give me another chance, I can impress you."

"All right then. Let's try it one more time." Hamilton stares up at me. "You're that boy from the paper, aren't you? The one who solved that kidnapping thing."

I nod. "We're the ones who found the missing money."

Ruby joins us, wrench in hand. "How are you, Mr. Hamilton?"

"I'm just fine, Miss Ruby. And you are looking prettier every day." He nods at me. "Is this that Yankee Zeke was telling me about?"

"This is him." She slides her arm through mine. "He's a good husband."

Hamilton eyes me critically. I hope I'm not about to face the business end of his shotgun, like I did Zeke's. I didn't even realize he knew Ruby.

"Say, Yankee. What would you think about working for me for a few races?"

I'm about to turn him down, but I have to do it nice and easy or I'll never hear the end of it. "I appreciate the offer, but—"

"That's all right, son. I can always find a spotter to fill in while Doggie has his knee surgery. Bobby told me you might be interested, that's all."

Did I hear him correctly? Did he ask me to be a spotter? I try to find words to tell him how much I'd like to do that without sounding like an idiot. "I could probably do that."

Hamilton smiles broadly. "Well, all right then. I'll see you all at Pocono."

GLAD AND RUBY'S
TRACK LOG

DOVER INTERNATIONAL SPEEDWAY

1131 N. DuPont Highway
Dover, DE 19901
Phone: 302-883-6500
Fax: 302-672-0100
Tickets: 800-441-RACE
www.doverspeedway.com

Track Specs

- Superspeedway: 1.0-mile oval
- Banking: turns—24 degrees; straights—9 degrees
- Straights: frontstretch—1,076 feet; backstretch—1,076 feet
- Pit stalls: 42 (1 shared), 15 feet wide by 28 feet long
- Grandstands: about 147,000 seats

The Dover racetrack, otherwise known as the Monster Mile, is a high-banked concrete oval that measures exactly one mile. It's the only concrete track in the NASCAR superspeedway circuit. The grooved surface allows for high speeds. But it also can play havoc with tires and nerves, as there isn't much room for error and the wrecks can be extremely hazardous.

NASCAR races are held on this track in June and September every year. Drivers typically love or hate the track. Fans enjoy the show. The track represents a challenge to even the best drivers in the sport. Different strategies are discussed and used at every race. The race has been won by hard-charging through the grueling four hundred laps. But it has also been won by taking it easy and saving your tires for the end. Some drivers have even won by using better fuel mileage to their advantage. You never know what's going to happen at Dover.

For fans, the view is good no matter where you're at in the stands. Traffic isn't too bad, with a number of alternate routes available, including Route 1. The city of Dover also offers the DART park-and-ride system, which will get you to the track on time.

In 2006, Dover announced plans for a five-year improvement project that will provide new and upgraded amenities for visitors and drivers. The multimillion-dollar-construction project began after the June 2006 NASCAR weekend.

Referred to as the "Monster Makeover," scheduled changes in the track include a luxury skybox and club for high-rolling fans; a new entrance for fans on the east side of the complex, which should ease congestion; upgraded food and beverage facilities; a new building to purchase tickets and merchandise; a larger vendor area; an outdoor arena for concerts; and more restroom facilities (fewer portable toilets).

Races

The first weekend in June is home to the NASCAR Busch Series race and the Neighborhood Excellence 400.

The end of September brings fans back to Dover for the Dover 200 and 400 races. Tickets range from $85 to $210. Seats on the Monster Bridge are not for sale.

Services

There are concession stands located around the track that serve hamburgers, hot dogs, Italian sausages, nachos, pizza, soft pretzels, beer, soda, and water.

Paramedics are on staff around the track during the races.

Souvenir trailers are located around the track and along the midway. You'll find sponsor souvenir trailers along the midway on the south side and northeast side of the track.

Mist tents are available for a quick cooldown at gates 2, 6, 9, and 15.

History

Dover Downs opened in 1969 with a unique idea: why not create a facility that could accommodate horse racing and stock-car racing? The idea turned out to be a good one, and the first event held at the speedway was a NASCAR Winston Cup Series race. The track seating was twenty-five rows, 10,333 seats. On July 6, Richard Petty in his number 43 car won the Mason-Dixon 300.

Other auto races, including Indy races, were held at the track, but in 1971, the other races were dropped from the schedule to play up the two five-hundred-mile NASCAR Winston Cup Series races held each year. This worked so well that no other changes were made until 1982, when NASCAR Busch Grand National races were added on the Saturday lineup during Winston Cup weekends.

Dover became NASCAR's first concrete-paved superspeedway in 1995, changing how drivers and fans thought of the track forever and earning it the nickname Monster Mile. Two years later, the NASCAR Winston Cup race became a four-hundred-mile event.

An additional 3,200-seat grandstand was added in 1986. Expansion continued through 2001, with grandstand seating capacity growing to over 140,000. The track had the largest seating capacity of any sports facility in the mid-Atlantic region at the time. That same year, the NASCAR Craftsman Truck Series began at the September race. Kurt Busch won the race from the pole.

Legislation legalizing slot machines at the facility didn't come until 1994. Dover Downs Slots opened on December 29, 1995.

Dover held the first Winston Cup race in the country after the September 11th terrorist attacks. Dale Earnhardt Jr. won that race and grabbed the American flag for his victory lap around the track.

The DuPont Monster Bridge was added on turn three in 2004 and remains a one-of-a-kind attraction.

DuPont Monster Bridge

With an incredible view of the track, the DuPont Monster Bridge provides fifty-six lucky visitors with custom theater-style seating. Each seat has audio and video coverage of the NASCAR race, along with access to the drivers' race-team communications. Flat-screen TVs are standard, along with wall-to-wall carpet and a full-service staffed bar.

The idea for the bridge was born in 2002. The reality is made of steel and concrete construction and juts out 110 feet across the track. Front and rear walls are made of laminated safety glass. It has an inside height of 10 feet and a width of 13 feet. It is poised 29 feet over the center of the track.

It's been called "the Miracle Bridge" and "the Most Exciting Seat in Sports." Visitors who are fortunate enough to watch the race from the bridge say the cars roar and scream beneath them. Probably not a seat for people with nervous tendencies. Besides media and dignitaries, some ordinary folks are given the opportunity to win a seat on the bridge at each race. You can win your spot by visiting the Dover Speedway website.

Miles the Monster

A hot new comic character has been created from the Dover track's nickname of Monster Mile. He's Miles the Monster, and you won't find him at your local comic book shop. *Miles the Monster* is a hit comic book from Insight Studios. He's affectionately known as the "heart and soul of the Dover International Speedway." He made his comic debut in June 2006. Dover is the only place you can buy a copy of issue number one of *Miles the Monster*. It's another fun way to remember the race.

Getting to the Race

Race-day traffic is as bad in Dover as it is at any other race. If you are camping at the speedway or staying in the posh Dover Downs Hotel next door, you won't have any problems getting to the track.

Tip: As you are coming into Dover, Route 9 is a great alternative to Routes 1 or 113. Of course, when you get close to Dover, you will still encounter heavy traffic. All routes within a few miles of the track will be full. On Route 1 South, drivers sometimes pull over on the shoulder. It will be bumper-to-bumper for miles.

If you are staying away from the speedway but you don't want to drive, you can consider the two options below.

The Race Express bus from the Blue Hen Corporate Center on U.S. 113 runs to Dover International Speedway. Service begins at 8:00 a.m. and runs until one hour after the race. It takes about twelve minutes, and exact change is required. The cost is $20 per car, which includes parking and round-trip bus service for everyone in your vehicle.

Another way to get there is the shuttle bus from Christiana Mall, off Route 1. Service begins at 7:30 a.m. There is limited seating on a first-come, first-served basis. The cost is $10 per person, which includes parking and round-trip bus service. **Tip:** Exact change is required, and all your belongings have to fit under your seat. Call 302-652-DART or visit www.dartfirststate.com for more information.

Staying in Dover

If you don't have an RV and would like to stay at a local hotel or motel, here are a few listings to get you started:

- Dover Downs Hotel (trackside): 866-473-7378
- Comfort Suites: 302-736-1204
- Dover Inn: 302-674-4011
- Hampton Inn: 302-736-3500
- Little Creek Inn: 302-730-1300
- Sheraton Inn: 302-678-8500

Area Attractions in and around Dover include:

- The Dover Downs Casino, which features slots and shows: www.doverdowns.com
- The Bombay Hook National Wildlife Refuge: www.fws.gov/northeast/bombayhook
- An eighteenth-century farm: www.agriculturalmuseum.org
- Museums and historical sites located in downtown Dover: history.delaware.gov/museums/sh/sh_main.shtml

Restaurants

There are a variety of restaurants for a change of pace from grilling or eating at the track. Some of these include:

- The Hub Rock Café, Route 13, Dover, 302-678-9885
- WT Smithers, 140 S. State St., Dover, 302-674-8875
- Hollywood Diner, 123 N. Dupont Hwy., Dover, 302-734-7462
- Atwood's Restaurant, 800 N. State St., Dover, 302-674-1775

GLOSSARY

If you are a new NASCAR fan or you've been trying to figure out some of the terminology, this part might be a big help for you. A few words can make the difference between understanding what's going on and being totally in the dark.

We're going to start with the Chase for the Cup. You might understand the basics of the NASCAR point system, but you may still wonder what the difference is between that system and the Chase.

Beginning in 2004, the NASCAR Nextel Cup Championship has been decided by a competitive system called the Chase. It's much like the playoffs found in football and baseball.

In the last ten races of the season, all qualifying drivers have their points reset. The points leader gets 5,050 points, the second-place driver gets 5,045 points, and so on. There are 5 points per position for all eligible drivers. Points are still assigned the same way as during the rest of the season to determine the champion.

Since any lead a driver had in the season points is erased, this guarantees the points battle will come down to the last race. Several drivers have a shot at winning the Cup until the last lap.

There are usually only ten drivers with a chance to win the Chase. The Chase begins after the twenty-sixth race of the season. At that time, all drivers in the top ten in points qualify for the Chase. Any driver within four hundred points of the leader qualifies, regardless of their point position.

NASCAR began using this system after Matt Kenseth's 2003 championship. He had such a large lead in the points, the rest of the season was a letdown for fans. This is what's known as a points blowout. NASCAR officials decided these bad point races weren't good for its growing television audience and ticket sales.

This discouraged some drivers, though most fans loved the innovation and competition. To win over the drivers who missed the Chase, NASCAR began to award a one-million-dollar bonus to the driver who finished eleventh in the points. That lucky driver gets invited to the banquet at the end of the year to claim his prize.

While this change in NASCAR policy has put extra zing into the race season, it also puts extra pressure on drivers to break into the top ten in points. Media attention generated by the Chase means big money from sponsors.

Terms

BUMP DRAFTING happens when a driver runs up close behind another car and pushes it. This makes both cars faster and is mostly done in restrictor plate racing.

The **CREW CHIEF** is the man in charge of the race team at the track. When a race team sets up, the crew chief is in charge of the car and mechanics. During the race, the crew chief makes the decisions about pit stops, tire changes, and chassis adjustments.

When a driver says his car is **LOOSE**, it means the back end of the car is losing traction and sliding around to the right, toward the outside wall. This usually happens when entering or exiting a turn.

PIT ROAD is the paved road leading across the apron from the racetrack to each team's pit area, where it services its car during a race.

The **POLE** position is the starting position of a race. A driver who qualifies with the fastest speed wins the pole. He starts the race at the inside (next to the pit area) in the front position. The second-fastest driver gets the outside pole (he starts on the outside, next to the grandstands) in the front row.

A **SHORT TRACK** is a racetrack that is less than one mile long. Rookies get their start on these tracks.

The **SILLY SEASON** is a time at the end of a season when drivers and crew chiefs are positioning themselves on different teams for the next season.

A **SPONSOR** is an individual or corporation that finances a race (Coca-Cola 600), race team (Roush), or racing series (Nextel). Corporate sponsors use racing venues as part of their advertising campaigns. Team sponsors have their logos on the cars, team trucks, and uniforms.

A **SPOTTER** is a team member who watches the race from a high position in the grandstands. The idea is to place spotters where they can see as much of the racetrack as possible. The spotter gives information to the driver using a two-way radio. He alerts his driver to unsafe activity on the track that the driver may be unable to see for himself and helps him maintain a good position on the track.

If you enjoyed *Hooked Up*, read on for an excerpt
from the first Pet Psychic Mystery by Joyce and Jim Lavene

The Telltale Turtle

Coming soon from Midnight Ink

"This is Mary Catherine Roberts, the pet psychic. You're live on Lite102.5 WRSC in Wilmington, North Carolina. Tell me about your pet."

"Hi. My name is Albert. I listen to your show every day, Mary Catherine. I'm calling about my dog, Ginger. She's getting older and has started chewing on things. Her teeth are falling out; that's how bad it is! I'm desperate."

"Well, we know she has a problem, don't we? She wouldn't just pick up that habit. We have to figure out *why* she's chewing. She's trying to tell you something. Dogs want to do what we ask ordinarily. What does she choose to chew?"

"Mostly my shoes. She won't leave them alone. If I hide them in the closet, she scratches on the door to get at them. If I accidentally leave a pair out, she chews them to shreds."

"I see. Do you walk her often? Besides the obligatory trip to the potty."

"I used to walk her several times a day when I worked for myself. But my new job keeps me for longer hours. I had to cut back. Now I only walk her once in the morning and once when I come home. Just until she goes; you know?"

"Dogs don't like change, Marty. None of us do. If you don't have time to walk her more often, hire someone to do it for you. Your dog needs some exercise. She's chewing your shoes because she knows you have to put them on to take her out. She wants your attention."

"Wow! That makes sense. I'll try it." Marty sounded relieved. "Thanks, Mary Catherine. You're a genius, like always."

"You're welcome. Good luck. Give my best to Ginger."

Mary Catherine looked at WRSC station manager, Colin Jamison, who stood outside the glass sound booth. He looked unusually stressed. That was saying a lot for a man who looked unusual when he *wasn't* stressed. "

"Good job," he remarked absently when she stepped out of the glass box. "Your ratings are looking great this month, by the way."

"Thanks." Sometimes she wished she understood humans as well as she understood other animals. She wouldn't have to ask ridiculous questions. "Is something wrong, Colin? You look a little under the weather."

He shrugged slender shoulders and adjusted his black wire-rimmed glasses which seemed to weigh heavily on his thin, sallow face. His curly brown hair was baby-fine above a high forehead and studious brown eyes. "I'm okay. I have a few family problems. But everything will work out. How's the clinic?"

"It's good. Too busy sometimes. But good. You should come down and volunteer for a few hours. You might like it."

He laughed uncomfortably, white teeth as even and straight as his childhood dentist could make them. "Wish I had time! You know my schedule."

"You're digging yourself an early grave." She flung her marmalade colored Batik shawl flamboyantly across one shoulder. "You should take some time to relax."

"I would. But *someone* has to keep the sponsors happy." He glanced at the man in the sound booth who'd taken Mary Catherine's place at the microphone. "Jimmy won't do restaurant openings, even though he's a food critic. Stacey won't endorse her sponsor's hair care products on the air even though she gives beauty tips."

"And I won't pitch Meaty Boy dog food. I know." She smiled at him. "I guess we're lucky to have you to keep it all together for us. You're a very talented man."

He tried to return her smile but his pursed lips wouldn't turn up at the ends and he finally gave up. It made him look like he had a nervous tick. "You could do one *small* endorsement."

The enormous orange colored tabby cat who sat on the green vinyl chair meowed loudly and shook his head.

"Quiet, Baylor," she admonished. "Stay out of this. You aren't a dog."

"Wow!" Mindy Evans, Colin's fiancé, looked at the cat as she joined them. "How do you get him to do that anyway? I don't think I've ever seen a cat that's trained like him. I didn't even know you could train a cat. Every time I see it, I'm amazed."

"You mean sit in one place for an hour?" Mary Catherine smoothed Baylor's plush fur with an absent hand. "That's what cats do best. And he wants to be here with me."

"You *tell* him where to sit every day and he sits there." Mindy took Colin's arm and smiled at him. She was a perfect foil for him; pretty, blond and mostly unconcerned about things. She was good at what she did and kept everyone on an even keel. She'd been at the station since Mary Catherine got there two years ago. "How do you do *that*?"

Before Mary Catherine could answer, a tall, broad-shouldered man in a gray western suit with a matching Stetson pushed his way into the room. "There's my psychic angel! Mary Catherine, you're looking mighty fine today!"

She rolled her expressive dark blue eyes. She wasn't sure if it was the terrible cologne he splashed on with a heavy hand, his obnoxiously friendly attitude, or the fact that he made his money being the Marlboro man on TV for years. Whatever it was, Clinton 'Buck' Maybelle irritated her. Just being in the room with him made her want to hit him with something.

Not a good sign since most of her intimate relationships with men started out that way. She'd only lost her fourth husband, Donald Roberts, two years ago, just before she moved to Wilmington, North Carolina. She wasn't ready to go through all that again.

"Mr. Maybelle." Colin shook the older man's hand, sucking up as always. Something *he* did best. "Glad you stopped by."

Buck played a short game of seeing which man could squeeze hardest (Colin *always* lost at this game), only giving up as he saw Mary Catherine head for the elevator. "Say, how 'bout some lunch? I've got my yacht tied up down at River Street. We could take a nice cruise while we're at it."

"I'd love to," Colin cleared his throat, "but I'm tied up in meetings all afternoon. Maybe next week?"

"Not you, squirt! I'm talking to Miss Mary."

"Please don't call me that." Mary Catherine held out her arms and Baylor jumped up into them. He blended in perfectly with her shawl and her shoulder-length hair as he snuggled in close and warily eyed the man in the hat.

"Sorry!" Buck winked at Colin. "The lady is *touchy* today."

She gave him a cold stare. "The lady is touchy every day where *you're* concerned."

"What else can I do to show you how I feel? Isn't it enough I pledge my faith by sponsoring your talk show even though you won't endorse my Meaty Boy dog food on the air?"

"Not really. You manage to sell your dog food without my help. Or should I say because people *think* I'm helping you."

"Now Mary Catherine, we've been over this. I took you to tour the plant. We use prime ingredients. There's nothing wrong with Meaty Boy!"

"Except every dog hates it."

"Dogs eat it!"

"You'd eat swill if you were starving too!"

"Please!" Mindy glanced nervously around the room. "Could you *please* move the discussion outside? I'm afraid you'll be heard on-air."

Mary Catherine ignored Buck. "Of course. Baylor and I were on our way home anyway. I hope things work out for you, Colin. See you tomorrow, Mindy."

The cat meowed again, face alert, whiskers twitching, ignoring everything to watch his prey. His blue eyes never strayed from Buck's florid face as the man followed Mary Catherine into the elevator.

"Meaty Boy is healthy *and* nutritious. I don't get it. Dogs don't care what they eat as long as it has meat in it anyway. What do you have against it?"

"The dogs I've spoken to hate it. They say it tastes like burnt turnips. The only reason you're still sponsoring my show is because you play golf with the station owner! Make a palatable dog food or I'll find a local sponsor who knows how to play golf as well as you do!"

Buck laughed. "You're really something when you're angry! Wee-haa! I like a woman with spirit! Why don't you invite your dog friends for a taste test? You know, like people do. They can try different kinds of food and see if they can tell the difference. If they can and they won't eat it, I'll change the formula, even though it's been in my family for a hundred years."

"Oh all right! If I can get any of them to come, I will. But don't blame me if no one trusts you."

He started to move closer to her and the cat on her shoulder hissed, warning him away. "If you can *really* talk to animals, darlin', I suggest you talk to that fur ball there. He's a mite testy!"

"He feels the same about you, Buck. Call me about the taste test later in the week. I'll see what I can line up. Maybe a few of the dogs at the clinic will volunteer. Although it hardly seems fair since some of them have *already* been abused!"

I'm only doing this for Colin because he looked so out of sorts today. Mary Catherine reminded herself of that fact several times as she left Buck in the Port City Java coffee shop downstairs from the station, grateful that Danny's cab was waiting at the sidewalk outside.

Baylor tossed his big head and looked unimpressed.

"You don't have to deal with him, do you?" she demanded of him. "He only called you a fur ball. He called me Miss Mary and his little psychic angel! How do you think *I* feel?"

"MC!" Danny greeted her as she opened the orange taxi door. "Buenos tardes! Como esta? How did the broadcast go?"

"It went fine until Buck showed up." She slid into the back seat. "You know how I feel about him."

"As always," he sympathized. "Where to?"

"Home. Baylor and I both need some lunch."

"We could stop by Raul's café for burritos." He grinned as he hyped his brother's café. His teeth flashed white against his dark skin.

"I don't think I'm up to spicy food today, Danny. Thanks anyway."

"De nada." He shrugged as he pulled out into slow traffic that moved along the river in historic downtown Wilmington. "Baylor, you want a burrito?"

The tabby cat meowed but Mary Catherine hushed him. "You don't need that either. The last time you sneaked out and got a burrito, we were both sorry. No more beans for you!"

Baylor slid down her lap and slumped on the floor.

"Oh now he's going to pout!" She shook her head. "It's not enough he's the only animal allowed into the radio station! It's not enough he does whatever he pleases!"

Danny laughed, his agile hands loose on the wheel as he negotiated walking tourists and sightseeing traffic along the narrow street. "Sorry, amigo. Maybe some other time."

A large yacht, the name *Blockade Runner* etched on the side, went slowly by, pine deck gleaming in the sun. Artists sat or stood beside easels all along the bank of the Cape Fear River in the old port town. They chalked and pasteled the picturesque river scene with the countless white sails against the warm blue sky. The new summer breeze shuffled through the streets, ruffling the leaves in the oak trees and drifted the smell of the river across the city.

Gulls followed the ocean-going ships, calling from the sky above them. It was hard to hear anything besides the racket their disordered cries presented. But there was *something* else. A faint small voice steadily called out for help in the midst of the louder shouts of the gulls demanding fish.

Closing her eyes, Mary Catherine focused her concentration on that voice, ignoring all the other sounds that assailed her through the open window. "Danny, we have to stop!"

The young Latino driver immediately put his foot on the brake, the taxi rocking as it squealed to stop. Other cars behind him pushed on their horns to get him going. "Que pasa? Are you okay, MC?"

"I'm fine. But Tommy needs help." Mary Catherine kept her eyes closed but Baylor grimaced, startled by the quick stop.

"Tommy?" Danny looked around, his black hair gleaming in the sunlight that came through the open window. "Who's Tommy?"

"I'm not sure yet." She held on to the sound of the tiny voice in her head. The breeze whipped her thick, tawny blond hair away from her face, blue eyes lost to the world as she stared out at the wide gray stretch of river.

ABOUT THE AUTHORS

NASCAR fans Joyce and Jim Lavene are a husband-and-wife writing team who co-author several mystery series, including the Sharyn Howard Mysteries and Peggy Lee Garden Mysteries. They live outside of Charlotte, North Carolina, just twenty miles away from Lowe's Motor Speedway. Find out more at www.joyceandjimlavene .com.